yours to keep

LC HEZEMANS

Trigger Warnings

Domestic Abuse is mentioned and portrayed throughout.

Book Playlist

California Girls - Katy Perry, Snoop Dogg

Cruel Summer - Taylor Swift

Cotton Candy - Nic D

Butterflies – Abe Parker

Bad Choices - Kode

Training Season – Dua Lipa

Never Be The Same - Camila Cabello

Iris - Jada Facer

Closer- Neyo

Flaws – Calum Scott

All I Ever Wanted - Dean Lewis

Antidote (feat. Sam Fischer) - Guy Sebastian

Home - Good Neighbours

Stargazing - Myles Smith

The Yours to Keep playlist can be found in Spotify.

L C Hezemans – Yours To Keep Playlist

To my grandmother, the strongest woman I know, who sadly lost her battle with cancer in the weeks prior to this books release.

There's always going to be an end to this thing we call life, and it passes us by quicker than you think.

Find that heart dropping, breathtaking, soul stealing, once in a lifetime love, and never let it go.

Chapter One

Cruz – Twelve Years Old

The cold chill that lives rent-free inside these concrete-colored walls in the prison I call home slowly suffocates me as the sound of my father's expensive designer loafers close in on my bedroom door.

He knows.

Backing up slowly toward the wall, sweat coats my skin. My throat aches as I try and swallow, looking around my room, ensuring it's flawless. My back hits the wall behind me as the footsteps outside my door come to a halt. Holding my breath, my eyes zero in on the doorknob when the sound of my father's ringtone brings everything to a standstill.

I can hear the muffled sound of his voice, but it's only when I hear the sound of his footsteps retreating down the hall that I let out the breath I've been holding. Walking over to my immaculately made bed, I sit down, letting my gaze drop to my shaking hands that rest in my lap. I try and think of an excuse not to go, but the thought of not going makes my chest feel heavy, and knots fill my stomach.

There's a knock at my door, and as I look up, my mother's soft, smiling face peeks into my room.

"You ready?"

Wiping my sweaty palms down the front of my navy jeans, I wince when they leave a mark.

I'll have to change before my father returns.

My mother must sense my hesitancy as she walks toward me, taking a seat beside me.

"You deserve a childhood, Cruz, regardless of what your father might tell you." Her hand brushes my dark hair off my forehead, and I do my best to absorb her words. "Come on, the car's waiting."

The short trip there feels like an eternity today. Half of me is still inside my bedroom, not being the disappointment my father expects me to be, but the other half of me, my favorite half, is here, watching the fire-red leaves float to the ground as the town car winds up the long driveway of the Barker residence.

A few months back, at the beginning of summer, after my father announced I'd be attending Crestwood Private in the fall, my mother started sneaking me out of our Beverly Hills prison to the park down the street. She told me it would be nice to make some friends before I started at the all-boys school. I was happy I didn't have to spend my days being home-schooled in that house anymore, but after a few visits to the park and a few failed attempts at making friends, I felt as lonely there as I did at the prison I called home.

Just wanting to leave, I headed for the town car when something caught my eye. A tall, blond man was smiling and laughing as his children tried to fly a kite. I watched on in amazement at how encouraging, kind, and gentle-natured he was when they couldn't get it to fly. If this were me with my father, I would have been scolded into oblivion by now for how pathetic I was. My mother must have noticed my staring, and before I knew it, she had set up a play date at the Barker house for the following week.

I barely slept that week. Excitement and fear crashed together, filling me with anxiety. If my father found out I was ignoring a direct order, there'd be hell to pay, but I couldn't shake the feeling of warmth I felt in their presence. The first visit was a little awkward; I didn't know how to function as a kid. My father had programmed me that there was no time for that kind of nonsense. If I wanted to be successful, I had to start early. Get a leg up on the competition was repeated to me more times than I could count. But as time went by, my weekly visits to the Barker house just got better and better, and as much as the repercussions terrified me if my father ever found out, the warmth inside my skin was too addicting to let go.

The car comes to a stop, and I'm pulled out of my head, but the feeling in the pit of my stomach won't go away. I try to ignore it as I slide out of the car where the tall, overly joyful Henry Barker is walking toward me.

"Hi, Cruz. Tristan and Taylah are down by the river. Do you need me to walk you down?"

I shake my head. "No, thank you, sir, I can manage." He nods at me, and I make my way down to the river that lies to the left of the property. With my hands in my jean pockets and my head down, I watch the colorful leaves crunch under my shoes as I try and ignore the anxious feeling that's creeping over me. The wind picks up, and I lift my head to see a burst of color fall from one of the many maple trees on the property. That's when I hear her laugh and instantly feel a wave of calm settle over me, causing a slight tug to my lips, which might have even formed a smile if I allowed it.

My eyes search the riverbank until I see her. Taylah Barker. I stop walking as my chest squeezes. Her smile makes my chest feel fluttery, and I lose my ability to take a breath. She's wearing her yellow sundress with little daisies all over it as her long blonde hair whips though the warm breeze. I've never met anyone in my entire life who projects so much sunshine from within. If she were a color, she'd most definitely be yellow.

As I make my way toward them, my mind starts to wander.

If I were a color, what would I be?

Grey is the first color that comes to mind. It feels the most opposite of yellow, which makes total sense.

"Hey! You made it." Tristan walks over to me, flicking his blond hair out of his eyes, readying for our handshake as Taylah watches from a picnic blanket nearby. "You get to meet Trey today. He goes to Crestwood Private too. I would've introduced you sooner, but he's been away with his family in Canada for months; his brother plays hockey for some team there."

"Tristan!"

I turn at the same time Tristan does to see a boy who looks around the same age as us making his way over. The same blond hair hangs over his forehead, just like Tristan, which makes me run my fingertips through my dark hair. His grin takes over his entire face, and I think to myself how easily these people give away their smiles.

"Hey, I'm Trey." He stands in front of me waving excitedly.

"Cruz." I wince internally at the abruptness in my tone. He draws his brows together for a split second before his over-the-top smile returns.

"Is that a rope swing?" He walks past us and over to the edge of the riverbank.

"Yeah." Tristan shouts running after him, "Come on, Cruz!"

I realize I didn't think to pack swim trunks, and jeans aren't the most appropriate swimming outfit. But when I see Taylah looking at me over the top of her book like I'm some kind of lost, scared animal, I pull my shirt off my body, toe my shoes off, and walk down to the water. I dive in, staying under for as long as I can, as I attempt to wash away the feeling of sympathy that was so clearly spelled out over her face. When I finally break the surface, I glance her way. Her eyes meet mine only for a second before she's buried back into the pages of her book.

After an hour or so of swimming and throwing around the football Trey brought with him, I get out of the water and walk over to where Taylah is seated next to a pile of towels. Wiping the water from my face, I see she's smiling at me. In a world where everything feels cold, even in the California sun, I'm becoming addicted to the way being near her makes me feel.

"Sandwich?" She points to the picnic basket beside her, her lips widening into a smile that makes my heart beat out of rhythm.

"Yes, please." I take a seat next to her doing my best to hide my nerves as she digs around inside the basket, handing me a sandwich and a bottle of water.

"Hey, Cruz, you want to go climb the fig tree?" A soaking-wet Tristan and Trey stare at me as they point a little further down the river. I shake my head and hold up the sandwich in my hand. They shrug before disappearing down the edge of the river. I almost regret the decision to stay as the silent minutes pass between us when I hear her speak.

"Why are you always so sad?" I stop mid-chew as my body stiffens at the question, torn between embarrassment and shame. I try and swallow the half-chewed food in my mouth but start to choke. "Are you okay?"

I nod as I wash it down with the water she handed me earlier. Turning away from her, I try and think of something cool to say. Something that's so far from the truth that it might make me seem somewhat normal.

A rustle of plastic brings me back to reality as her hand stretches out in front of me with an open packet of cotton candy. I almost tell her no thank you, it would be another rule of my father's I would be breaking. A strict no-sweets policy for as long as I can remember. But not wanting another reason to feel like the weird outcast, I pinch a handful between my fingers.

"Thank you," I answer as I turn to face her. She nods and smiles as she slides some of the candy into her mouth, and I mimic her movements.

"Does that make you feel less sad?"

There's worry in her voice that makes me look away, and when I finally glance back at her, I'm met with her steel-grey eyes. My eyes fall to the way she licks at the blue sugar stain that coats her lips, and I can't look away. I do the same, not sure who's in charge of my movements right now because it feels like my brain is malfunctioning. The next few seconds feel like everything moves in slow motion. Her lips are pressed to mine, and my heart explodes as I'm flooded with a joy-filled explosion of happiness. Warmth is pouring through my veins as my mind silences into a calm I've never known. She breaks away from me, and I try and fail to catch my breath, immediately feeling the loss of her as shades of pink fill her cheeks.

"Sorry. I thought it might make you feel better. I don't know why I..." She looks away from me, and I want to say something, but my brain has failed to catch up.

"Taylah, look what we found!" I hear her brother call her name, and before I can say anything, I'm watching her yellow sundress disappear into the trees that line the riverbank. I slowly lick my lips, letting the sweet taste of cotton candy explode along my tongue. A taste I'm sure I'll never forget.

The whole ride home I feel like I'm floating on a cloud. When her lips met mine, it was like I finally found a way to take some of her sunshine and bury it inside myself. I glance up at my mother, who's gazing out the window with a soft smile across her face, and I wish I could take this moment and freeze time. But as the tall iron gates open to our prison, reality forces its way back into my life. My mother stiffens beside me, and when I look out the window, I see exactly what's causing her distress. My father's silver Porsche... parked right there in front of us.

That means he's home. That means he knows.

I break out into a sweat as the tiny bit of sunshine I'd captured starts to slip away from me, making my bones feel heavy. My mother grips my face, pulling me to look at her, as a look of horror flashes behind her eyes.

"Listen to me. I want you to go to your room and shut your door, and no matter what you hear, you do not come out. Do you understand me?" I can feel her body shaking, and I don't know how to answer. "Tell me you understand, Cruz." Her grip tightens around my cheeks, and her tone is as serious as I've ever heard. I nod as a hot tear spills down my face.

"I understand."

I don't know how I made it to my bedroom. The entire way up the metal staircase and down the hall, my legs felt like they wanted to collapse beneath me, but I made it. It's silent for a long time, and exhaustion eventually overtakes me, my eyes growing heavy as the world starts to fall away.

"Stop!"

I'm jolted out of my sleep by the sound of my mother's screams. My first instinct is to run to find her, but her words replay inside my head as I reach for the doorknob, *"No matter what you hear, do not come out."*

I stand there with my hand on the doorknob, torn between obeying my mother's wishes and running to be by her side. Another scream, and I throw the door open, my heart pounding in my ears as I race down the hall. A thud inside my father's office, draws my attention. I almost trip over myself as I push my way through the threshold, my mother's eyes finding mine, widening with fear. But my attention is taken up by my father's hand wrapped around her throat. Heat flares inside me as I run to her, her panicked eyes screaming at me to stop, but I can't.

One more step, and I'll bury myself between them like a shield. That's my last thought before I'm laid out on the floor, my ears ringing as the glow of the golden chandelier twinkles above me. I see stars as I squint around the room. That's when I notice my father's phone lying on the floor next to his desk. It takes everything in me to lift my head off the ground, but I manage to roll over, grab the phone, and run as fast as my legs can take me as I dial 911.

I don't remember much after the operator answered my call. I know I must have given out our address because there are red and blue lights flashing outside my window. The house is quiet, too quiet, but my body is shaking so badly, I can't move. I hear footsteps outside my door and tighten the grip on my father's phone that's still sitting inside my hand.

The door clicks open, and my mother walks in. Pulling her golden silk robe tighter, she closes the door. It feels like an eternity passes before her eyes finally come up to meet mine, an empty look behind them that I've never seen before. She walks over to my bed and takes a seat, patting the space next to her. I want to ask her if she's okay, but I don't know how to say it.

I take a seat beside her as her cold hands slide my father's phone from my grip. She lets out a sigh as she stares out my window, her silence making me nervous.

"Calling the police was the wrong thing to do, Cruz."

I feel the world around me collapsing in on itself. I didn't know what she was going to say, but it definitely wasn't that. I sit there in silence, not quite understanding what I'd done wrong. "Your father only wants what's best for his family; success is something he has worked very hard for. His rules are in place to ensure you reach the same heights of success, and I realize that now."

No.

My heart sinks so deep into my stomach that I'm scared it's disappeared altogether. Sweat beads down my face as silent minutes stretch out.

"Your father will not allow you to spend any further time at the Barkers." My throat burns as tears threaten to fall down my face. "You will still be able to attend Crestwood, but your father needs you to get serious about your future."

A rogue tear escapes, rolling down my cheek, and that's when my mother finally looks at me. "Crying is a sign of weakness, Cruz." The lack of emotion in her tone terrifies me. She sounds exactly like my father right now, Mr. Jack Valentine himself. She doesn't look at me again as she leaves the room, and as soon as the door closes, I feel something tear apart inside me. Taking a breath, I walk over to my mirror and look at my reflection. My eyes are red, my hair is messy, and my face is wet and puffy from my tears. I look every bit as weak as my father says I am.

Enough is enough.

I wipe at my face, straighten my hair, and make a promise to myself never to feel anything again. It hurts like hell, and I'm not about to put myself through any of this again. Walking to my bed, the new me slips under the covers, and I feel the steel walls locking into place inside my chest. One summer. I got one summer where life didn't feel so heavy. And as I lie here staring at the ceiling, I know that the events of today have changed me forever.

Chapter Two

Cruz – Present Day

"**H**e's been a disappointment to the Valentine name since the day he was born."

I'm staring at the closed door to my father's office as he does his usual rant about me to my mother. I've been home from college for less than an hour, and I've already been summoned.

"Pathetic, worthless, weak, all from your side of the family, Elaine." My stomach twists with rage, listening to the way he talks to my mother, and I take that as my cue to walk in, allowing him to project the anger to where he wants to most.

As I step inside, his bright-red face comes up to meet mine as sweat glistens along his dark, pristine hairline. His office is modern, with twists of grey metal and black accents. Cold and sterile, just like his soul.

"You wanted to see me?"

His eyes narrow as his forehead creases, the crystal whiskey glass in his hand all but shatters as his body tenses at my presence. I side-eye my mother, who's standing against the far wall, a look of distress painted down her face and the remnants of a purple mark left on her cheek. As always, *I'm* the Valentine name disappointment, and it's *her* fault she couldn't have any more kids, so *he's* stuck with me.

"Sit." He nods to the chair that faces his desk, and as much as I'd love to give him a taste of his own medicine, he'll just take it out on my mother after I leave the room. He's never raised a hand to her in front of me again since the night I called the police, but the way she cowers in his presence says it all.

The silence is deafening as he stares at me in disgust, taking a long, slow slip from his whiskey-filled glass. "You've been accepted as a summer intern at Valentine Enterprises, that only accepts 150 people, and you want to spend the summer whoring around Malibu instead?"

Mr. Jack Valentine in fine form. CEO of Valentine Enterprises, one of the largest private equity firms in LA, is awaiting the day his only son graduates with an MBA from Colombia University, just like he did. I'll be thrown headfirst into working for him, and I need this summer for my fucking sanity. He waits for my fight, but right now, I don't feel like arguing; it's been a long day. Besides, I've only been accepted because he owns the fucking company.

"Tristan's parents are letting him use the Barker family beach house for the summer," I answer blankly. I met Tristan when I was twelve years old, and we've been inseparable ever since. He's also lucky enough to have a family the exact opposite of this shit show that's unraveling before me.

"You know how many people would love the opportunity to work at my company over the summer, and here you are, pissing this opportunity up the wall." His face contorts like he's just sucked the juice from a lemon. "Ever the disappointment, aren't we, Cruz?" He throws the rest of the amber liquid down his throat before slamming the glass down onto his sterile desk. I see my mother flinch out of the corner of my eye, and I need to wrap up this conversation before things take a turn.

I feel my phone vibrate in my pocket, and when my father shakes his head, I regret not leaving it in my room.

"I would have thought by your age, you would've learned some respect."

As much as I'd love to give him a lecture on what respect means, I also know there's no arguing with Jack Valentine, and I really need this summer break.

"Sorry." The apology feels sour as it rolls out of my mouth, especially when he smiles, satisfied he's produced an apology out of me, and that's when I use this moment to plead my case. "This summer break will be my way of leaving everything behind. The final pieces of myself to tie up before returning to New York to finish school." He stares at me intently before his left brow raises, contemplating what's just come out of my mouth. "I'll leave everything you despise about me in Malibu and focus on the man you want me to become." He narrows his eyes at me as a hollow feeling bottoms out in my stomach at what I've just promised. Like I've just sold my soul to the devil.

"Deal."

My black duffel bag is packed, and after I shower, brush my teeth, and throw on some grey basketball shorts, a white tee, and some runners, I'm ready. Slinging my bag over my body, I head down the metal staircase that leads to the bottom level of the house. I've barely touched down when I hear my father call me from the living room. Closing my eyes and gritting my teeth, I turn and head in his direction.

"Yes?"

He's reading the financial review and doesn't even look up to acknowledge my presence. Instead, he reaches beside himself before throwing a set of keys at my face. Luckily, I'm quick; otherwise, I'd be sporting a fat lip for the summer.

"Take the new Range Rover—your death trap stays here." I go to turn away when I hear him speak again. "One fuckup, and I'll have that car you love so much crushed, Cruz." I clutch at the keys and walk away before I make it any worse for myself.

Jogging down the slate front steps, I spot the silver Range Rover a few spaces down, my line of sight drifting to my 1967 Shelby GT500 parked a few spaces away. He was less than amused that I bought such a *"degenerate piece of shit,"* in his words. He's been waiting for an excuse to have it crushed. He'd probably chain me there to watch, knowing my father.

Throwing my bag in the back and sliding into the driver's seat, I open the sunroof and welcome the warmth. Being away at Columbia University during one of the coldest New York winters has made me miss the California heat.

I barely make it out of the driveway when my phone starts ringing. Seeing its Tristan, I click it to Bluetooth.

"I'm on my way."

"Dude, I've been calling you. I was worried your father cut you up into pieces and fed you to his pet snake."

Not wanting to rehash today's monstrosity of events, I change the subject.

"I'll be five minutes."

"Okay, just come straight through the house; we're over by the pool."

Five minutes later almost to the exact minute, I'm pulling up at the Barker's. One of the more expensive houses in Beverley Hills, with a driveway that winds up their estate lined with maple trees that turn fire red in autumn. Perfectly manicured lawns that stretch as far as the eye can see. The remnants of a lingering spring surround me, as the scent of wildflowers spill into the cabin. This place is as warm and welcoming as the family that fills its walls.

The white colonial-style house comes into view, and I park off to the side before heading up the stone steps, taking the heavy brass door handle into my hand and letting myself in.

As soon as I step inside, I'm filled with the familiarity of white walls lined with Barker family photos. As I walk through, one catches my eye. A very grown-up Taylah, on stage, standing in front of a grand piano. Long, silky blonde hair frames her face, and her steel-grey eyes sparkle under the bright stage lights that encase her angelic existence. The famous Barker bright white smile that I've seen her brother flash a million and one girls throughout the years sprawled across her perfectly symmetrical face. A familiar current of warmth zaps through my veins, a feeling I haven't felt in years, and the insurgent of it knocks the wind from my chest.

I hear Tristan's laugh from somewhere outside, but I can't seem to tear my eyes away from her; the feeling of seeing her again is like a heroin fix. The last memory I hold of her is when we were just kids. When my father found out my mother had been sneaking me out of the house, I was never allowed back. That was until I hit my teen years, but by then, Taylah was in New York at some prestigious music school. She may have grown into a woman, but the eyes looking back at me are the same ones that I used to dream about when life started slipping further into the dark. The summer I got to spend here at the Barker house is filled with the only moments of my childhood worth remembering, and she was a huge part of that. I know nothing about who she grew up to become, and she may never know the magnitude of the effect she had on my life. The girl in the yellow sundress, radiating nothing but light, saved me more times than she'll ever know.

Taking a step back, I clear my throat as I head in the direction of the outdoor pool where Tristan said he would be. Stepping out into the California heat, I see Trey and Tristan arguing about something before diving into the pool and I follow the cobblestone path to where Henry Barker is turning steak on the barbecue.

"Cruz. How's that business degree treating you?" He turns to face me, sporting the same bright white smile his kids inherited.

"It's going well, sir."

"Take a seat, this is almost ready."

I sit down at the outdoor dining table as Tristan's mother, Lauren, places a few different salads across the table in front of me.

"Nice to see you again, Cruz." She smiles, sliding a plate in front of me.

"You too, Mrs. Barker."

"Valentine." I look up as Tristan drops down into the seat beside me, shaking his wet hair all over me, as Trey takes the seat across from me. "This summer is going to be the complete brain reset I need."

Henry lets out a grumble as he slides a tray of meat onto the table. "Tristan, keep the parties to a minimum, please. You're a future doctor for god's sake."

Tristan just smiles without the slightest attempt at a response, while Henry playfully shakes his head, taking Lauren's hand as they retreat back into the house.

"I can't wait to get to the beach house. Endless parties, hot women, sun, and sand. Your parents are fucking legends, Tristan," Trey announces as he stacks his plate with meat. "You excited Valentine? Will we see that non-existent smile make an appearance this summer?" His sky-blue eyes flash with humor as he shovels a spoonful of potato salad into his mouth.

I stay silent.

"You definitely have that dark and brooding thing down pat."

Here we go. I roll my eyes and shake my head as Tristan buts in.

"Have we decided who's driving to Malibu?" he asks, leaning back in his seat, and glancing from me to Trey.

"I have my dad's new Range Rover; it has plenty of space if you want me to drive," I answer as I wash my food down with a glass of water before wiping the back of my hand across my lips.

"Why don't you have your car?" Trey asks. They both know how much I love my car, so I can understand the confusion on their faces. I just shrug, not wanting to get into it right now. Just the thought of talking about my father puts a sour taste in my mouth.

"That could work, considering you're the only one out of the three of us who doesn't drink," Tristan answers just as his parents make their way back over to us.

"Behave yourself and keep an eye on your sister, please," Henry states as he helps Lauren clear away our plates, before heading back inside the house.

Wait a minute, sister? My heart drops into my stomach and I break out into a cold sweat.

"So Taylah's coming to the beach house too?" Trey asks before I get the chance, leaning his arms over the back of his chair. "Is she driving down with us?"

Hearing Taylah's name leave Trey's mouth creates an agitation inside me.

"No, she's still wrapping up a final essay or something at Brown before she can take her summer break. She's meeting us there tomorrow night with Lexi."

A flush of heat assaults me as a thousand different thoughts run through my head, but all I manage is, "You didn't mention Taylah was going to be there."

Tristan gives me a confused look. "Is that a problem?"

"Will Meredith have an issue with you being at a house with another female? I know she's territorial, but I thought you broke up?" Trey cuts in.

"We did. There's no issue; I just didn't know, that's all." Their eyes are on me, and I need this conversation to end immediately.

"Damn, so a day and a half until I see Tristan's hot sister."

A wave of accelerated heat floods my body as pure rage threatens to break the surface. I can barely see straight as everything becomes a blur. It takes me a minute to register that Tristan is out of his seat tackling a remorseful Trey into the pool. Leaving me buried in a sea of my own thoughts. I'm thankful Tristan was out of his seat faster than me because, the way I feel right now, I seriously doubt I'd let Trey come up for air.

Driving down the California coast with the sunroof open, the warmth of the sun's rays, and the smell of salt in the air would almost be the peace I've been searching for if it wasn't for Tristan and Trey blasting "California Gurls" by Katy Perry, seeing who can sing louder. I'm five seconds from pulling over and throwing all their shit in the ocean. This is how our friend dynamic usually works. Tristan and Trey, the blond-haired golden retrievers, are all sunshine and rainbows. Meanwhile, I'm the dark cloud and complete outcast.

The sun is already setting as we pull up in the driveway. We exit the car as the accelerated bass coming from the house next door draws our attention. Add in girls laughing and screaming out "shots" has both Trey and Tristan snapping their necks at each other.

Dropping their bags, the race for the front door has begun as they fight for entry. Fixing my bag over my shoulder, I let out a sigh before following them inside, listening to them bicker as they trip over each other to get a glimpse of the girls next door.

This is gonna be one long fucking summer.

Chapter Three

Taylah

Taking a breath, I click submit on my essay about social justice before I finally get to leave for summer break. The door clicks open behind me, and I turn to see my roommate Skylar struggling through the door before dropping the cardboard box she's holding onto the floor. Her father is the mayor of New York City, but you'd never know it by looking at her. She's wearing ripped jeans and a band shirt splatted with red paint, accessorized with her maroon Doc Martens. She blows her wild cowgirl copper curls out of her face and drops to her knees as she rifles through the contents.

"What's in the box?" I ask as I close my laptop and get to my feet.

"Court transcripts from that case I told you about with the makeup company profiting off cosmetics that're still being tested on animals." The frustration on her face as she reads through some of the papers makes me smile. I know I'm passionate about making a difference in the world, but Skylar—she's on a mission to bring the world to its knees one corrupt CEO at a time.

"Is there anything I can help you with before I go?" I ask closing up my suitcase.

"Hold down this CEO and let me pour gasoline-based products down his throat?" Her trademark sinister smirk appears, and to be honest, she's a little scary. "I'm joking, Tay. Go have fun building sandcastles and suntanning or whatever normal people do at beach houses over summer break."

I laugh as I slide my suitcase off my bed. "You sure you don't want an extra pair of hands to help take over the world?"

She smiles and shakes her head. "No, thank you. That's an easy solo mission." I laugh to myself as I head out the door.

Exiting the building, I jog down the slate steps. Sliding my phone from my jeans pocket, I send off a quick text to my best friend Lexi, telling her I'm officially on summer break before shoving it back into my pocket as I head across the lawn.

There's one more place I need to go before I can leave.

I head west, walking past the fig trees I spent most of my free time reading under, and as much as I need this break, I'll miss it here.

About ten minutes pass when the building I'm looking for comes into view.

The library.

I walk up the stone steps, taking in the ageless white marble, and the worn oak doors add some much-needed warmth. I step inside and the beauty of the structure takes my breath away. In the center of the room, there are wooden study tables, each housed with halos of light emanating from green and gold table lamps. Oil paintings of a time long before watch over the room as the lighting from the golden chandeliers creates warm pockets of light, followed by the slivers of sun that creep in through window slots, sending rays of warmth to the bookshelves that encase the entire room. I'm pulled out of my musing by the buzzing of my phone in my back pocket. Sliding it out, I see Lexi's name flash across the screen.

"I am so ready to beach boy hunt." The excitement in her voice makes me laugh. I quietly slide the books I'm returning out of my bag, setting them on the front desk and ducking out the entrance before I answer.

"I'm just leaving campus now. My plane leaves at 5:00 a.m. tomorrow morning."

She lets out a groan. "Here I am, still wishing your first year would be so devastatingly boring that you'd run back to LA to be with me."

I met Lexi in high school at a prestigious music and acting school in New York. Since both of our families were back in LA, we immediately connected. Our plan was to finish school here and attend college together. But when I was offered a place at Brown, and Lexi got into an amazing acting school in LA, we've been running on a long-distance best friendship.

"And what exactly would I do in LA?"

"Serenade me daily with your piano playing skills."

I laugh. "You know my dream is to study politics, Lex."

She lets out a sigh of defeat. "I know. I just miss you."

"You get me for the whole summer. I'll see you tomorrow." I laugh as she ends the call with another melodramatic groan. With how theatrical she is, her career will take off in no time.

I swing my white Jeep into Lexi's parents' driveway and see she's already out front with her bags flanked on either side of her. She wears a bright-red bikini top with a short denim skirt as her sleek chocolate-brown hair blows in the breeze against her tanned skin. Her older brother walks out, and I take a moment to catch my breath.

Sam Summers.

He's three years older than us and is all tanned skin and muscles. He's training to be a firefighter, and as he picks up Lexi's bags for her in one easy swing, it shows. He slides them into the back of my car, and steps toward my open window. Leaning against my door, his dark brown eyes find mine.

"You sure someone as lovely as you wants to spend the entire summer with Little Miss Out of Control over there?"

The door slams beside me as Lexi slides into the passenger seat. "Out of control?"

I look back at Sam as he chuckles to himself, taking in his beautiful smile.

"How many vodka shots have you had?" His eyes are on me, but I know he's talking to his sister.

"Four." Lexi laughs out.

"My point exactly." He smiles shaking his head at her. He leans back, his hands still gripping my door as his biceps tighten.

"Have a nice summer, Tay." Tapping my door, he turns back to the house, peace-signing us away as I slide into reverse, willing my heart rate to return to a normal rhythm.

Lexi starts skipping songs on my playlist as we hit the California coast, searching for the perfect summer sound-track. Finally settling on "Cruel Summer" by Taylor Swift, she leans back into her seat, and starts singing.

"Sam would've been a nice addition this summer."

She shakes her head, turning the volume up. "Stop saying that. How would you feel if I obsessed over Tristan?" She turns and smirks at me, and we can't help but laugh. Lexi and Tristan can't stand each other. I've had to pull them both aside and make them promise me that they'll try and get along this summer for my sanity. They both swore they'd just ignore each other, but living in the same house for three months, I know it will only be a matter of time before things erupt.

"What are your plans when we get there?" Lexi asks as she applies another coat of gloss, smacking her lips.

"Soak up some sun with a good book."

She looks at me with raised brows. "Well, *you* can lay out reading about those fictional men who don't exist, and *I'll* be off finding one who wants to devour me all night."

"Good luck finding a man like that; those men only exist in books," I respond mid-laugh. She scoffs at me and leans back in her seat.

"They exist, Taylah. We just haven't found them yet."

I smile and nod at her, not wanting to burst her bubble on day one. Maybe she's right; maybe men like the ones in books do exist. I'm not sure where you would find one, but I seriously doubt a summer holiday house in Malibu with immature boys running around doing body shots is going to be the place.

We pull up, and it's unusually quiet. I can hear the waves crashing against the shore and birds chirping as I grab my phone from the console and slide out of the car.

"It's mid-afternoon. I would've thought Tristan and Trey would've had a raging party well established by now." I state, opening the back door and sliding my suitcase out. "I'm impressed."

Lexi doesn't bother grabbing her things; instead, she heads straight for the door. I follow her in, and as soon as we enter, I'm rendered speechless. Dropping my suitcase onto the floor, I take in the state of what I'm looking at.

It's a fucking mess.

"Well, this explains why they're so quiet. Hungover, guarantee it." Lexi shakes her head as she kicks a purple bikini top across the floor. Clothes are strewn all over the place, red drinking cups litter almost every surface, while ping pong balls scatter the floor.

"Why are boys like this?" She lets out a groan as she picks up a yellow thong off the white leather couch. "I can't do this." She shudders. "I'm going for a swim before I murder them all."

I watch as she storms toward the glass-paneled door that leads outside. I decide against following her, not ready to deal with her wrath. Picking up my suitcase, I head down the hall toward my bedroom. As my door comes into view, I pray that Tristan was not stupid enough to let anyone crash in there.

Cautiously, I open the door, relief washing over me when I see looks untouched. I head right for my timber canopy bed with sheer white drapes tied to each corner and lay against the soft white comforter. It faces floor-to-ceiling windows that watch out over the beach, and I feel my body giving into exhaustion as I watch the waves roll in. The early flight, then traveling here, combined with Lexi's impending outburst, have drained me.

Feeling sticky from the hot ride in, I slide off the bed and head for my ensuite for a quick refresh. The marble tiling with timber and gold accents really sets the coastal vibe. Taking the gold handle into my hand, I let the water steam up the room as I remove my clothes before stepping under its warmth and reaching for my shampoo. The smell of coconut fills the air, taking me back to my summers here with my family. I have to pinch myself sometimes at how lucky I am. I've been blessed with some of the most loving and understanding parents to ever exist.

When I was ten, I became obsessed with the piano. My father, being the supportive man he is, built a completely soundproof room here at the beach house so I could still practice throughout the summer. I spent more time in that room than I did on the sand after that. There's something so unearthly peaceful about music, and the way the notes hit the walls and vibrate back to me, enveloping me in peace.

Finishing up, I pluck one of the plush white towels off the marble countertop before wrapping it around my body and walking back to my room. Still lost in the nostalgic daydream inside my head, I slam straight into a solid body. Arms grab at me before I hit the ground in a panicked state. Confused, I look up, and my heart drops into my stomach as an overwhelming flood of heat butterflies through my chest.

"Cruz?"

Alarm flushes his face as he slides the headphones off his ears to link around his neck; those familiar honey-colored eyes study me, right before...

"My eyes are up here." It comes out more hostile than I intended as I grip the towel tighter to my body. He holds out his hand to help me to my feet, as the warmth of his fingers melt against mine.

"Sorry." Turning away, he grabs his bag off the floor, and heads for the exit, and for a moment, I'm rendered speechless at the sheer size of him. He's at least six foot two, with muscles that he definitely had to work for.

"Wait, why are you even in my room?" He pauses right before he reaches the door as I wait for a response that never comes. The door closes behind him, and I'm left with more questions than answers as Lexi slams her way inside my room.

"Your brother will be the death of me." She looks flushed as she drops down onto my bed, letting out a groan.

"You knew he was going to be here. This is as much his beach house as it is mine, Lex." I fake a laugh, my body still in a state of shock at what just happened. I knew Cruz was going to be here, too, but nothing prepared me for seeing those tortured eyes again. I distract myself, looking through my bag for something to wear as Lexi complains behind me.

"He's all like, 'I'm sorry, Lexi. Taylah told me you guys would be here later tonight. I thought I had time to clean up.'" She rolls over and buries her head into my pillow.

"Well, he's right... we did get here earlier than expected. Lucky you have your own room and don't have to curl up next to him." I joke, sliding on a pair of denim shorts and a white crop, letting my wet hair hang loose.

"I don't know how all the girls fall for that overly sweet attitude he's got going on. He makes me nauseous." She flips back over and sits up, her face twisting with frustration. I watch as she animatedly slides off my bed, before walking over to the window that looks out over the ocean as she continues to moan about Tristan.

If two best friends were total opposites, that's me and Lexi. She's always the life of the party. Tanned skin, brown hair, and dark eyes—a direct contrast to me. While I do tan up nice in the summer, her all-year-round natural glow is stunning. I have blonde hair and grey eyes, and most defi-nitely am not the life of the party on any occasion. It works well; she loves the limelight, and I hate it. We complement each other, and it just works.

"Wait." She turns abruptly and I'm met with curious eyes. "Did Cruz Valentine just leave your room? While you were naked?" Her grin transforms into a wicked smirk.

"One, I wasn't naked." I feel myself on the immediate defence.

"So, he was in here? Why?"

I shrug, not having an answer to give. To be honest, I'd actually like to know the answer to that myself. I haven't seen Cruz since I was ten years old. I checked in with Tristan from time to time to see if he was okay, but when he started dating LA royalty, Meredith White, daughter of famous movie director Richard White, I never asked again.

"It's a shame he broke up with Meredith. I could have asked him to bring her here so I could befriend my way into the Hollywood circle. Imagine meeting her father!"

A knock at the door interrupts her joyful proclamation, and she walks over to open it. "What the hell do you want?"

"Is my sister in there?" I hear Tristan's voice on the other side of the door as Lexi pulls it open aggressively, and heads to my ensuite out of sight.

"Sorry about the mess. Trey and I got a little out of hand last night. Exams kicked my ass, and I partied a little too hard. I thought you two were arriving tonight?" He apologises, running a remorseful hand through his messy hair.

"I finished my assessment early."

"Well, I've got Trey out there mopping as we speak." He walks over and brings me in for an apologetic hug. "Sorry, sis."

We break apart, and he goes to leave when Lexi steps out of the bathroom.

"We want a meeting. There needs to be rules in place if we're all going to be living together for three months." Tristan vibrates with irritation just from the sound of her voice.

"Fine, give me twenty minutes to finish cleaning up. We'll meet in the living room."

Chapter Four

Cruz

The boys got a little too carried away last night by the looks of this house. I've seen Trey pick up at least four different sets of bikinis. Tristan looks like death, but I'm not sure if it's the hangover or the wrath of Lexi Summers. And here I am, walking around with a black trash bag, cleaning up a mess I had nothing to do with. As soon as the house started overflowing with dramatic, loud, and heavily intoxicated women, I took my ass to bed. The last thing I need is my father catching a glimpse of one of these random chicks' Instagram with me in a compromised state to use this as an *I told you so* while crushing my car.

Not long after I left for bed, Trey fell into the room we share with a girl under each arm. Not wanting to witness whatever the fuck he had planned, I got out of there before his pants hit the floor, heading to the only room I knew would be unaccompanied throughout the night, Taylah's. One good thing about Tristan is his respect for his family, especially his sister. Even in his intoxicated state, he would never let randoms into her room, so I knew it was the perfect place to hide in peace. He told me she and Lexi were arriving later tonight, so when I got back from the gym, the last person I thought I'd see was a very grown-up Taylah Barker wrapped up in nothing but a towel.

I don't know a lot about who she grew up to become, but I always pictured her with that gorgeous smile as the warmth of the sun filled her pink cheeks with her face buried in a book. Seeing her today, with that same starry gaze, has ignited a craving to know everything there is to know about her.

"Can we get this over with? I have a tan to work on and guys to meet." Lexi strolls into the living room where I'm currently tying up the last trash bag before falling onto the couch with a very dramatic eye roll. Taylah walks in behind her and I take a moment to drink her in. I trail my eyes up the length of her, pausing at the way the curve of her hips fills out those tight denim shorts. She takes a seat next to Lexi and I look away as I dump the rubbish at the door.

"Can you not shout; my head's pounding," Trey whispers as he drops onto the couch opposite them, followed by Tristan. I head over to join them, taking a seat with the boys.

"So, we're all going to be living together for the next three months, and obviously, we want to spend the summer enjoying ourselves," Lexi starts.

"Yeah, we do." Tristan and Trey bump fists as Lexi continues.

"Anyway, if we could please just keep the orgies to the bedrooms, that would be great. I don't want to be removing women's clothing from the kitchen counter while I eat my granola, fair?"

Tristan and Trey look at each other and then back at Lexi. They start arguing about the pool area and bathrooms, but I'm distracted by my heartbeat pounding in my ears as my eyes travel up Taylah's long, slender legs. Her toned stomach that's bare, right before a white tank top suffocates her very round breasts as her hard little nipples peak through the soft material.

She has no fucking bra on.

"Good luck getting Cruz to dress up." Trey's voice unpleasantly ruptures my thoughts.

"What?"

"Tristan's birthday is in two weeks. Dress-up party. You could dress up as a Dementor from Harry Potter and suck the life out of the room, easy." Trey smirks, and Tristan falls into a fit of laughter. I don't even render a response; instead, I turn my attention back to Taylah, whose eyes are locked on mine.

"I'm so excited for this; what're you going to dress up as?" Lexi is jumping in her seat with eagerness. This girl can go from zero to a hundred in a millisecond. Wasn't she just mad? She's firing off costume choices at Taylah who's eyes don't leave mine in a stare off that neither of us want to break. "Maybe we could dress up as slutty nurses. What do you think, Tay?"

Taylah turns to her friend when she hears her name while I silently choke on the idea of an innocent Taylah Barker dressed up as a slutty nurse. The images in my mind make my body flood with heat.

"Let's get some sun." I jolt as Lexi jumps to her feet, grabbing Taylah by the arm before disappearing down the hall.

"Where'd you take off to this morning? Your car wasn't here when I walked some of the girls out," Trey asks as he pops some pain relievers into his mouth, following them down with a glass of water.

"Gym."

"You know there's a gym here, right?" Tristan adds, nodding to the back of the house.

"It's hard to do a full-body workout when the gym equipment is littered with red cups and push-up bras."

Tristan leans back onto the couch as his features flood with regret.

"Yeah, we really lost control of the party last night. Knowing my sister is going to be here for the rest of the summer, I think I tried to really let loose before she arrived." He sits up and rests his head in his hands. "Oh god, I think I'm going to be sick."

As Tristan and Trey head back to their rooms to sleep off the remnants of their hangovers, I feel my phone vibrate in the pocket. As soon as I retrieve it, I wish I hadn't. I'm flooded with agitation when Meredith's name flashes across my screen with an incoming text.

> **Meredith:** You left without saying good-bye. You're really giving up on us so eas-ily?

I leave her on read and slide the phone back into my pocket when Taylah and Lexi walk back out, my eyes finding, then proceeding to undress Taylah's white bikini from her toned body. She doesn't glance in my direction, but by the way her cheeks heat up as she passes me, she knows I'm staring. My phone vibrates again, sending irritation up my spine, but when I slide it out, it turns to hatred as I see my father calling me.

"Hello?"

"When were you going to tell me you broke things off with Meredith White?" I close my eyes and lean my head back over the couch, gripping the phone so tight my fingers start to cramp. "Not that I'm surprised." He sighs. "Can you do anything fucking right? I handed that relationship to you on a silver platter."

My father has been pushing this relationship to progress further the entire time I was away at college. A relationship that imploded the day before summer break, where I walked in to find her on her knees with the captain of the basketball team shoved down her throat.

"Do you have anything to say for yourself, Cruz? Or is this just another fuckup to add to your ever-growing collection?"

"It's not going to work out." Shattering glass rains out, and it takes everything in me not to end the call.

"Enjoy your summer, Cruz, because when this is over, you will fix this." He ends the call, and I drop the phone onto the couch beside me. Before I can sink too far into the dark depths of my mind, I hear footsteps, and my eyes spring open, only to find a soaking-wet Taylah for the second time today.

She side-eyes me, that pink flush returning, only this time I feel my cock harden as I stare at the stream of water that drips from her hair, down her spine, and into the curve of her back.

The way my erection lies hard against my thigh, straining against my sweats, has me wishing I hadn't decided to go commando.

I watch intently as she heads into the kitchen, thankful for the open plan living that my line of sight can follow her every movement. She opens the stainless-steel fridge and grabs two bottles of water. But it's when she turns around to face me, and her magnetic eyes find mine as her pouty pink lips part, that causes real fucking damage.

Jesus Christ.

Both locked in a stare-off, my eyes drift to the subtle dip of her throat where her pulse point is beating erratically, finding some solace in the fact she's just as affected as I am right now.

"Taylah, you have to come see this!" Lexi's high-pitched voice rings out through the room. She jolts, and the bottles of water in her hands drop to the floor. She rushes to retrieve them as Lexi continues to talk. "Two blond-haired, panty-dropping surfer boys just ran into the ocean, and I feel the sudden urge to be rescued."

Before I know what's happened, Lexi is dragging Taylah out the glass door, and I'm left readjusting myself, once again alone with my thoughts.

"What a waste of a day." Tristan has finally ventured from his room, looking warily out to the sunset that's encasing the sky before lying down on the couch. "What'd you get up to today?"

"Went for a drive along the coastline," I answer without looking up from my phone as I delete all traces of Meredith from my socials.

"Bet you wish you had the Mustang instead. V8 engine, rumbling down the California coast. Wind in our hair." Pretty sure he's mocking me. I look up and meet his gaze as he lays with his arms behind his head.

"You wouldn't understand." I turn my phone back to silent and rest it face down on the glass coffee table.

"Is Trey awake yet?" he asks, glancing around the room.

I shake my head. "Haven't seen him."

"I'm starving," he counters, and as if right on cue, Taylah and Lexi walk into the house carrying bags of groceries. When I got back from the drive to clear my head, they weren't here, so I hadn't seen Taylah since our intimate stare-off until now. She has her back to me as she unloads the groceries onto the countertop and something inside me wills her to turn around.

"So, we got steaks and stuff to make a salad. Who's grilling?" Lexi looks from me to Tristan and back again. Tristan rolls onto his stomach and buries his face into the couch pillow.

"I'm all but dead." His muffled excuse makes Lexi's eyes roll into the back of her head.

"Cruz?" She stares at me, arms folded against her chest, with a look that she's going to stab me in the face if I say no. I get to my feet and make my way over to the kitchen, taking the steak from the countertop before heading for the exit.

"I'll take that as a yes," she shouts after me as I step out through the sliding glass door.

Chapter Five

Taylah

"He's such a hard person to read," Lexi announces as Cruz leaves the room and walks across the back deck, past the pool, toward the barbecue. "Maybe the breakup is taking its toll on him," Lexi adds as she shuffles through items inside the fridge.

I ignore the comment that his recent breakup is having a negative effect in him, as it flushes agitation over my skin. Instead, my thought process narrows in on the fact that while I haven't seen Cruz in years, it worries me to think that the sad boy I once knew grew up to be a sad man too. He never did tell me what was wrong all those years ago, but I'll never forget the haunted look behind those beautiful amber eyes.

"Can you ask Cruz to throw these on too?" Lexi asks, thrusting a container of chicken wings into my arms, and I take a moment to gather myself before working up the courage to head for the door. There was something unsaid between us today, and I know he felt it too. I'm not gonna lie; he really grew up over the years, and while I've yet to see him without a shirt on, the cuts of his muscles projecting through the thin cotton shirt he's wearing today, gives my libido a workout.

He has his back to me as I approach, and I'm thankful for the sound of sizzling steak that drowns out the sound of my hammering heart.

"Lexi asked if you could please add these." I say it so fast, I'm not sure he understands what falls out of my mouth. He's so dominating in his space as he stands there, tongs in hand, staring at the smoking steak. "Is that okay?" He barely acknowledges my existence, and my skin becomes clammy as I stand there waiting for him to respond.

"Never mind." I turn to leave, and feel his hand grab my wrist as streams of electricity coarse through my veins. Rattled and completely overwhelmed I rip my arm out of his grip. Before I can comprehend what happens next, he takes the chicken from my hands and adds it to the barbecue, all without his eyes ever meeting mine. I turn my back and rush for the house, as my heart bashes against my ribcage. Without looking back, I don't stop walking until I'm back inside the house staring at Lexi as she dices up a salad. She takes one look at me and freezes as her brows pinch in curiosity.

"Is everything okay?"

"What?" I'm unsure if she's focusing on the erratic pace of my heart or the confusion stamped across my face?

"Your face is flushed. You're not sunburnt, are you? Summer has barely even started." She looks back down and continues to dice up some tomatoes. I'm spared from responding when

I feel a body slide past the back of me, causing my heart to take a dive into my stomach. But from the smirk I see when I glance over my shoulder, I realize it's just Trey. He slides the painted white wooden stool away from the bench before taking a seat. His grin widens as he leans on his elbows, watching Lexi throw the salad into a bowl. I can see the frustration work its way over her features, knowing how much Trey is pushing her buttons.

"Is there something I can help you with, Trey Whittaker?" Lexi snaps, keeping her eyes on the salad she's tossing together, and I just know it's taking everything in her to not slap the smirk right off his face.

"One week," he announces, leaving Lexi and me both looking at each other like he's lost the plot.

"Excuse me?"

"I said one week." He repeats as his smirk widens.

"I heard you," Lexi snaps back.

"That's all I give you."

"Until what?"

"Until you and Tristan fuck."

This isn't going to end well.

I watch on as Lexi picks the knife back up, taking a cucumber, and slicing it aggressively into small pieces before tossing it into the salad.

"He comes anywhere near me, and that's what I'll do to his unwanted cock." She says it matter-of-factly as she snatches the bowl off the bench and heads for the back door.

"Jesus, why is she always so damn hostile?" Trey asks as I gather some plates and cutlery.

"Let's just go eat before I have to help her bury a body," I answer as I head for the door. He slides off the stool and jogs after me, throwing his arm around my shoulders as we make our way over to the outdoor dining table. I find myself searching for Cruz as we approach, but he's nowhere to be seen. I take a seat next to Lexi, and Trey sits across from me while Tristan jumps out of the pool before racing over and shaking his wet hair all over Lexi's back.

"Tristan Barker!" Lexi shrieks as Tristan proceeds to snatch a tomato off her plate before taking a seat next to Trey.

Dinner is relatively silent, apart from the constant vibration of Lexi's phone, and by the smile on her face, I assume it's the surfer boy she gave her number to today.

What was his name again? Oh, right, Jacob.

"It's rude to text at the dinner table, Lexi. Didn't your parents teach you any manners?" Her eyes roll at the sound of Tristan's voice, but she doesn't respond. It's only when we finish up and start to clear the plates away that Tristan snatches her phone out of her hands, running off toward the house.

"Tristan!"

"This, I've got to see." Trey is out of his seat just as fast, sprinting after the both of them.

I continue packing up when I see the glow of a phone in the distance down on the beach. It's only when the phone screen moves to light up his face that I see it's Cruz. The moon casts a beacon of light, just enough for me to watch as he runs a stressed hand down his face before bringing the phone to his ear. He looks tense.

Having not eaten with us, I make him up a plate of food and start down the wooden staircase that leads out onto the sand. His back is to me as I approach.

"Do you hear yourself? Why do you agree with him?" The tone in his voice to whoever is on the other end of the line is a cross between anger and desperation, his thick shoulders tensing under the fabric of his tight shirt. "What's it going to take for you to leave?" His voice breaks, and I suddenly feel horrible that I'm witnessing such a private conversation. I quickly turn around and head back toward the staircase when I hear him end the call.

"Taylah?" My heart drops into my stomach as the sound of crashing waves breaks up the silence that follows. I close my eyes and take a breath before turning around to face him. It's when his golden-laced eyes find mine, locking me in a state of panic, that I rethink my plan. He obviously wanted to be alone. He left the house and came down here to take a private call, and I stood there and listened.

"You missed dinner." I take a step closer, holding the plate of food out to him. His piercing stare intimidates me, my focus falling on the roll of his throat as he swallows. I take a step closer, with the plate of food still out in offering, but his eyes won't leave mine, threatening to pull me undone. I hold my composure and close the distance between us focusing on the way his eyes search mine. Like he's staring directly into the depths of my soul. His lips part as if he's about to say something when his phone starts ringing in his hand. Stepping away from me, he glances down at the screen then back up at me, before sliding the plate from my hands.

"Thank you."

I manage a smile, before turning to leave. I don't look back as I jog up the stairs toward the house, the break in his voice on repeat as my mind wonders who's managed to upset him so deeply.

"You missed one hell of a fight, Tay," Trey announces as he carries a stack of plates back toward the house.

"Who won?" I ask, following him inside, and finding the living room in disarray.

"If you go by the bite marks that litter Tristan's back, I'd say Lexi won that round."

I'm seated next to Lexi on the couch as we share a bowl of popcorn, with Trey and Tristan sprawled out on the couch to the left of us. The boys are flicking through the horror section since we lost a game of rock, paper, scissors. Lexi hates horror movies, so of course, that's exactly what the boys are putting on. I see them click play on the movie *Saw*, and I feel Lexi stiffen beside me.

It's only been playing for a few minutes when I see Cruz walk into the living room in a pair of grey cotton shorts slung low on his hips, showing that defined V that dips into his pants. He rolls a black T-shirt down his chiseled body, his hair tousled and damp like he's just come from the shower. I keep my eyes on the TV, but I can see him scanning the room for somewhere to sit. With Trey and Tristan's large bodies spread out over one couch, that means the only spare spot is right next to me. He stands still for a moment as if considering going back to his room, before making those few steps toward me, lowering his freshly showered body next to mine.

Immediately, I'm hit with the scent of jasmine and bergamot. It takes me by surprise that someone so dark and mysterious smells like a garden of flowers on a warm spring day. My eyes are drawn to his hands that are locked together in his lap. Huge, and manly and delicate all at once—like he has the ability to be soft and hard-handed at the same damn time.

I hear him clear his throat as his legs part slightly. His thick, muscular thigh brushes against mine, and that's when I see the outline of his cock. It's resting against the inside of his thigh, and without it even being hard, I can see the trace of it so clearly I suddenly forget how to breathe.

"Fuck!" I jolt so hard it feels like my soul jumps out of my body as Lexi screams and curses beside me. I turn my attention back to the TV just in time to see a man's body slicing apart in a maze of razor wire. "I can't watch this; I'm going to bed," Lexi states as she gets to her feet and stomps down the hall. Her empty space provides me with room to move but shifting away from Cruz is the last thing my body wants me to do.

Chapter Six

Cruz

Not even the fact that a grown man is being tortured on the TV right now in pure gore can bring my mind away from the fact that after Lexi went to bed, Taylah stayed with her body pressed against mine even when there was room for her to shift away from me. Maybe I'm overthinking it; maybe she's just comfortable where she is. A million thoughts are running through my head, but most of them consist of the way her body feels against mine. She's wearing a pair of short, pink silk pajamas that sit so snug to her body that it took me a minute to gather myself when I first walked into the room. Thinking about the tight pull of the material across her round, perfect breasts makes me start to harden. I adjust the way I'm sitting in an attempt to hide my growing erection. All I need is a moment fixated on the gore in front of me to push her out of my head, and slowly I soften.

The ending credits roll in, and I sit up and stretch, feeling the tug of my shirt ride up my body as my arms lift into the air. I side-eye Taylah, whose eyes are fixated on my bare stomach while she slowly slides another handful of popcorn into her mouth. Her eyes drift up my body before finding mine. She realizes I'm watching her, and pink highlights her cheeks. She doesn't look away, and I don't either.

The light in the hallway flicks on, prompting me to break eye contact as I get to my feet. Trey and Tristan are arguing down the hall over who was right about the plot twist in the movie, and I feel her move behind me. I turn to see her cleaning up the spilled popcorn, and I lean down to help. She smiles at me before heading toward the kitchen. Grabbing the empty beer bottles off the coffee table, I follow her in. She dumps the uneaten popcorn into the trash before placing the bowl into the dishwasher, keeping her back to me, and I toss the beer bottles into the garbage and go to leave when I hear her say my name.

"Cruz?" I stop walking and turn to face her. She's leaning up against the kitchen sink, her arms resting behind her, with her shoulders pulled back. It takes everything in me to not allow my eyes to drift down her tight body that's trapped in the stretch of the material. "I'm sorry," she whispers as she nervously bites at her bottom lip. I raise my brow in confusion. "I wasn't trying to hear your private call. I-Is everything okay?" Worry flashes behind her eyes, no scrap that, sympathy.

She feels sorry for me? Fucking déjà vu.

"I'm fine." Before this conversation can go any further, I trek back to my room, or Tristan's room, to be exact. It makes more sense that the two blond-haired, party animals share a room, so we traded. As soon as I close the door, I'm engulfed in embarrassment. Taking my phone from my shorts pocket,

I'm reminded of the sound of my mother's cries from earlier. Her begging me to just get it together, pleading I take back the cheating, piece-of-shit ex because it's what's good for the family. How the fuck is a cheating girlfriend not a fucking embarrassment? I'll never know. Her billionaire family name must mean that I'm supposed to turn a blind eye to her behavior.

Well, fuck that.

I'm doing everything my father has asked of me. I'm getting my MBA at Columbia just like he did. I'm on my way to be his special little protégé, all because I'm trying to protect my mother from his wrath. Because at the end of the day, she's always to blame.

My fist is wrapped so tightly around my phone that the screen starts to crack, and when another reel of my mother pleading with me to stop asking her to leave rushes through my head, I throw it across the room and watch it shatter down the wall.

I'm suffocating and need to get out of here.

All the lights are off when I walk into the hall. Taylah's door is closed, and I stand there for a moment. The warmth I feel in her presence is so calming in the chaos that lives rent free in my soul. I want more than anything to open the door and... I shake the thoughts before they have enough time to embed too deeply in my mind and hurry out the back sliding glass door.

Jogging down the staircase, I jump down onto the sand and take off in a sprint. The sound of the waves crashing against the shore is drowned out by an incoming storm. Thunder rumbles in the distance as lightning lights up the night sky, but it's not enough to drown out my father's voice in my head. *Always the disappointment, aren't we Cruz?*

I run faster as my chest starts to burn, *Tears are for the weak; you let your emotions get the better of you. So fucking pathetic.*

The clouds open up, and it's a downpour. I can barely see as rain hammers down my face and into my eyes. Thunder roars above me like the sky is in direct communication with what's taking place in my head. The rage I feel inside is blinding, consuming, suffocating, and I can't breathe.

I stop running as one leg gives out, followed by the other, until I'm on my knees facing the ocean. The rough sea is lit up as lines of static rip through the sky in shades of purple, making the darkness of it all look somewhat beautiful.

I grip my wet shirt and slide it off my body, letting the rain beat down on my bare skin. It's almost soothing. Closing my eyes, I lift my head to the sky, and let the sounds of chaos rupture around me.

The rain is still pouring as I jog up the back stairs toward the house. It's still in darkness as I quietly slide in the back door and make my way down the hall. I come to a halt outside Taylah's door, and before I can comprehend what happens next, my hand is on the doorknob, and I'm inside her room.

I stand there for a moment as her shocked face meets mine. Her eyes widen as she takes me in, and it's then I realize I'm soaking wet and dripping all over her floor. She sits up and leans back against the headboard, her blonde waves framing her perfect face.

"Are you okay?" Her voice shakes as her sympathetic eyes slowly look me up and down. My chest heaves as cold drops of water drip from my hair and slide down my chest. The static energy between us has nothing to do with the storm that's raging outside. "Cruz?"

"Don't feel sorry for me, Taylah. I don't need your sympathy." I cut her off, her eyes flashing with a mix of emotions as she takes a deep, shuddering breath that makes my heart speed up. It's at this moment I know I need to remove myself from her room before I cross a very forbidden line. I turn around and fumble with the doorknob, before heading back to my bedroom as my heart sprints off into oblivion. She's off limits, I tell myself as I let go of the breath I'm holding.

The darkness I hold already consumes me; I won't let it consume her too.

Chapter Seven

Taylah

"Are you listening, Taylah?" I glance up from my book as Lexi rolls over on her towel to look at me. "That book must be enthralling for you to be so deeply buried inside it." She lies down on her back, shading the sun from her eyes. I look down at the book in my hands and see I'm on chapter eight, having no clue what I've just read. My mind is still stuck on what happened last night when Cruz walked into my room soaked and shirtless. The cuts and ridges of his torso dipping into his low-slung cotton shorts lit my entire body on fire. But that's not what my mind keeps getting stuck on; it was the static energy that completely engulfed the room. The rasp of his tortured voice when he told me not to feel sorry for him. The heave of his chest as his abs tightened with every strained breath. He's always been rough around the edges. Always walked around like a dark cloud followed him. But something about him feels different, like whatever has been eating away at his soul is finally breaking the surface.

"What're you reading?" I hear Trey's voice and peek over the top of my book to see him standing in front of me, reaching down for his towel with Tristan and Cruz behind him.

"Porn," Lexi blurts out, her hand still hiding her face from the sun. Cruz and I glance over at each other at the same time, his brows raised in curiosity before we both look away. Trey drops his wet body beside me, smiling. "Read us a paragraph then."

I close the book and nudge him away. "Things boys like you wouldn't know anything about."

He rolls over and playfully grips his chest. "You wound me, Taylah." I laugh and shake my head, my eyes trailing back to Cruz, who's wiping water from his face. His wet hair drips onto his sun-kissed chest, and I'm immediately taken back to images of the same wet body in my room last night.

"So, don't be mad, but we've organized a party for tonight, and before you yell, I promise it will not be a repeat of what you walked into the day you arrived." Tristan barely finishes his sentence as Lexi sits up so fast, it gives me whiplash.

"You remember the rules, right?" she snaps as she glares at him.

"Yes, Lexi, keep the orgies out of the kitchen, I understand." He throws his wet towel onto her face before heading in the direction of a group of girls sunbathing further down the beach.

"How someone like Tristan is going to be a doctor is beyond me." Lexi huffs as she lies back down. Trey laughs getting to his feet and racing after Tristan. "You coming, Cruz?"

I can't look away as Cruz makes his way down the beach, a twist of jealousy stirring in my stomach. I try and focus on the book in front of me, Zane and Tessa's age-gap forbidden romance, but my eyes keep drifting to where Cruz is standing. While Trey and Tristan are smiling and laughing, Cruz is standing back, his focus lost somewhere out in the ocean.

"Did you ever call that surfer guy we met the other day? What was his name... Brad?" Lexi asks as she rolls onto her stomach.

"No, I haven't really had the time," I lie.

"Well, I'm going to invite them to the party tonight. You know the boys are gonna be inviting only girls, and where's the fun in that?" Before I can protest, I see Lexi shoot off a text as my eyes drift back down the beach to Cruz. A tall, brunette woman stands next to him. She's smiling up at him, and by her body language, I can tell she's flirting. He doesn't look interested, but Cruz only has one facial expression, so it's hard to tell.

Lexi gets to her feet and dusts the sand off before gathering her things.

"Let's head inside and get ready."

I take one last glance down the beach as the brunette runs her hand across his chest, and heat erupts up my spine. Grabbing my bag and towel, I follow Lexi up the stairs toward the house. The only thought running through my head as I rush to my room is the need to become the distraction Cruz Valentine can't bear to look away from.

"Lipstick or lip gloss?" Lexi calls from my room as I run my fingers through my loose waves.

"Gloss," I shout back, sliding on the white dress I decided on before inspecting myself in the mirror. The dress is cut into a deep V at the front—deep enough that my navel is visible while the thin material barely covers my breasts. I can see the tight stretch over my nipples and contemplate whether or not I should use a nipple cover, but I decide against it. My entire back is on show as I turn, the top of the dress linked around my neck, the bottom stretched tight around my ass, falling mid-thigh. The tan of my skin is further highlighted by the contrast of the white material strained against it.

I hear something drop behind me, and I turn to see Lexi standing there with her mouth agape, staring at me.

"Is it too much?" I ask as she breaks out into a smile before picking her phone up off the floor and snapping a picture. She walks toward me, tapping at her phone, her smile now bordering sinister. "What're you doing?" I hear the familiar sound of her message tone, and she smirks before turning the phone to face me. There's a picture of me with the caption, "*She'll be the one in white,*" followed by a message from Brad – Surfer boy, that reads, "*White is my new favorite color.*"

"You're trouble, you know that." She follows behind as I walk to my closet and search for my favorite black YSL heels.

"Don't even try to tell me you dressed like this to not be obsessed over, Taylah." She's right about that, but what she's wrong about is who I want to be obsessing over me, and it's not Brad – Surfer boy.

As soon as I walk outside, I immediately feel out of my depth. There are people everywhere—in the pool, in the spa, playing beer pong on the grass, taking shots at the table where we eat our dinner. I slip my shoes off and decide to go barefoot as I follow Lexi to the table where a shirtless Greek god wearing sunglasses is pouring out shots of what I assume is either vodka or tequila.

"Which pretty face needs a drink?" The Greek god's biceps flex as he continues to pour.

Lexi raises her hand. "Me." Her tiny halter top almost allows a free peep show. The guy smiles and hands her a shot glass, and in one quick toss back, she's ready for another. He looks over at me and holds one in my direction. I shake my head. "No, thank you, I don't drink." Lexi takes it from his hand and tosses it back before throwing both arms in the air.

We head over to where Tristan and Trey are teaming up against two of the girls they met at the beach today while an intense game of beer pong plays out. If those girls are here, I wonder if the brunette who was all over Cruz is here as well.

Wait, where is Cruz?

I scan the yard, sifting through the sea of bodies jumping around to "Teenage Dream" by Katy Perry.

"Found you." Arms wrap around my waist as a foreign scent engulfs me. Turning around, I see Brad. His light-blue eyes find mine as his soft blond hair falls across his forehead. "You look amazing." I take his hands in mine and gently remove them from my body, as I'm riddled with guilt. Lexi made it seem like I was interested, and this poor guy is just doing what he thinks I want.

"Drink?" He holds up a red cup, which I know contains some type of alcohol. I'm about to say I don't drink when I see the brunette who was flirting with Cruz earlier today walk past us in a tight red dress, leaving very little to the imagination. Before I realize what I'm doing, I grab the cup and down its contents. The burn that runs down my throat and through my chest makes me wince and cough. "You okay?" Brad's eyes widen with concern.

"She doesn't drink," Lexi answers for me as she takes the cup from my hand.

"Shit, I'm sorry." Brad goes red as he apologizes, but I shake my head at him.

"No apology necessary. I needed that."

His brows shoot up in an attempt to read the situation. I can tell he's confused, but we're interrupted when Lexi has her arm around mine, dragging me toward the grassed area where the speakers are blasting and most of the crowd are grinding on each other. She stops and turns to face me, surrounded by a sea of highly intoxicated bodies.

"Something's wrong, tell me." She holds my gaze as I stand there, contemplating what to tell her.

"Nothing, I'm fine. I'm just letting my hair down." She scans my face as I watch my lie sink in.

"Well, just be careful. One drink for a non-drinker is a lot, Tay."

I feel a body press up behind me, and when I see Jacob behind Lexi, I know it's Brad. We dance through a few songs, and seeing how happy Lexi is right now, grinding up on Jacob, makes me smile.

Hands grip my hips, and I'm flipped around so I'm facing Brad. He moves in closer so his body is flush with mine. That's when my line of sight catches those amber eyes. Cruz is a few feet away, leaning against the fence line with his eyes focused on Brad's hands sliding toward my ass, and suddenly I feel suffocated.

"I'm sorry, I need some air." My heart's beating rapidly in my chest, and the contents of my stomach crawl up my throat like acid. My legs feel like jelly as I head toward the house, darkness licking at my vision. The living room is full of people, and my eyes settle on a dark corner beside the house, enclosed by a large hedge. I take the few steps into the darkness and welcome the rush of cool air that falls over me.

Closing my eyes, I press my back up against the house, embracing the cold shiver that wraps up my spine. My heart is beating so fast my chest aches as the knots in my stomach tighten. I'm filled with such an array of emotions that I'm completely overwhelmed. "Bad Choices" by Kode starts to play and I try and focus on the beat of the music to stabilize me.

I feel the air around me shift, and I open my eyes. There, dressed in a tight black shirt and a pair of black jeans, is Cruz. His animalistic eyes are locked on mine as he takes a step closer.

"Are you okay?" The moment feels like déjà vu, except now he's the one asking me that question. Another step, and I'm flooded with the clean scent of flowers and citrus, and my heart clenches tight. He takes another step, and he's so close I can feel the warmth of his skin as I drown in the liquid honey of his eyes.

One hand is pressed to the side of the house next to my head, then the other, caging me in. His face hovers over mine as my eyes trace the shape of his lips. His tongue slides over them, drawing my attention to the way they glisten, filling my vibrating core with need.

"Taylah, are you okay?" The rasp of his voice cuts through me, making me gasp. "Do you need me to take you to your room?"

My entire body flushes with heat, sending a hot rush between my legs. I can't move as my erratic breathing accelerates, his hand coming down to cup my face as the pad of his thumb runs tortuously slow along my bottom lip. My body trembles as his fingers slide gently down my neck, pausing at the pulse point, as a shuddering breath vacates his lips. The purposeful brush of his fingers runs down the center of my body where my dress is parted open, sending my insides into an explosive mess. His hand runs back up, and it's when his fingers brush over my hard nipple through the fabric of my dress that I completely come apart. My eyes close and my head tilts back, as an uncontrollable moan slides out of my throat. I feel him pull away from me, and I open my eyes, trying to catch my breath. He has his back to me as he stares up into the sky right before he storms away from me, cursing into the wind.

I take a minute to fix my dress and gather myself before I attempt to sneak past everyone and up to my room. I barely make it in the back door when I hear Lexi shout my name. I look over and see her running toward me. "Jesus, I looked everywhere for you. Is everything okay?" She looks me over as I nod.

"I'm just tired. I shouldn't have drank." I regret the words right after they leave my mouth when I see Tristan's head snap in my direction.

"You drank tonight?" He looks pissed. "You're underage, Taylah." Yep, definitely pissed.

I look around the room, and that's when my eyes fall on Cruz. He's unreadable, but coming from someone whose usual facial expression mimics irritation, I don't think much of it.

"It was one drink; leave her alone," Lexi snaps back as she takes my hand and walks me over to the couch to take a seat. Brad and Jacob are flanked on either side of us while an angry Tristan is glaring at me. The blonde from earlier sits on his lap, running her hand up and down his chest, right next to Trey, who's making out with the other blonde.

"I don't think I've ever seen you scowl Tristan. Is blondie ruining your mood?" Lexi shuffles the deck of cards in front of us, while the blonde on Tristan's lap glares at her like she wants to scratch her eyes out.

"Her name is Katie," Tristan spits back.

"Oh, you've stepped up in the world, getting on a first-name basis these days, are you?" She throws Tristan's cards at him and smirks, and it's actually quite entertaining to watch my brother's mood sour. It's a rare occasion that he's not the happiest person in the room.

"Now, who's ready for a game of *give and take?*"

Chapter Eight

Cruz

It takes everything in me to keep it together when I find out Taylah was drinking tonight before whatever happened between us... happened. The way her body responded to my touch. The tremble of her lips, the flush of her skin, her hard nipples, and that mind-blowing moan that escaped her body, setting me on fire, were all in an intoxicated state.

When I saw her dancing with Brad tonight, I couldn't think, and when he gripped her hips, pressing himself against her, I wanted to break every one of his fingers. Then something changed in her eyes, a look of panic. I watched as she scanned the yard for somewhere to calm herself down. And when I saw her duck into the shadows at the side of the house, I couldn't stop myself from following her.

I rounded the corner, seeing her lean up against the side of the house with her eyes closed. The erratic beat of her heart pulsed in her throat as her breaths expelled rapidly from her chest. It's hard to see someone who's the literal definition of the sun fall apart in front of you. And now, I'm standing in the kitchen watching her as she nervously plays with her hands, knowing I crossed a line with her tonight, and I'm angry with myself.

"You want to play, Cruz?" Lexi looks up at me as she's handing out cards. I shake my head and glance at Taylah, who's avoiding looking my way.

Fuck, I really can't read her.

I watch on as the game starts.

"What's give and take? I've never heard of it before." The blonde, now known as Katie, questions as she looks over the hand she's been dealt.

"It can get complicated, so let me show you." Lexi places a card down on the table, and it's a queen of hearts. "Anyone got another queen?" Lexi looks around the group, and I see a very smiley Jacob place down a queen of diamonds. "Okay, so that means I've paired with Jacob. He can either ask me a question to get to know me better, or he can take a kiss." Tristan leans forward, slamming a queen of spades onto the table as Lexi rolls her eyes. "And now we have the reason for why the game is called give and take. Everyone has to vote on which card I give back and whose card I take. Raise your hand if I should give Tristan's card back." I watch as Taylah raises her hand, along with Brad, Jacob, and Katie. Lexi scans the room, seeing Tristan's outvoted. Smirking at him, she throws his card back at his face before grabbing Jacob and pulling him in for a heated kiss. Tristan looks more annoyed than I've ever seen him, and I'm unsure how this is going to play out. Before things escalate, I see Taylah throw one of her cards onto the table.

Ace of spades.

Trey jumps out of his seat and places an ace of clubs on top of hers. "I have no questions, so I guess I'll take a kiss." His date grabs his shirt and pulls him to sit back down, and Tristan gives him a warning look. But that's nothing compared to the fire that's ripping through my conscious state at what I'll do to him if his lips go anywhere near hers.

Brad leans forward, and I watch as he places an ace of hearts on top, and I feel my heart drop into my stomach.

"Okay, let's vote. Who thinks Taylah should give Brad's card back?" Trey raises his hand sky-high, and so does his date. I turn my back to them and white-knuckle the kitchen sink.

"Guess that means I win this round, right?" The sound of Brad's syrupy voice makes me nauseous. I keep my back to them as I step out toward the hall, removing myself from a situation I know will only end in my fist shoved so far down Brad's throat he'll wish he stayed home and made love to his surfboard.

I don't stop walking until I get to my room. When my mother asked me to come home for the weekend to celebrate my father's birthday, *"No fucking way"* had never left my mouth so fast. But as painful as that might be to deal with, somehow, I feel like staying here right now will be worse.

I curse at myself for smashing my phone as I'm unable to let my mother know I'm coming home, when a soft knock drums lightly at my door. I turn around and open it to see Taylah standing there on the other side.

"Can I come in?" Her voice is like fucking silk. I take a step back, holding the door open for her, taking in her candy-coated scent that makes my heart skip as she steps past me before closing the door. She looks around the room, her eyes resting a little too long on my bed. The cut of her dress shows off her bare back, and my eyes fall to the dip of her hips, before slowly taking in the tight material that's hugging her ass. I bite at my bottom lip hard enough it draws blood.

Fuck!

"What's going on with us?" she questions without turning to face me.

What I want to say is *you're all I think about*, but what comes out of my mouth is, "Nothing."

She turns to face me, her eyes searching mine as if to get a read on me. Good luck with that. I was taught from an early age to barricade my emotions behind solid, impenetrable steel.

"Nothing?" It's a seductive whisper, and my cock throbs painfully between my legs. There's a look on her face that makes me want to throw her on my bed and watch her take every inch of me. But the fact that she's been drinking and is a line I know I shouldn't cross, pulls me out of my inappropriate thoughts.

"We can talk when you're not intoxicated." I walk past her, feeling the heat of her gaze follow me as I sit down on my bed.

"So, your hands on my body was nothing?" The anger in her voice throws me.

"And I'm sorry about that. I shouldn't have done that, and if I knew you were intoxicated, I would've never laid a hand on you."

"Oh my god, it was one drink. I didn't realize you had so much regret." She throws her arms up in frustration before she turns and heads for the door. I get to my feet so fast that I trip over myself as I race to reach her.

I can't let her leave like this.

"Taylah, wait." She pulls at the door, but with my hand pushing against it, there's no chance she'll get it open. "Don't leave like this."

"Please just let me go, Cruz. This is embarrassing enough as it is." Her voice breaks, and I have no idea what to do. I take a step back, giving her space, and within a matter of seconds, the door slams shut in my face.

Walking back to my bed, I fall onto my back and let out a deep sigh as I stare up at the ceiling. I can feel my heart racing under the hand that rests on my chest.

I care too much about her to let someone like me destroy her, no matter how much I want to know what her mouth tastes like or how soft her skin would feel underneath me. Just thinking about her body under mine has me harder than I've ever been in my life.

Life with me is a death sentence, and someone like her deserves more than I would ever have to offer. Tristan has been there for me through some of the darkest moments of my life.

He's made it very clear his sister is off-limits, and he's one person in my life right now I can't afford to lose.

Rolling onto my stomach, I bury my face into my pillow, letting out a groan that expels the pain from my chest.

A few days away from here is exactly what I need, even if the next two days will be spent in hell.

I park my father's Range Rover and pull my dark hood over my head. I spent the drive back to my parents' house telling myself to do anything I could to blend into the background and avoid my father at all costs. Sliding out of the car, I grab my phone from the cup holder in the center and take a breath as my father steps out onto the front porch. He's dressed in a dark grey suit with a black silk tie, his signature glass of scotch in hand.

Let's get this fucking over with.

I walk toward him as a twisted smile spreads across his face.

"How nice to have my only child home for my birthday." His grin widens into a sickly smirk, creating an unease inside me and slowly filling me with regret. I nod, and he dips out of the way, motioning me inside. Walking through the foyer, I notice a few new abstract paintings on the dark grey walls. Everything in this house screams sterile, cold, and unemotional.

Just as I'm about to climb the staircase, I see my mother seated in the living room with a glass of red wine in her hand. It's only been a few days, but she looks more fragile than ever. I walk toward her, and a small smile forms across her face when I remove my hood. "I'm so happy you decided to come home this weekend. Your father was hoping to see you." Her eyes flicker with sadness as she brings the glass of wine up to her lips, her hand shaking slightly.

"Are you okay, Mom?" I know better than to ask this question, but I can't help it. Maybe I am weak, like my father says. Maybe I do have an issue handling my emotions.

Her hand reaches out and brushes down my cheek. "You grew up before my eyes, Cruz."

"Stop wasting time." My father's voice echoes behind us, my mother jolting so hard that her wine spills into her lap. My blood boils at her reaction. Taking a deep breath, I rein in my emotions and plant my game face back on, just like I've been taught. "I'll need to have a tailor come and fit you with a new suit."

I turn around to face him as he throws the last of his drink down his throat. "You represent the Valentine name, and you never know who you might run into." His sadistic smile returns, and dread works its way through the hollow pit of my stomach.

Chapter Nine

Taylah

I groan awake as Lexi opens my blinds, the morning sun blinding its way into my room.

"One drink and you can't get out of bed. No wonder you don't drink!" She laughs as she drops down beside me, resting her head next to mine. I'll let her assume me hiding out in my room is because of the one drink I had when the truth is I'm avoiding Cruz. Replaying last night in my head coats me with a fresh dose of embarrassment.

"So, Brad's just not it?"

After Cruz walked out of the room last night, I told Brad I wasn't feeling well and left before the game we were playing got out of control. Even something as innocent as a kiss feels deceitful, and I don't want to be leading anybody on until I know what's going on in my head.

"He's a sweet guy, it's just..."

"He's not the book boyfriend you're after?" Lexi cuts me off laughing. "Girl, your future is a world of politics, late nights, and deadlines. These kinds of summers won't last forever." She slides off the bed, flicking her long brown locks over her shoulder. "Let's go costume shopping for Tristan's birthday party. We don't have long to find the perfect outfit."

I stare at her for a moment, watching her squirm with impatience as she waits for my answer.

"Give me twenty minutes to get ready." Her smile beams across the room as she swings her hips and exits.

After a quick shower, I slide on a white maxi dress and sweep my blonde locks into an effortless ponytail before heading down to meet Lexi.

As soon as we step outside, the first thing I notice is Cruz's car is no longer parked in the driveway.

"Did you see Cruz leave?" I ask Lexi as we slide into my Jeep.

"No, I haven't seen him since last night. He's probably at the gym. Have you seen how tight that boy's body is? I'm surprised he doesn't live there to maintain all that manly perfection." Lexi fans herself dramatically, and I keep my eyes focused on the road in front of me because, yes, I have, in fact, seen how tight that boy's body is.

We pull up at the shopping mall and head for the best costume shop in LA: Darcy's. As we enter, my mind is thrown into chaos. It's a large square room with rows and rows of costumes, from Halloween outfits to superheroes to Disney characters.

"Where do we even start?" I let out a breath as Lexi claps her hands together excitedly.

"Sexy Disney princess." She points to the back wall and heads in that direction. I follow behind, looking around to see if anything grabs my attention. There's a cute Little Red Riding

Hood one, but when I hold it up and am met with the wrinkle of Lexi's nose, I slide it back onto the rack.

Three hours later, and a thousand and one costume changes, we finally settled. Lexi as a sexy princess Jasmine from the movie *Aladdin*, and I decided on a sheer white Greek goddess dress that leaves little to the imagination. Paired with a gold leaf crown and a pair of gold strappy sandals and I'm all set.

We spend a few more hours in our favorite designer shops before heading to Starbucks for a reset.

"Do you know what the boys are dressing up as yet?" Lexi asks as she circles her straw through her iced latte.

I shake my head and bring the mug of hot coffee to my lips. "Probably something where they can be topless, like a lifeguard maybe."

"I wouldn't mind a shirtless Cruz walking around. I just wish I had the chance to meet Meredith before they broke up. Oh my god, let's stalk her Instagram." I watch on as she types and scrolls through her iPhone. "Jesus, she really is gorgeous, isn't she?"

She holds up a picture of Meredith in a cut-out one-piece red bikini. Her long dark hair is wet and effortlessly slicked back from her face, as her piercing blue eyes hold my attention for longer than I'd like.

"Yes, she's beautiful."

She continues to tap at her phone until I see her brows draw together before bringing her eyes back to meet mine.

"What did you find?"

"I think I know where Cruz is," she says, flipping the phone to face me. Right there on her screen is a picture of Meredith posing in a strapless red gown with the caption, "Weekend with my Valentine."

"What?" I snatch the phone from her hand and search the background, but nothing looks familiar.

"Valentine has got to be code for Cruz Valentine. Guess they didn't break up after all," Lexi states, taking her phone back out of my hand. "I do hope he comes back soon though. His abs are my favorite in the house. Hopefully, he brings her with him. Oh my god, can you imagine if I got to meet her dad and he asked me to audition for one of his upcoming movies?" She sips animatedly on her drink with a smile that looks like Christmas morning. I give her a smile back, but the thought of Cruz showing up with Meredith makes me feel sick to my stomach.

We head back to the house with the windows down as the quickened beat from the song "Prada" blasts through the speakers of my car. Ironic since most of the afternoon was spent restocking our designer wardrobe. Lexi throws her hands in the air as the wind whips through the car. The afternoon sun soaks our skin, and the entire cabin is filled with a combination of bad singing and laughter.

I realize now what Lexi was trying to tell me earlier about the memories you create before you dive headfirst into adulthood. The ones you find yourself reminiscing about when you're eighty years old, and I intend on making this summer something my heart can hold onto for the rest of my life. Whatever I thought was happening with Cruz was nothing, or so he's told me, and it's time to have some fun. Switching the volume up and bouncing along with Lexi, I smile to myself.

It's time to let my hair down.

We get back and start unloading the car when I hear Trey's voice shouting, "Nugget, no!" right before a golden retriever jumps up onto Lexi, knocking her down.

"What the hell!" Lexi is shocked as Tristan walks over and hands the dog a snack.

"Good boy." He smirks before walking the dog back into the house. I step over and help her get back to her feet while she dusts herself off.

"Whose dog is that?" she snaps at Trey, who's still laughing at her.

"The Malcolm's a few houses down. They asked us to dog-sit for them for two weeks while they spend some time in Florida." He walks toward us, taking our shopping bags from the back seat. "Let me help."

As we enter the living room, I see Tristan and Nugget on the couch watching TV.

"What's wrong, Lexi? Not a dog person?" Tristan laughs as Lexi shakes her head in disgust.

"Just add you and Trey, and we have three golden retrievers living in the house now," Lexi snaps back.

"Wow, she has jokes."

With every comment that falls from Tristan's mouth, I can sense the hostility warming up next to me, so I decide to cut out before I have to witness yet another exhausting fight between them.

Carting my shopping to my room, I close the door and take a seat on my bed. I take my phone into my hands and scroll to Cruz's number. Something in me still refuses to believe this situation was completely one sided, and I need to know if he really did go home to spend the weekend with Meredith.

I click dial, and before the phone even reaches my ear, I'm hit with his voicemail. I throw my phone down next to me when a text chimes through.

> **Brad:** We're having a party tonight. Would love to see you.

I stare at the text message from Brad as I replay Cruz's words to me that there's nothing between us, and I type my reply.

> **Taylah:** This time, I'll come find you.

I feel a rush of nerves as I watch the text bubbles.

> **Brad:** I'll be the one in white.

Chapter Ten

Cruz

Staring at myself in the mirror, I adjust the cufflinks on the black suit jacket, when I hear a knock at the door. I watch in the reflection as the door slowly opens, and my mother appears. She's wearing a champagne-colored cocktail dress that barely clings to her fragile structure. It's hard to watch your mother waste away in front of you, and it kills me that no matter how many times I beg for her to leave, she doesn't.

I turn to face her as she walks toward me, taking the black tie from my bed and linking it around my neck.

"You look very handsome." She smiles as she tightens the tie until it sits perfectly flush against my black silk shirt. "All I want is for you to have a wonderful life, son. You might not agree on much with your father, but you can't deny he's not an extremely successful man." It's hard for me to stand here and look at the state she's in while she compliments the monster I've grown to hate.

"You know I do all of this for you." As soon as the words leave my mouth, it's like I can't stop. I take a step back and run a frustrated hand through my hair. "You really think a business degree and working at Valentine Enterprises is what I pictured for myself? Everything I do to be less like the ever-growing disappointment is to save him from taking it out on you." I see her flinch at my words, knowing every word I'm saying is true. I shake my head and beeline for the door. As I enter the hall, I'm not ready for who's standing before me. Meredith fucking White.

Closing my eyes, I let out an aggravated sigh. *This is not fucking happening right now.*

"Hello, lover." Her voice grates over my skin, and I'm praying the floor opens up and swallows me whole. I feel her hand on my arm, and I open my eyes as I pull away from her.

"Don't touch me."

"Ahh, the couple of the hour," my father announces walking toward us, with his shit-eating grin plastered on his plastic-looking face. My mother steps out of my room behind me and closes the door and a hint of annoyance flashes across my father's face.

"Happy birthday, Jack." Meredith leans forward and air kisses my father, who's lapping up the attention like a dog in heat.

"There's a car waiting for you two downstairs."

Meredith holds her arm out for me to take, but I ignore her and head for the stairs. The clicking of her heels against the floor quickens as she hurries behind me. Sliding into the back of a town car, I feel her follow in after me.

"What's your problem?" The irritation in her tone satisfies me as she slams the door shut.

"Why're you here?" I stare out the window, focusing on the incoming traffic I'm about to be stuck in.

"Because I'm your girlfriend." Her hand slides across my thigh, which I brush off immediately, invoking an oncoming tantrum.

"You are definitely not my girlfriend, Meredith."

"You didn't seem to mind me being around when you got to bury your cock inside me."

"And even then, it was less than average." I turn back to look out the window, waiting for her to explode, but I'm surprisingly met with silence.

We don't speak again the rest of the trip, and my mind wanders back to Taylah and that fucking white dress. The way I left things with her has been playing in my mind, and not having a functioning phone right now to check in on her is killing me. I make a mental note to buy a new one first thing tomorrow morning.

The car comes to a stop as a sea of reporters await outside the building. Knowing my attention-seeking father, he's probably paying them to run a story on him. Taking a deep breath, I open my door as Meredith follows me out.

"It's the couple of the hour," I hear a balding man with thick wire-frame glasses shout as cameras start flashing in my face.

What the fuck?

I hold my hand up to my face in an effort to block myself as I head to the entrance that more reporters barricade.

"Just one good shot please?" I don't see who says this because the next thing I know, hands are around my neck, and a set of lips are attached to mine. I freeze momentarily in shock before pulling her off me, and as soon as I see her smirk, I know this was a setup.

"I would've thought you'd try harder, knowing that's the last time your lips will be anywhere near mine." I walk away before she has the chance to say another fucking word. Cool and calm on the outside, just like I've been taught, but underneath, my body is warring between rage and resentment.

As soon as I walk into hall, I head straight for the onyx bar situated under dim lighting against the back wall.

"Shot of vodka." The petite bartender with kind eyes nods as she pours the clear liquid into a shot glass and slides it across to me.

"Will that be all, Mr. Valentine?"

With the shot glass gripped tight in my fist, I head for the men's bathroom. I kick the door open as two older men dressed in suits jump at my abrupt entry. They wipe the coke residue from their faces and fumble with their pockets as I walk over to the sink that's molded into brown marble. I turn the faucet on before throwing the contents of the shot glass into my mouth and rolling it around like mouthwash. Anything to remove the vile taste of poison that coats my tongue, thanks to a Meredith White and Jack Valentine PR stunt. Spitting the contents into the sink, I take a mouthful of water from the tap to rinse the remnants of lingering vodka from my mouth. Bringing my eyes back up to my reflection, I stare at myself before adjusting my tie and rolling the stress from my neck as I wipe my wet lips with the back of my hand.

I barely make it five steps from the bathroom when Meredith interrupts my view.

This girl doesn't know when to give up.

"Can I speak with you?" I look over her shoulder and see her parents standing with mine in the distance, clinking glasses in a cloud of laughter.

"Speak."

She looks over her shoulder and back at me. "Somewhere in private?"

"No, thank you." I stare at her, waiting for her to say whatever the fuck she thinks she needs to say, and when nothing comes out of her mouth, I go to step around her.

"Wait."

I stop walking and look at her over my shoulder. I don't really want to be anywhere near her right now, after the stunt she just pulled, but I don't particularly feel like being stuck in a room full of people who lick my father's ass for a living either.

"I miss you, and your father told me you miss me too." She reaches for me, and I recoil from her touch.

"It's over... leave me alone." I go to walk away, when I feel her hand grip my arm.

"But I love you."

I freeze on the spot, agitated at how freely people throw the word love around. It's almost fucking laughable. I turn around to face her and find tears in her eyes, and even as one rolls down her cheek, I feel nothing. I take a step away from her, removing her hand from my arm.

"If you loved me, Meredith, you wouldn't have invited someone who wasn't me back to your room to bury his cock down your throat. Great acting though. Your father would be so proud."

I storm back into the dining hall and find a darkened corner of the room to wait out the night. I watch as my father parades around the room like he owns the place, as people worship the ground he walks on. It's full of men in suits talking about the latest and greatest investment on the market, and as I look down at the black tailored suit that suddenly feels suffocating, I realize this is my fucking future.

"Ah, there you are. Come with me; I have some people I want you to meet." My father's voice notches aggressively up my spine, making me shudder. I don't answer as I follow behind him through the sea of suits. He takes a seat at one of the round tables where a bunch of other men are seated. After one quick skim of them, I recognize the two who I saw in the bathroom doing blow, and the rest look just as entitled. I take a seat next to my father, who pours another glass of amber liquid before sliding it across to me. My stomach lurches, and I push the glass back, not bothering to meet his eyes.

"It's a celebration, son." He slides the glass back toward me just as Meredith's father sits down across from me. I ignore it as he continues his speech, banging on about how proud he is that I'll be joining Valentine Enterprises when I graduate.

Proud?

The longer he talks, the more tempting it is to down the glass of whiskey that sits in front of me, but not even this is enough for me to take the alcohol into my hands and drown in it like he does. He introduces the table to me, which I've come to know is the COO, CFO, and majority members of the board.

"Do any women hold any positions of power?" I can't keep the agitation out of my tone as the table falls into silence right before they erupt into fits of laughter.

"That's a joke, right?" cokehead number one asks as he wipes a tear from his face, unable to contain his hilarity.

I'm washed with relief when most of the men get to their feet before making some fucked-up comment about how "Whores wouldn't know how to run shit," and excusing themselves to go smoke their cigars. That relief soon turns to dread when I see Meredith sit down in front of us. And when my father's grin widens into the stratosphere, I know he has something up his sleeve.

He leans back in his chair, resting his hand on my shoulder. "Can I start by saying how proud I am that my son has found someone as amazing as you, Meredith."

Proud? He's been throwing that particular word around all night, although we both know he's talking shit out of his ass. Meredith's father sits taller, smiling as he wraps his arm around her shoulders.

"I couldn't have thought of a better family for my little girl to be married into."

My entire body becomes rigid, and the urge to vomit creeps over me, making my body run cold.

One, this is the last fucking family you would want your daughter marrying into, and two, why the fuck is marriage even being brought up right now?

"I was over the moon when Cruz told me she was the one."

Heat courses through my veins, and I've lost all ability to speak. I glance over at Meredith whose eyes are gleaming at me like I've just given her the world on a silver platter.

"I can't fucking do this." I slide my seat back so hard across the tiled floor that it makes a high-pitched squeal before I storm across the room toward the exit. I shove the door open and welcome the crisp night air on my scorched skin.

I barely make it down the front steps when I hear my father's voice behind me. "Cruz Valentine, you keep walking, and you'll regret every fucking step."

I do, in fact, keep walking. I'm not doing this anymore. "Your mother won't like this, Cruz."

Anger has now turned to blinding rage as I whip around so fast his face actually resembles shock before sliding into a sickening smirk. "Thought that would get your attention."

Before I can stop myself, both my hands have formed fists with the collar of his shirt as I walk him backward, not stopping until his back smacks the wall behind him, emptying his lungs of air.

"I'm. Not. Fucking. Doing. This. Anymore," I say through gritted teeth, my chest heaving so violently, I'm running short of oxygen. "I'm not marrying Meredith. Fuck, I'm not even dating her. I'm done with your fucked-up games."

It's a stare-off as energy heats up between us. Pure hatred pouring out of us both.

"You'll do as you're fucking told."

That's the moment that sends me over the edge as I draw back my fist and throw it toward his smug fucking face. But before it connects, I hear my mother scream.

"Cruz!" The distraction is enough to dismantle me, my fist hitting the brick wall instead of my father's face. Pain sears up my arm as I step back, right before glass shatters across my face, and I drop to the ground. My head throbs as I watch blood drip from my face onto the concrete, with remnants of my father's whiskey glass scattered out in front of me. My vision is blurring as blood runs into my eyes, and hear my father's footsteps retreating as I slowly get back to my feet.

"You're better than this, Cruz." I feel my mother's hand on my shoulder as she uses her handkerchief to help clean off the blood. Her face slowly comes into view, but the raging headache makes me squint.

"He deserves a lot more than that, and you know it." She winces at my words, but right now, she needs a dose of fucking reality. "I can't keep doing this shit, Mom." I hear my voice crack open, and even I'm surprised by the emotions that are barreling through me. "I'm begging you to leave him. If you don't, it's only a matter of time before I'm attending your funeral."

She just stares at me like she can't hear a word I'm saying.

"Spencer, can you please take Cruz home and have Alice stitch him up?" She can't even look at me as she calls over one of my father's drivers. I just told my mother I didn't want to have to bury her, and she looks at me like she doesn't even know who I am.

I'm emotionless as I slide into the back of the town car as it drives back to my father's hellhole. Alice is waiting for me as soon as I walk through the door, and as much as I need the cut across my brow stitched up, I can't stay here another minute.

Jogging up the stairs and down to my room, I slam my door and head to my bathroom to inspect the damage. There's blood smeared on my cheek, chin, neck, and all through my hair. The cut is right above my right eye and definitely requires stitches. Overwhelmed at the state I'm in, I try an inhale a steadying breath. I don't even bother changing as I grab my car keys from my dresser, and head for the garage.

My Mustang rumbles to life beneath me, as a hunger ignites inside my soul. A starvation for the girl who makes me feel... everything. And as I effortlessly slide through the gears, listening to the roar of the engine as I head right for to her, my damaged soul has never craved anything more.

Chapter Eleven

Taylah

"Bikini to a party?" I ask as I try and wrangle my breasts into my yellow bikini top.

"Would you stop fidgeting. It's not weird to go to a pool party that backs onto the beach in a bikini, Taylah."

I shake my head as I grab a pair of denim shorts and slide them up my legs. "Fine, but if we don't go swimming and you made me wear this for no reason, I'm telling Tristan you had a dream about him last night."

Her face glows red, and I'm unsure if it's from anger or embarrassment.

"I knew I shouldn't have told you that."

"Hey, if there's something you need to tell me, I won't care if you're completely in love with him. I always felt like you were sister material." I barely get the sentence out when I'm hit in the face with a black lacy bra.

"He disgusts me."

"Right."

Lexi is three shots in as we walk up the timber staircase toward the "surfer boys" party. Lady Gaga is playing as we reach the back of the house, and I take a moment to look around. There's a DJ to the right, where a few people are grinding away on each other. A beer pong table sits behind a long, rectangular pool that's lit up with deep-blue lighting. There's what looks to be an entertaining area further up near the house. All in all, it's very similar to our backyard. I assume most of these beach houses are decked out somewhat the same.

"I need a shot." Lexi grabs my arm, and I jolt forward as she tugs me toward a group crowded around a beer keg. When we get there, I see a small glass table to the right littered with clear plastic shot glasses, all ranging with different colored alcohol. Lexi scans them, bringing one to her nose, before shrugging and throwing it back. I mimic the scrunched-up look on her face as she does another.

"Hello, beautiful." I watch as Jacob wraps his arms around Lexi's waist from behind. She giggles as she turns to face him. She looks back at me as if questioning if I'll be okay alone for a minute. I smile and nod and watch the happy little development they have going on, making out all the way to where the DJ is currently banging out "Training Season" by Dua Lipa.

A cool breeze picks up as the sound of boys shouting "Chug, chug" fills the air, and I immediately feel out of place, taking a few steps back into the shadows. I look around at the drunken bodies, laughing, dancing, even undressing, and for a moment,

Cruz's face flashes through my mind stirring up a craving for his presence in the pit of my stomach.

"Yellow, huh?" I jolt at the sound of Brad's voice. Even though I was expecting him, it weirdly takes me by surprise. Everything about meeting him here feels wrong. I turn to face him and watch as his eyes travel the length of my body, letting out a soft whistle.

"Yellow?" I mirror. He points at my breasts, letting out a small laugh.

"Your bikini. You seem more like a red kind of girl to me." He winks as he brings the beer bottle to his lips. I look down at the triangle material that barely covers my nipples, surprised boys actually care what color anything is. Like it mattered what color the material was that hit the floor of their room that night. And why red? What's wrong with yellow?

"Is everything okay?" he asks, raising his brow at me. I nod my head slightly, unsure exactly why my mind had just spun into a world of complete nonsense.

"I'm fine."

"Swim?" Before I can answer, he's removed his white T-shirt from his body and stands in front of me in a pair of tight white shorts that leave little for the imagination. He lifts his arms animatedly, flexing his muscles. And while he's definitely got some tone on that tanned skin, Cruz buries him in a heartbeat.

Cruz. Why is he so present in my mind? *Nothing*. I repeat his own words back to me, bringing myself back to the reality of the situation, and link my arm in Brad's.

"Can you get over the fact I'm wearing yellow, or is that a deal breaker?" I joke as we head toward the pool.

"You could always just remove the bikini altogether; problem solved."

"If I said I don't like white, will you remove your shorts?"

"Already trying to get me naked on our first date."

My stomach churns, and a sinking feeling swallows my lungs. *Was this a date?*

We reach the pool, and I slide my denim shorts from my body, kicking them under the nearest sun lounger. Brad takes a few steps toward the water and dives in. I don't give him a chance to break the surface as I dive in after him. We barely get five minutes to ourselves when the pool starts filling with laughing bodies. Lexi is next to me in minutes, with Jacob not far behind her. He grabs at Lexi, pulling her close, before diving in for a kiss. I feel Brad move in closer, and I turn my face to look at him. His wet blond hair is pushed back from his face, and his piercing blue eyes are staring right at me. His hands slowly wrap around my waist as he pulls me closer, with the heat of his breath fanning across my face. The sound of the bass-filled music and drunken shouting is drowned out by the thumping of my heart that's making its way up my throat. I feel a tug in my core to back away as he leans his face closer to mine.

Cruz

Blood from the cut across my brow is dripping into my eyes, distorting my vision. I blink a few times to clear it out as I weave my way through the LA traffic. I welcome the high that folds over me while I change through the gears and accelerate until everything around me becomes a blur. The rush of adrenaline clings to the tortured parts of my soul, dragging me out of the darkness that resides in my head. The roar of the engine beneath me silences his words of shame that haunt me, and I revel in the moment.

I pull into the driveway and kill the engine. It's dark and quiet as I enter the house, and without a second thought, my feet take me to Taylah's door. I stand there for a moment, just staring at it, as the pain from the gash in my face makes me wince. Holding my breath, I softly knock on her door and wait a few moments, but I'm only met with silence.

Heading down the staircase that leads to the beach, I drop down onto the sand and start walking—where to, I'm not sure. I soon regret not removing my dress shoes as they slowly and uncomfortably fill with sand, but I keep walking until something tells me to stop. I look out into the ocean as it crashes against the shore, the reflection of the moon shimmering like a beacon of peace among chaos. I wonder what it might feel like to have something like that. Something that could shine over a chaotic mess and make it look *beautiful*.

Her laugh fills my head, and for a second, I'm unsure if I imagined it in the moment or if it was real. My question is soon answered when I hear it again, my heart swelling inside my chest as I turn around and set my eyes on her. Her yellow bikini glows like a beacon of light against her sun-kissed skin. Her blonde hair is wet around her face as she splashes around in the pool, her head tilting back as she laughs again. I take a step toward the staircase that leads up to the house but stop abruptly when I see Brad wrap his arms around her. Her back is to me now, so I can't read her face. For a few brutal minutes, they're both staring at each other as water splashes around them and when I see him lean forward, his lips finding hers, it feels like someone has belted me across the chest with a sledgehammer. I bring one hand to my chest, gripping at my shirt as if that might somehow ease the pain, falling to one knee as I struggle to remain upright.

Looking down at myself, embarrassment heats my skin as I process the situation. I'm on my knees watching Taylah kiss another man while blood rolls down my face from an open cut that clearly needs medical attention. Reality sets in as I watch blood pool in the sand. Why did I think it was a good idea to see Taylah in this state? That would require an explanation, and one I'm nowhere near ready to give. I choke on my next breath as I get back to my feet, refusing to torture myself any longer.

Closing the door to the shared bathroom where I know the first aid kit is, I assess the damage. Blood has dried in my hair, making it stiff, as the open wound produces a slow trickle down my face. I lean in closer to my reflection and open the cut, gauging how deep it really is. Crouching down, I retrieve the first aid kit from the wooden cabinet and rifle through the contents until I find some Steri-Strips. Squeezing the cut together, I manage to secure one in place right before I hear the sound of a door closing and voices in the hall. My heart drops when those voices sound very much like Taylah and Brad. I hear her laugh again as I stare at myself in the mirror. I need to take a shower, but I can do that in the ensuite attached to my room. Less of a chance of someone seeing me in this state. I wait for the voices and joy-filled laughs to silence, before I step out into the darkened hall.

Chapter Twelve

Taylah

"I don't think I can do it." I grip the surfboard between my legs as Brad sits on his across from me, laughing out words of encouragement. Last night, when he kissed me, I froze. Nothing, I felt absolutely nothing. I so desperately wanted to be that girl who could just let her hair down and have some harmless fun, but kissing leads to other things. And while I'm not entirely untouched, I still haven't given myself over completely to another man before. Something always pulls me back. Lexi tells me it's the unrealistic men I have clouding my head from all the books I read. If that's the case, I've friend-zoned yet another one as I look over at Brad, who's still trying to explain the secrets of the ocean to me.

"I promised you when I walked you back to your room last night that, as an apology for kissing you without your permission, I would teach you how to catch a wave." He shakes his wet hair out of his eyes as the sun highlights his burnt cheeks. "This one has your name all over it, Taylah." He nods to a small wave rolling in, and I lie down and start paddling like he showed me. "Okay, stand up." One foot barely hits the top of the board, and I'm tipped under, with saltwater forcing its way up my nose. Luckily, the stupid board is attached to my ankle, because there's no chance I'd be able to save it along with myself. His arm grips just under my shoulder as I break the surface.

"You, okay?" he asks with a chuckle.

"My nose burns like I've just snorted battery acid, and this wet suit is so far up my ass it feels like it's cutting me in half. Other than that, I'm bloody excellent." He giggles at my humor and it makes me smile as he guides my board toward me, helping me back up.

"Let's try again."

A couple of hours pass, and I've eaten shit on every single attempt. My eyes and nose are burning, and I'm completely out of breath.

"Come on, let's head in."

We paddle back in until we can stand and begin the walk back to his house. We get to the stairs that lead up to his yard, and he takes the board from me, tucking it under his arm.

"I'll run these up, then walk you back."

"No, I'm fine. The house is literally a five-minute walk."

He eyes me over before his eyes square off over my shoulder.

"Hi, Lexi." He grins, and I turn around to see my best friend making her way toward us, wearing nothing but a flossy white bikini.

"How did the surfing lessons go?" Her eyes flick between us as if trying to read the situation.

"I suck." They both laugh.

"Is Jacob here? He hasn't been answering my calls," Lexi questions awkwardly. A look of worry flashes over Brad's face as he runs his hand up the back of his neck and through his hair. "Umm, I think he might've gone to the gym." Something feels off about his behavior as he glances from the house to Lexi.

"Okay, well, if you see him, can you tell him to call me, please?"

"Mhm," he answers as he turns and jogs up the staircase.

We start the walk back to the house, and it's a few silent minutes before I hear Lexi speak.

"That was weird, right?"

I let out a breath and nod. "Yeah, I'm not buying it."

"Fucker." She kicks her foot through the sand as she curses into the wind. "We fucked last night at the party. He took me into the bathroom, and we fucked." She stops walking, planting her hands on her hips, as a groan of frustration jerks from her chest. "He told me he was tired and fucked off to bed right after. I walked back alone, and now the motherfucker's ignoring my calls." She glances down at the house and then back at me.

"Don't even think about it, Lex. You want to get under his skin, then act like you used him. There's a bonfire tonight... plenty of hot guys to take your mind off it."

She smiles up at me and nods. "You're right. How's that saying go again, get under someone to get over someone, or something like that?" She laughs as she grabs my arm, pulling me down the beach, babbling about how she's going to destroy *spaghetti dick surfer boy.*

Showered and changed out of that suction cup of a wet suit, I let out a breath of relief. Lexi wants to go down to the beach and get some sun before we have to start getting ready for the bonfire tonight, so I slide on my yellow bikini and walk over to the books that litter my nightstand. I pick out a few different genres and slide them into my cotton beach bag, grabbing some sunblock and a towel and head out to find her.

It doesn't take me long, I just have to follow the arguing coming from the kitchen, and as I round the corner, I see Trey on the couch with the dog, watching in utter amusement as Lexi and Tristan go at it.

"Just look at this, Tristan." Lexi throws a sneaker at his face, but he's too quick and catches it before it makes contact. It's when Tristan laughs and holds the sneaker up that I can see it's been chewed to pieces.

"Why are you throwing the dog's chew toys at me?"

Lexi's looks like she's about to explode, and I'm considering an intervention.

"They're the only pair of running shoes I brought with me, Tristan."

"You don't even run."

"Not the fucking point. The dog needs to stay outside."

"Here's a fucking idea, why don't you fuck off down the beach to the surfer boy's residence. I didn't realize you were the type of girl who fucks people they barely know in bathrooms."

Lexi's eyes widen in shock, and I see her swallow hard. The room falls silent. I've never seen Tristan behave like this. His chest is heaving, and he looks really fucking angry. I've barely snapped out of my state of shock when I hear the back door slide open as Cruz steps inside. Breaking out in a nervous sweat, my stomach squeezes tight. He slides his headphones off his head to link around his neck as he stares at the awkward situation he's just walked into. His sweaty black shirt sticks to the defined muscles of his torso. His eyes find mine for a brief second, and butterflies explode through my stomach. Without a word, he slides his headphones back onto his head and looks away as he brushes past me, heading for the hall.

"You're a fucking dick, you know that." Lexi's broken voice pulls me out of my reverie, and I'm brought back to the present moment where Tristan seems to have lost his damn mind. Tears roll down Lexi's face, and I'm confused to what alternate universe I've stepped into.

I rush to Lexi's side and pull her toward me. "Are you okay?" She wipes her face and nods before drawing away and heading for the back door. I turn back to Tristan and shove at his chest. "What's wrong with you?"

He doesn't answer; instead, he turns his back to me and opens the fridge door, leaning down and grabbing some water. I don't have the energy to try and figure out what the fuck is going on with him right now, so I walk toward the exit, grabbing my beach bag on the way, and head down to the beach in search of Lexi.

I see her laid out not far from where the staircase drops into the sand, and I make my way over to her. Laying my towel next to hers, I barely sit down when she jolts upright.

"Did you tell him?" I'm unsure if the tone in her voice is anger or hurt.

"Tell who what?"

"Did you tell Tristan I slept with Jacob? I only told you." I rear back in confusion.

"Lexi, are you seriously asking me that question? Why would I ever do that to you?" I feel shattered that question was even apart of her thought process.

"Jesus, I'm sorry. I have no idea what's going on with me right now." She runs her hands through her long chocolate locks. "I can't believe I let enemy number one see me fucking cry." She lets out a frustrated groan.

"Tristan was out of line." I say, reaching down and sliding a book from my bag.

"Maybe I need one of those in my life." She nods at the book in my hand.

"A book?"

"A book boyfriend. At least they don't fuck you in a bathroom and pretend you don't exist."

I laugh. "That depends on which book you read."

She raises her brow at me, and I reach for a book by romance legend Mia Sheridan and hand it to her.

"No bathroom fucking in that one, just pure heart-melting romance." She takes it from me as we both get settled, with book boyfriends in hand.

After about an hour in the blistering heat, indulging in a red-hot forbidden romance, I'm in desperate need of some water. Getting to my feet, I glance down at Lexi, who's completely captivated with her current read.

"I'm just going to run up to the house and grab us some water."

She waves me off, not bothering to glance my way. I guess a good romance book is enough to take her mind off recent events.

Sliding in the back door, I freeze when I see the Tristan and Trey seated in the living room. Tristan throws his head back and laughs at something Trey says, and I'm happy to see him back to his usual happy self, although his behavior is concerning. I make a mental note to have a conversation with him later to try and see where his heads at as I beeline for the kitchen.

"Cruz can say they aren't together all he wants, but a picture doesn't lie."

Wait, did he say Cruz? A nervous hum skims over my skin. What picture? I open the fridge and pull my phone from my back pocket, typing 'Cruz Valentine' into the search engine. Boom.

Sweat starts to form in irritating droplets over my skin, as my heart falls abruptly into my stomach. It's a photo of Cruz, dressed in a black suit, in a complete lip lock with Meredith White. The heading screams at me in bold letters.

"Rekindled romance of a young powerhouse couple in the making."

My hands are shaking so badly, my phone slips from my grip.

"Taylah? You okay back there?" I hear my brother's voice, and I'm flooded with embarrassment. Here I am, freaking out over a photo of a guy kissing his girlfriend, who, by the way, is not me. The self-mortification is eating me alive. "Taylah?" I hear Tristan repeat my name, and I turn to face him with a perfect fake smile slapped across my face.

"Fine, just dropped my phone."

I head for my room, but as I enter the hall, I see Cruz's bedroom door is open, and it's as if my legs are running on pure emotion, taking on a mind of their own. Before I can slide some rationality into the moment, I'm standing inside his room, closing the door and staring at a shirtless Cruz, lying on his bed.

My body engulfs in an inferno of heat as my eyes slide down the length of his body. He has one arm resting behind his head, accentuating the bulge of his bicep. My mouth runs dry as my eyes fall to his chest, then down past the defined ridges of his stomach to the V-shape of his torso that slides into his grey sweatpants. I can see the outline of his thick cock, and heat rushes between my legs as I try and swallow. He clears his throat and I bring my eyes back up to his, and that's when I notice the cut across his brow.

"What happened to your face?" He sits up and leans against the headboard, running a finger to ghost over the cut. It has some Steri-Strips holding it together, but you can tell it's deep. The silence stretches out between us, and his intense stare makes me nervous.

I see the first aid kit on his nightstand, and without thinking, I head toward it, taking a seat on the edge of the bed. Fumbling through the contents, I grab some antiseptic wipes and some butterfly bandages.

Turning to face him, my heart was not ready for those whiskey-colored eyes to be staring right at me. My breath catches in my chest, making me cough from the lack of oxygen. I ignore the thumping of my heart against my ribcage as I lean forward and remove the blood-soaked dressing. Opening an antiseptic wipe, I clean the skin, the sting making him flinch.

"Sorry." The apology is almost a whisper. My ability to speak through the lump lodged in my throat is difficult. I apply fresh strips, my face flooding in sympathy, when a drop of blood slides down his cheek.

"Don't do that." His eyes narrow down on mine as his body pulls tight in agitation.

"Do what?"

He slides to sit on the opposite edge of the bed with his back to me. "Stop feeling fucking sorry for me, Taylah." The aggravated tone in his voice stabs me in the chest. Frustrated, I get to my feet and march toward the door, but something stops me from exiting through the threshold. The photo of him kissing Meredith launches itself through my mind as an unfamiliar feeling whips through me, like my stomach has started to disintegrate. And when I turn to face him, the next sentence that spills from my lying mouth confirms the sickening feeling I'm being assaulted with is jealousy.

"Brad's an amazing kisser, by the way." I have no idea what's gotten into me or why the hell he would care, but I can't stop as heat barrels through my body, completely overwhelming my ability to think like a decent human being. His eyes are on mine, a look of torment rupturing his features as he slowly gets to his feet.

Okay, yep, he cares.

Every step closer, his stare intensifies, and the room feels like it's closing in on me. I can't think or speak. Overwhelmed, I take a step back. It's when his hand starts to close the door, I realize I've stepped out into the hall.

"Enjoy your summer, Taylah." That's the last thing that leaves his lips before the door closes in my face.

"Fuck."

❧

Chapter Thirteen

Taylah

Disgust. That's the feeling that's soaking its way into my bones as I pace my room. My nervous system is shot to shit, and I'm filled with so much remorse, that it's making my skin crawl. I've never acted out with such malice before in my life, but the feelings Cruz is making me feel are overwhelming and unfamiliar, and I'm not really sure how to get a handle on myself.

As soon as he closed the door in my face, intense shame started pooling in my stomach. In the heat of the moment, I wanted him to feel just like I'd felt after I saw the photo of him kissing Meredith. It was spiteful and cruel and...

"Jesus, there you are." My door clicks closed as Lexi's voice fills the room. "I am *not* reading another page of this. My heart is broken in half, and my expectations of men have skyrocketed." She drops onto my bed and lets out a groan before pulling the pillow over her face. "I'm going to be single forever now."

Knowing the minute Lexi sees my face, she'll be able to read me like a book, I head for my ensuite. "Just having a shower; have to freshen up before the bonfire tonight." She makes a grunting noise with her head still buried in the pillow in acknowledgment.

I head straight for the shower, bypassing the mirror. I can't even bear to look at myself right now. All I can think about is the look on Cruz's face when those spiteful words left my lips, and I know I need to apologize. I feel like a complete lunatic. In the fit of an embarrassing jealous rage, I wanted an answer to the question that had been plaguing my mind for days. And when I saw exasperation flood his features the second that mortifying lie left my mouth, I had my answer. He cares.

With a tub of Ben and Jerry's cookie dough ice cream each, we take a seat on the couch in the living room.

"You sure you want more fictional men in your day?" I ask as she scrolls through the romance section, stopping on *The Notebook.*

"I'm just going all in at this point."

The movie barely starts when I see Tristan walk in with Trey, a beer in each hand, as they head in our direction.

"Ryan Gosling does it for you, does he, Lex?" Lexi lets out a groan, and Tristan's smile only widens.

The front door clicks closed behind me, and when I look over my shoulder, I see Cruz. His head's down, and he's scrolling through his phone, and the lack of eye contact does nothing to calm my racing heart.

"Well, for one, he knows how to treat women, unlike a certain blond man-whore I know."

"Hey, don't talk about Trey like that." Tristan jokes taking a sip of his beer.

Not in the mood to hear these two go at it again, I interject, "Any woman would be lucky to find herself her very own Noah Calhoun."

Trey drops down beside me and throws his arm around my neck. "Please enlighten us as to what this Noah character has that the men in this room fail to possess?" He smells like stale beer, and his words are slurred.

"Are you kidding me? The guy's the definition of perfect. He gives his one true love his heart, making it impossible for him to move on, and lives on the hope that the love of his life will walk back into his arms." I finish talking and for some reason my eyes find their way over to where Cruz is standing.

"So right person wrong time, bullshit. I don't fucking buy it. If you love someone, you aren't letting that person slip through your fingers." I hear Trey's voice and I turn back to face him.

"Sometimes it's not as simple as that." He rolls his eyes at me and turns to face Lexi.

"By the way Lexi, I just had a nice little chat with your little surfer boy. Funny, the girl on his arm didn't look like you." His antagonistic tone grates over the room.

"What is wrong with you?" This is not the Trey I know. His red eyes burn into mine as he takes another sip of his beer.

"Firefighters."

"What?" I'm so confused at this point if this is a question or a statement or just drunk babble.

"That's your type, right, Taylah?" He laughs and looks from Lexi back to me.

"I don't have a type," I answer, with absolutely no idea what the fuck is going on right now.

"You sure about that?" The smug grin on his face makes me feel uneasy. His eyes are glazed over like he's had a lot to drink or maybe something else. I'm not even sure at this point.

"Is there something you need to say?" The hostility in my voice doesn't go unnoticed, and he raises his hands in surrender.

"The sun will be going down soon; don't you boys have a fire to start?" Lexi's interjection is a welcome one. Trey nods, getting to his feet, and downing the rest of his beer. I look over to where my brother is standing in an effort to understand what the fuck is going on, but his face is buried in his phone, clearly not even listening to a thing that's just been said. Cruz follows them out, clicking the door closed behind them.

"What the hell was that?"

Lexi shrugs and gets to her feet. "He's drunk... don't listen to him."

The sun is fading away by the time *The Notebook* ends, and we make our way down the staircase to the bonfire. A cool breeze has picked up, making me thankful I opted to wear the grey hoodie I received from Brown University. We drop down onto the sand and head over to where the boys have set up a fire surrounded by picnic blankets and seat pillows. I don't see Trey as we approach, and I'm flooded with relief.

"Taylah Barker." I hear my name and turn to see Brad jogging toward us. Lexi stiffens beside me as if she expects Jacob's to pop out from behind him. Brad looks at her, and the agitated look on her face must say it all, as he raises his hands in surrender. "Don't look at me like that. You'll be happy to know I told his ass not to come down here tonight. I didn't know all the details, Lexi. I didn't know he used you, in a spare bathroom of all places, and let you walk home alone."

"Jesus Christ, I need a drink," Lexi states, heading off in the direction of the coolers filled with beer.

"He's an ass." Brad runs his hand sheepishly up his neck as he stands there waiting for me to speak.

"He is an ass," I agree, walking over to the nearest picnic blanket and taking a seat. Brad drops down next to me bringing his beer bottle to his lips.

"Are we still friends?" He bumps his shoulder to mine, and I playfully bump him back.

"The actions of your friend have nothing to do with you, so I guess we can still be friends."

He chuckles while finishing off his beer.

"Good, because I really enjoy watching you slide off a surfboard for hours on end."

I laugh as I shake my head and glance out to the ocean. The sun is well and truly gone as the moon takes its place as the only other light source besides the bonfire that's crackling away in front of me. Waves crash against the shore, as the smell of salt fills the air and I let the feeling of summer wash over me.

A storm brews in the distance as lightning ruptures across the ocean, sending my mind running to the last storm and a soaking wet Cruz in my bedroom.

"What're you thinking about?" Brad's voice breaks through my daydream.

"I was just watching the storm play out over the ocean. Hopefully, it's not moving toward us."

"Hopefully not." He says as he gets to his feet dusting the sand off his hands. "I'm just going to get another beer. Would you like anything?"

I shake my head and watch him walk away. Scanning the bodies, I look for Lexi. My eyes stop and my heart seizes inside my chest when I'm met with Cruz's burning stare. He's seated on a log on the opposite side of the fire. His dark hood shadows his face, but the glow of the fire crackles along the agitated pull of his features. There's something else flaring up behind his eyes, and I can't tell if it's anger or disgust.

I break our eye contact as Brad returns with Lexi by his side. They take a seat on either side of me, and I tilt my body to face Lexi.

"See anyone you like?" I ask as she takes a long drink of the beer in her hand, possibly in an attempt to get her mind of recent events. Her eyes are laser-focused on something in the distance, and when I follow her line of sight, my stomach bottoms out as Trey comes into focus. He stumbles slightly, and Tristan grabs his arm before he loses his footing completely.

"Take a seat, bro."

Lexi stiffens beside me when they sit down seat across from us. After the way both of them treated her today, she has good reason to be annoyed. There's a nervous energy circulating around us, and as the storm continues to assault the sky out at sea, unease starts to consume me. I feel Brad's hand rest on the small of my back, and I turn to face him.

"Are you okay?" His soft blue eyes reflect concern. I don't answer because I actually don't know what to say other than something feels off.

"It's nice to see you here, Brad, but I do wonder where your mate Jacob is?" Trey's voice grates over me, and I watch as Brad shifts uncomfortably as he turns to face him.

"I'm here to see Taylah, that's all." Brad's voice is tense, and I'm worried about where this is heading.

"I didn't realize you were seeing each other."

"We're just friends," Brad snaps back, bringing his beer to his lips and taking a sip as his eyes narrow in on Trey.

"And I'm sorry to say, but that's all you'll ever be."

"What is your problem? You're being a real jerk." I snap.

"I'm just spitting facts."

I glare at him as I get to my feet. I've had enough of his drunk, inexcusable behaviour, and as I turn to walk away, his next sentence knocks the wind out of me.

"You're in love with Sam Summers, right?"

I can't breathe. I snap my face in Trey's direction, whose smug grin makes me feel sick. Turning to where Cruz is now on his feet, my heart collapses into my stomach when sheer devastation filters through his features. Heat prickles at the base of my neck and trickles of sweat accumulates over my skin.

"What?" My voice cracks as emotion crashes through me. The only person who knows about my crush on Sam, is Lexi. I turn to her as she gets to her feet and grabs my arm.

"Let's leave." There's a slight tremble in her voice, but I'm not leaving until I know the truth.

"Did you tell him?" She looks at the sand for a minute before bringing her eyes back to mine, and the look on her face tells me everything I need to know. "Fuck, Lexi."

This is all too much at once, and I need to get out of here immediately. Pulling back, I turn to face Brad, who's on his feet. I link my arm with his as we turn and head off down the beach. With each step, my heart starts to settle until we get to the staircase that leads up to his house.

"You want to come up? We can talk if you need to?" A crack of thunder booms above us, sending me into silence. I feel his hand slide into mine in an attempt to comfort me, but something about it just feels all wrong. Dragging my hand from his, I take a step back.

"I think I need some time by myself right now."

He nods at me, pulling my hood up over my head. "It looks like that storm is closer than we think. Don't stay out too late." He smiles before turning and jogging up the staircase. I turn to face the ocean as another thunderous crack roars above me. The sky is seconds from opening up into a downpour, but there's no way I'm going back to the house right now. Scanning the beach,

I see the wooden jetty in the distance. Keeping my hood up and my head tucked low, I start to run in that direction as the clouds break open and rain crashes against me.

I step under the protection of the jetty, right as a crack of lightning lights up the entire night sky, highlighting the silhouette of a man towering in front of me. And as if right on cue, lightning flashes around us, and those devastatingly beautiful honey-colored eyes find mine.

Chapter Fourteen

Taylah

Seconds drag into minutes, and the only decipherable sounds I can comprehend are the chaotic storm cracking around us and the thump of my racing heart against my rib cage. I watch as rain slides down his face, dripping onto his chest, which even though covered with his hoodie, the pattern of his uneven breathing is obvious. I bring my eyes back up to his face, and the tortured sorrow that plays out behind his eyes steals my breath, as an overwhelming feeling of guilt courses through me.

I can't be here.

Sucking back a rush of air, I turn to run. But something keeps me from moving my legs. The rain has turned torrential, and my wet clothes are sticking to me as my body starts to shake. I can't think, can't move, and can't for the life of me understand what my heart is screaming for.

I turn abruptly, only to smack right into a tall, solid wall of muscle. His scent fills me, and my heart plummets into my stomach as he lowers my hood. My eyes are stuck, staring at his thick chest, and I'm finding it hard to bring them to meet his.

His height towers over me, partially sheltering me from the rain, as water droplets roll down his face and slide onto mine.

Slowly, I lift my eyes and trace them up his chest, stopping at his throat to watch his Adam's apple bob as he takes a harsh swallow. I keep moving up, pausing at his full lips. His mouth parts slightly, and droplets of rain slide across his lips and drip onto mine. His warm breath ghosts over my mouth as another bolt of lightning sends static through the air.

"Is it true?" His voice is barely audible. "You're in love with Sam Summers?" His eyes captivate me with their movement, so the question doesn't register right away. The pain in his voice sends tremors through my chest. Confusion has my stomach in knots, leaving me incapable of forming any kind of response. I feel the warm rush of his exhale slide over my lips as he lets go of the breath he was holding as he leans into me.

Tilting his head to the side, his cold wet nose slides up my jaw, igniting my entire body with heat. I close my eyes and welcome the cool rain against my scorched skin as he buries his face into my neck, breathing me in. My entire world is spinning as his hands brush over my shoulders and slowly slide down my arms. The urge to be closer, to bury myself tight to his chest, is overwhelming, and I lean into his touch.

I open my eyes as he slowly pulls back from me. Lifting my arms, I slide the hood off his face and link my arms to rest around his neck. His earth-shattering eyes stare back at me, ablaze in the storm. His tongue slides across his bottom lip, and his hands glide down my back to rest on my hips, leaving a trail of fire against my skin.

He shifts toward me, and I lean in, mirroring his movement, as the warmth of our uneven breathing ignites the space between us. My body starts to tremble when his lips brush across mine. An involuntary moan rushes from my lips, as pure ecstasy coats my skin. My eyes flutter closed and I wait for him to take my mouth completely.

A crack of lightning hits the sand behind us, breaking the moment clean in half as the static-filled air sends my hair into the stratosphere. Cruz steps away from me, pulling his hood back over his head, and I drag my fingers through my wet hair, doing my best attempt to pull myself back together. I watch as his eyes dart up to the house and back to me.

"We need to get out of this storm."

I nod in agreement. He looks up at the sky as if deciphering the best moment to make a run for it, before stepping forward and linking his fingers through mine.

I lose myself in the warmth of his palm against mine as we make a run for the house. The living room is lit up where I can see most of the bonfire participants have taken refuge out of the rain. Cruz stops in his tracks as he analyses the situation.

"This way." His grip on me tightens as he tugs me toward the sycamore tree that splays out against the back of the house. Before I can grasp the situation, his hands are around my waist and I'm hoisted onto a thick branch that conveniently leads to Tristan's bedroom window. I laugh to myself, as it finally falls into place how Tristan managed to sneak out to meet girls while we summered here as a family.

I push the window open and slide through, dropping onto the floor as Cruz follows me in. I keep my back to him as the window locks shut behind me. My body is shaking and it's unclear whether that's from the soaking wet clothes I'm wrapped in or sheer adrenaline. I fail to get my breathing under control when his arms wrap around me from behind.

"Arms up." His deep voice ricochets over my spine, and I want to drown in it. I do as he asks, and he drags the hoodie from my body, letting the wet material drop to the floor. He steps around me, and I lower my arms down as he drops his gaze, drawing his bottom lip between his teeth. I follow his line of sight when it suddenly dawns on me: I'm standing in front of him in a drenched white T-shirt with no bra on. I become overly aware of my hardened nipples pulled taut under the thin material. His fingertips slide under the hem of my shirt, drawing his soft touch over my stomach as I lose myself in the sight and smell of him.

He takes the bottom of my shirt into his hands and slowly slides the wet material up my body as our breathing clicks up a notch, mingling together like an electrically charged cloud of pure fucking heat. My entire body is screaming for his touch, for his mouth to find mine and suck every erratic breath gasping from it.

His eyes roam over my body as the gentle slide of his fingers cascades effortlessly down my spine. I'm all in at this point as the sexual tension sucks up the air around us. It's overwhelming and erotic and... he takes a step away from me, before reaching for a dry hoodie and sliding it over my body. He leans in and I soak up the smell of him as he places a soft kiss to my forehead.

"You should leave."

"Why?"

"You know why." The tortured ache in his voice makes my clit pulse with need. "Good night, Taylah." He moves away from me, and the loss is brutal. I stand there for a few moments, as my libido screams at me to drop to my knees, and beg him for release. But my brain soon catches up, and I leave the room with my dignity still intact.

I barely make it inside my door when Lexi appears behind me.

"I'm sorry. I didn't mean to tell Trey about Sam."

I pull Cruz's hoodie tighter to my body, coating myself in his scent.

"It's not ok, Lexi. You were outraged when you thought I told Tristan about you sleeping with Jacob. I trusted you." I'm hurt and she knows it. Her actions tonight stirred up unnecessary drama and hurt, which at some point I'm going to have to deal with. "I need a minute."

She's devastated with herself, that's clear. But I'm too exhausted to continue this tonight.

"Okay, I'll see you in the morning."

I toss and turn, but my mind won't stop as I stare up at the sheer drapes wrapped around my four-poster bed. I think of how I feel when I'm around Sam. It's fun and flirty and comforting. It's everything I thought finding someone to spend your life with should feel like. Then Cruz Valentine walked back into my life, no scratch that, exploded, like a god damn supernova. He's confusing and torturous, and with the way my heart-rate accelerates in his presence, he's dangerous. *Very fucking dangerous.*

Letting out an exasperated huff, I throw my comforter off my body and head for the only place I can think of to try and settle the chaotic mess inside my head. As soon as I enter the room, I'm filled with a calming sense of safety. To the left is a white wooden bookcase. It starts with books from my childhood, followed by my teen years, ending with some more recent additions. There's a huge bay window on the far wall that looks out over the beach, and directly in front of that sits my white grand piano.

Taking a seat on the smooth wooden bench, I let my fingers settle over the ivory keys, and bask in the instant warmth that travels up my fingertips. Closing my eyes, I let the melody float through the room, as I slowly piece myself back together.

Chapter Fifteen

Cruz

Sam Summers. As soon as that sentence left Trey's mouth, the look on Taylah's face told me everything I needed to know. It hurt, boy did it fucking hurt, and seeing her under the jetty in the raging storm with those fascinating silver eyes locked on mine, the ache in my chest only multiplied.

Visions of her wet body under my fingertips plague my mind, like an erotic rush spilling through my veins. I've never been so turned on in my entire life at the thought of my mouth on her skin. She smells like a mix of marshmallows and cotton candy, and my god, I want to taste every inch of her.

Sliding one arm under my head, I stare up at the ceiling, and let out an deep exhale. She's in love with Sam Summers, the sweetest fucking guy I know. If Taylah's sun-filled personality had a twin, it would be him. I want her so fucking bad it hurts, but at what cost?

How can I take the sun away from her only to deliver her nothing but rain?

I'm pulled out of my sleep by the sound of my phone vibrating on the nightstand. I reach over and pick it up, glancing at the name flashing across the screen. *Jack Valentine.*

Oh, for fuck sake.

I hesitantly answer and place the phone to my ear.

"It's Meredith's birthday in a few weeks. I was thinking you could take her somewhere tropical, perhaps Tahiti?"

Closing my eyes, I suck back the urge to tell him to go fuck himself as I contemplate hanging up.

"That's not going to happen."

"Tahiti it is. I'll inform the pilot."

He ends the call as anger coils through me. I sit up and take a breath as the room slowly suffocates me.

I need to get out of here.

I throw on some jeans and a shirt and grab my keys, but as soon as I step through the threshold and into the living room, I'm smacked in the face with Taylah's scent, stopping me in my tracks.

That familiar wave of heat floods through me as my heart starts to race. I turn my head to the couch where she's seated, staring at me. Her blonde hair is braided away from her face, and she's wearing a white strapless dress that molds tight to her toned body. It sits mid-thigh, and my eyes trace down her long, tanned legs. My palm twitches, and I flick my keys to distract myself from walking over to her and running my hands all over her body.

"Oh, for god sake." It's only when I hear Lexi's voice that I realize we're not alone. The back door slides open, and when I see who steps inside, I realize the cause of Lexi's frustration. Tristan walks in, letting Nugget off his leash, followed by Trey. After last night's drunken episode, this is my first time seeing Trey, and by the look on the girls' faces, this is their first time too.

Tristan drops onto the couch across from the girls, pulling Nugget to sit next to him as he scratches his head.

"You know that's not your dog, right?" Lexi states, doing her best to ignore the elephant in the room. Tristan ignores her, but my eyes draw to Trey, who's taking a step toward Taylah. Heat explodes in my core as anger crashes through me in waves. Her eyes look up at him, and something that reflects sadness flickers over her features, making my stomach recoil.

"Don't go fucking near her." The ice in my tone makes the entire group glance my way. Trey stands still and raises his hands.

"I'm just trying to apologize," he stammers as his voice breaks. It's evident he's ashamed of his drunken behavior, but right now, I'm struggling to forgive him. He takes another step closer, and I see red. How fast I get to him surprises even me as I wrap my hand around his arm and drag him away from her before pinning him against the wall.

"I said, don't go near her." The sentence barely slides out through my gritted teeth as Trey's eyes pool with a cross between fear and confusion. The room is silent for a few minutes, and I can feel the heat of their eyes on me. I take a step back as Tristan gets to his feet and walks between us with his hands up.

"Okay, I think we need a time-out." The emotion in his voice is laced with worry, and I want to feel remorse, but I'm struggling to find it. He turns to look at Trey. "You definitely need to apologize to the girls. What the hell was with you last night?"

Trey's face goes sheet white as he runs his hand through his hair.

"I wasn't myself last night, and I apologize from the bottom of my heart." The sorry in his tone is obvious, and the room falls into silence.

"Kitchen, bathrooms, including all toilets for a week." Lexi's stubborn tone cuts through the moment.

"Just a week?" I watch as Tristan walks in front of Trey and playfully nudges his shoulder. "Make it a month."

"Mean." There's a slight grin in Trey's response as if welcoming any kind of reaction as a win.

Glancing back at Taylah, I see a smile on her face. Her eyes look up to mine briefly before leaving me, as she gets to her feet.

"I think we need to spend the day together. There's so much tension in the group, and a day of fun, food, and laughing, sounds like the perfect remedy." She smiles at Trey, and I can't help but feel a jealous turmoil slide around in my stomach.

"Does Tristan have to come?" Lexi asks sarcastically.

"Didn't realize you were so interested in whether I come or not?" His sexualized response gets Lexi to her feet.

"I didn't mean it like that, and you know it." She shouts, shoving her finger at his chest.

"Nope." Taylah steps forward and holds out her hands. "You two aren't allowed to argue for one whole day."

"That's fine. Just tell Lexi to stop thinking about me sexually all the time."

Before I know what's happening, Lexi is chasing Tristan out the back door as Trey grabs Nugget and follows behind, and everything feels back to normal.

The room is suddenly filled with awkward tension as Taylah looks over at me, drawing her bottom lip into her mouth. She's flushed with arousal, as her mouth parts ever so slightly, delivering a soft rush of air across her lips, and I hold my breath to stop the rush of air that's trying to force its way out of my lungs.

I know I should walk away.

I'm trying to relay that message to the rest of my body, but no matter how much I tell myself to leave, my feet stay glued to the ground.

"Wherever we go, make sure there's lots of ways I can torture your brother." Taylah jolts as Lexi comes barging back through, and I use this moment to head for my room. My mind has had enough filth-filled moments, for the time being, and I need to cool the fuck off.

The sun has started to descend as we make our way into the carnival gates. The smell of popcorn and freshly cut grass fills the air as we cross through the field and head toward the ride section. Lexi is talking animatedly as she drags Taylah toward the rollercoaster that houses most of the back section of the field. I can't look away as Taylah's long blonde hair flickers in the afternoon breeze in gorgeous waves from the braid she was wearing all day. The tight, little white dress that hugs her body to perfection is sending me insane, as her sweet scent drives the final blow to my heart.

"I'm not fucking doing that." Tristan's terrified voice forces me from my daydream. "You know I hate rides." I draw my attention to Tristan, who's paled significantly. Taylah steps forward and nods behind us.

"What about the Ferris wheel?" The sun is setting behind her, making her skin glow, and my mind is struggling to comprehend anything else that's been said as we head in that direction.

I slide my hands into the pockets of my jeans as we stand in line. Taylah is standing with Tristan, still trying to convince him that the ride isn't dangerous, given its mostly enclosed carriage structure, and Lexi's with Trey, who's been apologizing for his behavior for the last ten minutes.

We get to the front of the line, and Tristan takes a leap back. "Nope, I can't do it."

"Tristan!" Frustration pours through Taylah's voice, and agitation heats my skin.

"Get on the damn ride, Tristan," I call out after him, but he doesn't even look back as he storms toward the food vendors. I hear Taylah let out a sigh, and my head snaps back in her direction as Lexi and Trey take a seat together. She turns away from me and steps onto the stairs that lead to the next seat when a tall, lean man dressed in dark-blue overalls grabs her arm.

Fire explodes up my spine as I launch forward, gripping his wrist in my fist. "I suggest you get your hands off her." The words sound savage as they punch out through clenched teeth. The man's eyes widen, and he nods and lets go.

"I'm sorry, it's just that it's two per seat, for safety reasons." The tremble in his voice makes me feel bad for terrifying him, but the thought of anyone putting their hands on her makes me want to...

I don't finish that thought because I'm visibly distracted by the way she's looking at me. The flecks in her eyes sparkle like a fucking galaxy, and my chest tightens with every breath intake. The need to be close to her is physically suffocating me.

I look at the ride attendant and nod as I take Taylah's hand in mine, pulling her into the vacant seat with me.

Chapter Sixteen

Taylah

The adrenaline that's pumping through my veins creates pulses of heat through my body as the ride starts up. I'm confused by Cruz's behavior, and for the life of me cannot read the situation we're currently in. He grabbed my hand and dragged me onto the ride with him, but as the carriage door closed, his grip left my body, and we're seated so far apart it's driving me insane.

As the ride creeps toward the incline, I try and keep my eyes focused on the sun slipping out of the sky, but when I hear him clear his throat, I can't help but glance his way. His legs are slightly parted as his big hands rest in his lap. His dark jeans sit so snug to his muscular thighs, which makes me wonder what it would feel like to be pulled into a lap that looks like that and...

"What're you thinking about?" His voice is like warm honey, and I want to close my eyes and savor every word. But the way his eyes are devouring me right now, is intimidating as hell.

"Nothing," I answer, sitting further back in my seat and trying to focus on the ribbons of pinks, blues and purples encasing the sky.

He slowly closes the space between us, leaning into me, and sliding his face into the dip of my neck. My heart races as his hot breath cascades across my neck and into my hair, creating currents of pleasure, and my core aches for more.

I close my eyes as his soft mouth brushes against my neck, making my clit throb between my legs. His hand is suddenly cupping my face while his tongue traces up the side of my throat before dragging the bottom of my ear between his lips. The carriage shakes slightly, and my stomach bottoms out as warmth travels through my veins, activating every single nerve ending and making me gasp for air.

"Fuck." The way those four letters softly blow out of his mouth against my skin, edges me closer to my release. His hand leaves my face, and I'm instantly swallowed by an empty feeling from the loss of his touch. I want to open my eyes and beg him to put his hand back on me, but before I work up the courage, his fingers start tracing up the inside of my thigh.

I part them slightly to solidify my consent, as his fingers continue to skim the inside of my leg. The wait is torturous, and my panties are ruined by the time his fingertips brush softly at the outside of my thong.

"Oh my god." The gravel in his voice almost sends me undone, as I widen my legs even further. His fingers dip inside my panties and slowly find their way to my throbbing clit. I take short, sharp, delicious breaths as he circles a finger agonizingly slow. Over and over.

My body is so hot and overstimulated I forget where I am as I reach out for something to ground me. Finding the bottom of Cruz's shirt, my body starts to pull tight as an overwhelming rush of pleasure threatens to rip through me at any given second. I tighten my grip on his shirt as I welcome my impending high.

"Open your eyes." His voice is the last thing I hear as my body shatters into a million euphoric pieces, and I open my eyes. The cotton candy sunset creates the perfect backdrop to the peaceful feeling that's engulfing me, while I slowly float back down to earth.

It's silent as we touch back down to the ground, both of us looking straight ahead as the sun finally dips out of sight. The enclosed cage starts to feel suffocating and overwhelming as the reality of what I've just done with my off-limits brother's best friend starts to set in. The ride attendant opens the latched door, and I'm on my feet as quickly as humanly possible, jogging down the steps and taking off in a run.

"Taylah?" I turn around at the sound of Tristan's worried voice. Are you okay?" he asks, placing a hand on my shoulder, and I'm suddenly filled with guilt. I nod and give the best fake smile I can muster, as the rest of the group catches up to us. Just having Cruz this close to me again makes me struggle to catch my breath.

"Are you sure?"

"I'm fine. The ride just made me sick, that's all." I regret the words as soon as they leave my mouth. I didn't mean it how it sounds, and I can't bring myself to look at Cruz for his reaction.

"Maybe you should eat something."

The colorful carnival lights flicker as we weave our way through the food vendors, stopping at a hotdog station. I scan the rest of the line and see a man whipping up cotton candy at the end of the aisle.

"I'll be right back." I head in the direction of the stall, as the sweet familiar scent surrounds me.

"Hello, miss. How many?" The older gentleman with grey hair smiles at me, as he finishes packaging up the pink, purple and blue candy, and handing it over to a young blonde girl with pigtails.

"Just one, please." He nods at me as he spins a fresh batch together.

"The boys are finding a seat over by fireworks." I turn to see Lexi a few feet away holding a tray of drinks. "I'll just take these to them."

I nod to her as she rounds the corner out of sight.

It doesn't take me long to find them all sprawled out on a large picnic blanket, with hotdogs and beers in hand.

"Does anyone else want some cotton candy?" I ask as I approach. Cruz's face whips around to look at me, and I'm met with a look that resembles... fear?

"I'll meet you guys back at the house," he stammers as he struggles to his feet.

"You sure? It's like an hour walk," Tristan shouts after him, but by this time, Cruz has already broken out in a run.

Glancing down at my phone, I check the time for the millionth time. It's been an hour since Cruz left, and while the rest of the group seems to be laughing and bonding like we planned, my mind won't stop thinking about, Cruz, and what happened on the Ferris Wheel tonight.

"Have I mended our friendship, Tay?" I'm pulled from my delicious recollection of events as Trey throws his arm over my shoulder. "I'm so sorry." He's mimicking puppy dog eyes, and I can't help but laugh.

"I guess you're forgiven." I give him a playful shove, and we break apart. "Where's Tristan and Lexi?" I ask as I scan the area where I last saw them.

"Went to get drinks," Trey responds.

'Wait, like together?"

Trey grins as he nods, letting a chuckle escape his lips. "I think they like each other more than they let on."

"No, we fucking don't," Lexi snaps, shoving a red cup into his chest, as the contents splash onto his grey shirt.

"Okay, my bad." Trey laughs as he takes a sip.

The fireworks are minutes away, and I sit there in silence, sipping on the homemade lemonade Lexi brought back for me. Lexi and Tristan are arguing about the golden retriever that Tristan doesn't want to give back, and Trey is talking to a cute redhead wearing cowboy boots.

My thoughts get the better of me, and I get to my feet. "Lexi, can you catch a ride with the boys? I'm not feeling the best and want to go home." She looks at me with concern as she rises to her feet.

"You don't want to watch the fireworks?"

"Some other time."

She turns to Tristan and slams her cup into his hand. "I'll come with you."

"No. I'm fine. You stay with Tristan and Trey. Enjoy your night. Besides, I think Trey has more apologizing to do, anyway." I smile as I wait for her response.

"Okay, well, drive safe and text me as soon as you get back to the house."

I nod, turning on my heel, and heading in the direction of my Jeep.

Chapter Seventeen

Cruz

By the time I get back to the beach house, my chest is on fire. When the words *cotton candy* left Taylah's mouth, memories of us together crashed through me like a freight train. That life-altering day by the river when we were just kids. A memory I've held onto, to guide me through some of the darkest days of my life.

Throwing back a glass of water, I stand shirtless in the kitchen in nothing but a pair of sweats. I've managed to shower and change, and I still can't seem to catch my breath. So much has happened in one night, and I'm struggling to get my emotions in check. Placing the glass in the sink, I lay my palms flat against the counter as I lean against it, struggling to bring my heart rate back to earth.

As soon as my eyes close, I'm filled with images of Taylah's flushed skin as her body contracted and released in my grip. The way she come apart in my arms, dragging me close while the glow of the sunset lit her up like an angel, made my heart stop, and I reveled in every fucking second of it.

Remembering how wet and responsive she was to my touch sends blood rushing between my legs, clearly draining from my brain, as I grip the counter in an attempt to not pass out.

Fuck.

I'm soon reminded of the sentence that left her mouth about how sick the ride made her feel. It knocked the wind right out of me then, and repeating it over in my head does the same amount of damage.

I down another glass of water before heading back to my room, but as I step into the hall, I hear the front door open behind me. Glancing back, I watch Taylah step inside the living room. She stands alone as her eyes move to my direction, and when they finally meet, she draws that pouty bottom lip of hers into her mouth. The urge to take that bottom lip between my teeth becomes so overwhelming that I turn and walk toward her. Her eyes widen with every step closer until we're inches apart. The sweet smell of her skin enraptures me, and I can't fucking think of anything but tasting her. Leaning in, I close the distance between us.

"Wait." The word leaves her lips and stabs me in the chest with so much force, it knocks the breath from my lungs. I take a step back, leaving my eyes on hers as I try and read her. She starts to pace the room, and I take a few more steps back to give her some space.

She runs a frustrated hand through her hair as she attempts to form a sentence that I know I'm not gonna want to hear.

"What happened tonight was crossing the line."

There it is.

My legs hit the couch behind me, and I slowly take a seat as my heart disintegrates inside my chest. Her frantic pacing is making me dizzy, and watching how distressed she's becoming fills me with guilt.

"You're Tristan's best friend, Cruz. If he finds out what we did…" The tremble in her voice is unbearable to hear.

"Come here, Taylah."

She stops pacing and turns to look at me, pausing for a moment before taking a step toward me. Then another, and another until she's standing right there in front of me. It takes everything in me to stay focused on her face as my disobedient mind screams at me to take in every delicious inch of her. But I can tell she's at war with herself, so I keep my focus on her beautiful face.

"It can never happen again, Cruz." The words leave her mouth. But the way her eyes trail over my lips before finding their way back to my eyes makes what she's saying hard to believe. "We can't." The emotion buried behind those two words is enough to make me want to grab a hold of her and never let her go. So, when she turns to leave, my hand finds her wrist, and I tug her onto my lap. She falls into me, with her legs on either side of mine, as a rush of air blows out of that perfect mouth. Her body molds to mine like it's made for me, and I let my eyes focus on the quiver of her lips. The thought of crashing my mouth against hers is all I can think about, making my cock grow painfully hard beneath her.

Her breathing picks up as she feels me hardening against her core, and the wriggle of her hips almost makes me come in my pants. I slide my hands down either side of her back, bringing my eyes back up to meet hers. The vibration of her body under my touch is achingly satisfying as my hands rest on her ass. She places her hands on either side of me, leaning in as she grips the back of the couch, and I watch as a fire erupts behind her eyes. Our erratic breathing mixes together as she grinds against me, her magnetic eyes not once leaving mine. The quiet gasps and breathless moans are pouring off us as I grip her tighter, my hips falling into sync with hers.

Since when has dry humping been so fucking erotic?

Her cheeks become flushed as her body pulls tight. I know she's close, and I brace myself to watch her fall apart for the second time tonight.

Her mouth parts slightly as she sucks back a rush of air, and I watch intently as she brings herself closer to the edge. Her head tilts back slowly, and her body starts to tremble.

"Eyes on me, Taylah. Watching you come apart is the best part."

Her eyes snap open and find mine, and I'm rendered speechless while her body shudders against me, sweat rolling down her face. The moans that pour out of her make me want to place my lips to hers and catch every fucking sound, but I'm too mesmerized to move. She falls against me, her mouth almost colliding with mine, as we sit chest to chest. I can feel her racing heart pounding against my chest, as her eyes fall down to my lips.

"Cruz." My name leaves her lips in a breathless whisper, and the entire room melts away.

Fuck.

The sound of the front door unlocking sends us both barreling back into reality. She jumps off my lap so fast, she loses her footing and falls directly onto her ass. I stand and hold out my hand to her, but she shakes her head at me, embarrassment coloring her cheeks as Lexi and Tristan step through the threshold. Lucky for us, they're off in a world of their own, giving Taylah time to get to her feet.

"Where's Trey?" Taylah asks straightening her dress.

"He left with some hottie at the carnival," Tristan answers, heading for the kitchen. I take a seat back on the couch, and surprisingly, Taylah takes one next to me as Lexi sits across from us. Beads of sweat trickle down the back of my neck as Lexi looks us over in curiosity.

"Everything okay with you two?" she asks, but before we have to find the words to answer, I see her roll her eyes when Tristan walks into the room with Nugget.

"I thought we agreed that the dog stays outside!" The arguing commences, and I am thankful for the distraction as I link my fingers through Taylah's and squeeze to get her attention. Letting go, I get to my feet and head for the hall. I feel her presence behind me as we walk down the darkened hall. We get to her bedroom door, and she reaches for the knob.

Fuck it.

Adrenaline fills me as I turn and reach for her wrist, pushing her against her door. In one swift movement, I lift her arms above her head, pinning her beneath me. Her chest is heaving as I gaze down at her and feast on the way her eyes search mine. I want her so bad it hurts, but after her freak-out moment earlier, I need to know where her head's at.

Keeping her hands pinned, I lean my face to hers, letting my lips ghost hers while I devour the way her uneven breathing washes across my mouth. I hold still for a moment, working up the courage to speak.

"Are you sure we can't cross that line, over and over, until you can think of nothing but what I feel like pressed against you?" I whisper into her mouth as pure torment detonates between us.

"We can't."

With that, I let go of her wrists and take a step back as her eyes fill with tears, and it takes everything in me to walk away from her.

Chapter Eighteen

Taylah

"Earth to Taylah." Lexi's voice carries me out of the echo of my mind, and I turn to look at her. "Well, how do I look?" She does a twirl in her adults-only Princess Jasmine costume that leaves very little to the imagination.

"Beautiful, obviously." I smile at her as she bats her long, dark lashes at me.

"I'm going to make myself a drink; there's not a chance in hell I'll be able to handle your brother on his birthday sober." She closes my door behind her, and I look up at myself in the mirror. I'm seated at my mirrored dresser, sliding the gold leaf headband into my curled hair, taking a moment to look at myself. The last few days here at the beach house, I've felt a shift in me, and for the first time in my life, I feel utterly lost.

For as long as I can remember, I've been the type of girl who knows exactly what I want, and exactly where I'm heading in life. Get into Brown, move to New York, career in politics, and marry the love of my life. There was a time when I thought that maybe Sam could have been that guy. Sweet, kind and dedicated, not to mention drop-dead-gorgeous. But the moment Cruz walked back into my life, it stirred up something inside me that I can't explain. Like I've been living dormant, just going through the motions of life, and suddenly... I'm alive. There's so much confusion going on between my heart and my head, but what I do know for certain is that no one has ever made me feel the way Cruz Valentine makes me feel.

Taking a breath, I get to my feet, letting the sheer white material of the almost transparent gown gather at my feet. There's a slit up the left side of the dress that opens the gown mid-thigh. I slip into my tan gladiator style sandals and slide on some gold bangles to finish the look. When I open the door and almost crash directly into a waiting Cruz, as he stands there with his fist up, as if about to knock at my door. Shock fills his features momentarily before that emotion is replaced with a sexual hunger as his eyes roam over my body.

"Wow." The warmth of the exaggerated whisper rushes over my collarbone, sending shivers down my spine. He's wearing a plain cotton black T-shirt with black jeans and a pair of black Vans. It takes a moment for it to register that he's not dressed up for the party tonight, and saying it saddens me would be an understatement.

"You're not staying for Tristan's party?" Disappointment fills my voice, and a quizzical look brushes over his features. He looks down at his outfit and back up at me.

"Because I'm not in some ridiculous costume?" he asks, and I suddenly feel the need to taunt him.

"So, this, what I'm wearing is ridiculous?"

He narrows his eyes at me, sensing the playful tone of my voice, stepping forward and leaning his body against mine. His lips brush the sensitive spot just below my ear, sending goosebumps racing across my skin.

"If I say yes, will you take it off?"

Holy fuck.

My entire body ignites with so much heat that my brain struggles to retain any kind of self-control, and what I do next surprises even me. Somehow, in the moments after those words left his lips, I've managed to drag him into my room and onto my bed. His fresh, clean scent surrounds me, and the familiar aroma of soap and freshly cut flowers consumes me. I want to pull him into me and suffocate on his smell, and as my hands grip the bottom of his shirt, I do just that. His hard body is pressed against me as his hands slide their way slowly down the sides of my body. The way his fingertips gently caress, search and explore my skin electrifies me, and I feel myself opening up for him.

Oh my god, I want this.

His hands grip my thighs, and he pulls my legs to wrap his waist. His hard cock presses against me through the denim of his pants, and a sharp rush of air escapes my chest. My mind is racing, and I want to scream at the top of my lungs for him to rip my clothes off, but he's in no hurry as his eyes remain focused on mine. The air is so heavy it's hard to pull a breath, and the way his eyes sparkle with desire only adds to my inability to breathe when he's this close to me.

My hands are pulling at his clothes to bring him closer. I need him closer. It's all I can think about while our uneven breath intermingles together, sending my heart racing into oblivion. I've lost all control, which is new for me. Like I'm freefalling, but know, beyond any doubt, he'll be there to catch me. It's the most freeing moment of my life, and that's the moment I blurt out...

"Do you want me in the way I want you?"

He draws back from me slightly, drawing his brows together, and I worry that I've lost the moment. His eyes scan back and forth between mine, and I'd do anything to be able to read him right now. The silence between us only fills me with dread as my stomach launches into a summersault.

Oh my god.

The room suddenly feels overwhelming, and I go to move out from underneath him when I hear him whisper under his breath.

"Yes."

That one little word has warmth soaring through my chest, and I take a second to absorb the moment in its entirety. The way he's looking at me right now, with so much adoration and desire, kicks my arousal into overdrive, and I drag him into me until his mouth is hovering over mine. I can smell the fresh, minty aroma from his face being so close, and I want to devour his mouth with my own. The desire burning through me to have his taste coat my mouth is blinding.

"Taylah, your roommate from Brown is here." Lexi's voice slices the moment clean in half as she pounds her fist against my bedroom door. We scramble apart so fast it makes me dizzy, and I'm thankful I had the foresight to lock the door. "Taylah?"

"Yes, I'll be out in a minute," I do my best to hide the tremble in my voice as I shout back, fixing my dress. Cruz has his back to me as he tilts his head up to the ceiling, letting out a breath.

"I'll go out first; she'll be there waiting for me."

He doesn't answer me, and I should probably ask if there's anything wrong, but I'm too distracted by the incessant banging on my door.

I whip the door open and step out into the hall, swiftly closing it behind my back.

"Finally." Lexi links her arm in mine and tugs me down the hall and into a sea of drunken costume covered party animals. I see Skylar in the kitchen with one ankle crossed over the other, leaning up against the fridge, and the unamused look on her face makes me laugh.

God, I've missed her.

Her fiery curls, linked with that dark jacket, matching mini skirt, and signature maroon Doc Martens, make her stand out in a crowd of dressed-up cartoon characters.

"I'm so happy you made it." I smile as I bring her in for a hug.

"So, this is what a normal summer break looks like?"

I laugh as I start to ask her how her summer's been, when Trey slides between us dressed as Tommy Shelby from *Peaky Blinders.*

"Skylar Rhodes, I'm Trey Whittaker." He holds out his hand as he introduces himself but quickly pulls back when a look of pure annoyance envelops Skylar's face.

"Let me stop you right there, playboy. No, I don't want a drink. Yes, I'm aware I'm not in a costume at a dress-up party, and no, I don't let strangers into my vagina after five seconds of conversation. Now, if you'll excuse me, I need to use the bathroom."

The look on Trey's face as he watches Skylar walk away could only be described as dumbfounded.

"You okay over there, Trey?" He turns to face me at the sound of my voice, planting his hands on the counter to keep himself steady.

"I think I'm in love."

I laugh and slide him a red cup of liquid courage. "She has that effect on most men."

The mix of colorful strobe lights and the smell of tequila is wreaking havoc with my senses as I lean against the countertop in the kitchen. Skylar left about an hour ago to do some more *"research gathering,"* and I was more than tempted to join her. Instead, here I am, watching overly intoxicated cartoon characters grind against each other while Chris Brown blasts through the speakers. Every now and then, the crowd parts just enough that I get a glimpse of Cruz seated on the couch in the living room.

Fuck, he's hot.

"Shot?" A very drunk boy in a Mickey Mouse costume holds out a shot glass of clear liquid in front of my face.

I shake my head. "I don't drink."

His brows lift in complete confusion before he shrugs at me, throws the shot back, and disappears into the sea of bodies on the dance floor. I scan the room looking for Lexi. The last I saw, she was running after Tristan after he asked if he could take a shot from her breasts, and that was more than an hour ago.

"Once again, you're the one in white," a familiar voice rings out behind me, and I turn and see Brad standing there dressed as a cowboy.

"Finally, a familiar face." I laugh as he cracks open his beer and takes a sip.

"You don't know these people?" He nods to the very crowded house laid out in front of us.

"No." I shake my head. "Tristan and I went to completely different schools and had completely different friend groups."

"I see. Well, this is my last hurrah. Heading back to Ohio in the morning."

"I didn't know you were from Ohio."

"Born and raised." It might not have worked out between us, but I can't deny he's turning out to be a great friend. We talk for a while, and I welcome the comfort he brings me until I see a wide-eyed Lexi walk between us and take a shot off the kitchen counter. She downs it fast, then reaches for another.

"Are you okay?" I ask when she reaches for a third. Her silence, combined with the flushed look on her face, has me slightly worried. "Lex?" I reach for her, but her eyes dart past me.

"Holy fucking shit!" she bursts out and starts to jump up and down excitedly. "Meredith White is here."

My chest seizes as my heart falls into my stomach.

Why is Cruz's ex-girlfriend here?

I slowly turn around and see her walking toward Tristan, who looks absolutely ridiculous in his Tom Cruise from *Risky Business* outfit. She leans in, smiling, as she hugs him, her naughty nurse outfit creeping further up her thighs.

"Oh my god, do you think she might know any inside gossip about what her father will be directing next?" Lexi is way too overexcited... top that with her liquid courage, and she's on her way over to her. "I'm going to go ask her."

She only makes it a few steps away from me when I see Cruz's tall, broad body parting through the crowd as he makes a beeline for Meredith. I watch fixedly as his hand wraps around her wrist, and everything falls into slow motion as he pulls her down the hall with him. I want to ignore it, but my feet have a mind of their own, and I take a few steps in their direction. It's when I watch him pull her into his bedroom, and close the door, that my body runs cold.

I'm filled with so many different emotions as rage, embarrassment and hurt, flood through me in waves. I'm not sure how I make it back to the kitchen counter where Lexi and Brad are standing without losing my shit, but I do. I plant both palms against the white marble to steady myself as I take a long, static breath. But the pain in my chest is only getting worse. I'm hurt, and I need something, anything, to make the pain tolerable.

I reach out and grab one of the shot glasses of tequila and throw it down my throat. The burn makes me gag slightly, but as the warmth floods my chest, it's somewhat relieving. So, I grab another.

"Taylah! Stop!" Lexi grabs my arm, but I pull out of her grip and throw the second shot back. The burn is not as bad as the first one, but it still makes me gag. I reach for another, but when I grab hold of it, Brad's hand wraps around mine, halting me from bringing it to my lips.

"Taylah? What's going on?" I look up at his sincere blue eyes, but I can't find the strength to pull myself together.

"Let go of me." It comes out harsher than I mean it to, but right now, I just want to numb the pain barreling through me. He nods at me with a worried look in his eyes as I bring the shot glass to my mouth. The warm liquid barely touches my lips when I feel arms wrap around my waist. The shock of the movement makes me drop the glass onto the floor as I'm hoisted up over someone's shoulder, and I'm hit instantly with his scent... Cruz.

"Put me down." I kick and scream as liquid courage courses through my veins, but he only grips me tighter. Stepping inside my music room, he kicks the door closed before placing me on my feet. He reaches for me, but I step away from his grip.

"What're you doing?" There's so much desperation laced in his tone, but I'm too annoyed to care.

"Me? What am *I* doing?" I don't mean to shout, but fuck it, this room's soundproof, and I need to get this out. "You're sending me mixed signals, Cruz." I'm pacing, and I'm frantic, but the cocktail of emotions that's buzzing through my veins has me spiraling out of control. "You tell me you want me in one breath, then the first chance you get, you run back to your fucking ex." He reaches for me again, but I take another step back, hitting the wall behind me. "Don't touch me." Visions of him with his hand around Meredith's wrist as he pulled her into his bedroom assault me, and I'm mad... really fucking mad.

"Don't be like that." He runs a stressed hand through his hair as a labored breath breaks from his chest.

"Was she worth it?" The thought of them being together breaks me, and silent tears soak my face.

"Taylah."

"Was she!" The sentence barely leaves my mouth when Cruz's lips crash into mine. In the heated frenzy, an involuntary moan vibrates out of my body as a rush of euphoria fills my veins. His tongue slides into my mouth, and I wrap my arms around his neck, pulling him closer. He pushes his body into me, pressing me against the wall. His hands grip my thighs, and he hitches my legs around his waist before his hands find my wrists, pinning them above my head.

"Nothing happened with Meredith." We barely break apart as he speaks into my mouth. "I grabbed her, took her to my room, and told her she wasn't welcome and needed to leave without causing a scene." I can feel the desperation flooding from his mouth into mine with every word he says. "It's you Taylah." I moan into him as the way he says my name vibrates from his lips and imprints onto mine. "It's always been you."

Locking my legs tighter around his waist, I lose myself in the heat that's filling my core as his thick cock pushes against me. Letting go of my wrists, his hands cup my face, sucking the breath from my lungs before pulling back to look at me.

"This room's soundproof, right?"

Chapter Nineteen

Cruz

Taylah's hands wrap around my neck as I carry her toward her piano at the back of the room. Warmth floods my veins just from having her close, and with the way those cosmic grey eyes are staring up at me, I would do anything to pause time right now.

My heart is beating out of my chest as I slide her onto the top of the piano. She unlocks her arms from my neck and leans back onto her hands. Her head tips back slightly, the movement leaving her exposed. I feel myself fall into her as I draw my tongue up the inside of her throat. The soft moans that spill from her lips as I suck at her skin only heightens the electrically charged moment as I lock my fingers in her hair.

She gasps as I lean her into me and devour her mouth, reveling in the warmth that's pouring out of her, and into me. Everything about her sets my soul on fire, and right at this moment, I'd move heaven and earth to keep her.

Taking a seat on the wooden bench that sits between her legs, I watch as her head tips to look down at me. She's panting, and her heart is racing, as my hands slide down her thighs, and lift them over my shoulders. The sheer material of her dress pools at her waist, and her shiny gold thong comes into view.

Her legs open wider as I slide my hands back up her thighs. Linking my fingers into the sides of her thong, I tug it down her legs. Her breathing shallows, and goosebumps erupt over her skin. Lifting one leg, I slip her thong over her foot, then the other, as I drop the gold material onto the floor.

I draw my eyes from hers as I look down at her, completely exposed before me. The only light in the room is from the full moon that's glowing through the floor-to-ceiling windows. It's just enough light to see she's slick with arousal, and the hunger inside me to devour every inch of her is maddening.

Cupping her ass in my hands, I lean into her, her legs squeezing around me as I kiss slowly up the inside of her thigh.

"Cruz."

Her back arches when I reach her core, her entire body opening up to me, and I slide my tongue between her silky folds. Her sweet juices coat my mouth, and as much as I want to close my eyes and appreciate every mind-blowing second of this moment, I can't look away from the way she's responding to my touch. I wrap my lips around her swollen clit, and she rolls her hips chasing more.

Slowly and beautifully, she falls apart as I eat her like a starved animal. Drowning in her taste, I keep my face buried between her legs as her juices soak me completely. I continue my wrath on her clit, consumed by the way she moans and shakes as her body reels in pleasure. I let my teeth graze over her clit before tilting her slightly, giving me better access to slide my tongue inside her while her hands slide their way into my hair. Her grip tightens when I bring my mouth back up to play with her clit, getting off on the way it throbs blissfully against my lips.

"Cruz!" My name screams from her mouth as her body lifts into me. Her hands are now fists in my hair while her body powers through its climax. Her mouth falls open, and the most delicious sounds fill the room as her body trembles beneath me. I could watch this girl cum every second of every day for the rest of my fucking life.

Her grip on me slowly loosens, her eyes fluttering open as she looks down at me. I pull back from her and wipe the back of my hand across my soaked lips while we stare at each other, unable to voice the moment that just passed between us. And then, as if the reality of what just happened dawns on her, she slides off the piano and scrambles to her feet. She's frantic as she grabs her thong off the floor and hurriedly tries to pull it up her legs.

"Taylah." I get to my feet and walk toward her, but she keeps her back to me. "Are you okay?" I'm met with silence before she nods her head and races for the door.

I head back into the party and see her standing with her back against the kitchen counter, but my heart pulls into my stomach when I see who she's talking with.

Sam fucking Summers.

We make eye contact so briefly; I struggle to read her before she turns away.

"There you are. I have to talk to you." The serious tone in Trey's voice manages to pull me from the destructive thoughts in my head.

"What's happened?" I ask as he nods for me to follow him. We head down the hall, and he kicks open the door to his room as I follow him inside. Closing the door behind us, I watch as a sadistic grin spills across his face.

"Something huge happened tonight." His laugh is borderline manic, and I start to panic.

Does he know?

"Tristan hooked up with Lexi." It takes me a minute for my mind to catch up with the words that just came out of his mouth. He drops down onto the bed laughing and takes a sip of his beer, shaking his head. I stand there, letting it all process when the door flies open, and Tristan falls into the room with a tall brunette dressed up as a Playboy bunny under his arm. He tugs her toward his bed, and I take that as my cue to vacate the room. Trey falls out the door not far behind me, and we head back toward the living room.

We've barely sat down when two blondes I don't recognize in matching bumblebee outfits sit down next to us.

"You're Cruz Valentine, aren't you?" blonde number one slurs out mid-hiccup.

"Yes, he is," Trey answers smugly, as blonde number two slides into his lap. I glare at him, drowning in the smell of stale alcohol. They're talking and laughing, but I block them out, letting my thoughts wander back to the piano room when I see

Taylah make her way through the crowded dance floor and out the back door... alone.

I pull myself to my feet and head in her direction. But as I step outside and scan the yard, I've lost sight of her. Heading for the stairs that lead down to the beach, I squint into the distance, where I see her white dress blowing in the wind. I jog down the stairs and slide my shoes off before dropping onto the sand. As I make my way down the beach, the sound of intoxicated party goers fades away, slowly being replaced with the crashing of the ocean. With every step closer, she comes into focus, and my heart pinches tight at the sight of the way the moon saturates her skin as she stares out to sea.

Closing the distance between us, I position myself behind her. I'm still so unsure of how she feels about us. Her reactions are conflicting, but my god do I want to hold her. I want to feel the warmth of her skin against mine while she melts the ice that's cemented in my veins.

"Do you remember the last time you saw me?" I'm taken aback for a moment.

"Do you mean the day at the river when we were kids?" She nods, and I take a step closer, letting my arm brush hers. "Yes."

"What do you remember about that day?" she asks, keeping her focus forward. I stand there for a moment as I relive every detail of that day.

"Everything." The word leaves my lips, and I feel her hand slide into mine as she slowly turns to face me. And when her eyes finally find mine, it feels like my heart stops beating. Her fingers trace my other hand before she wraps her warm palm against mine.

"Tristan would never be okay with this; you know that, right?" She douses me with reality, and a selfish part of me wants to scream out that *I don't care what Tristan thinks*, but I know deep down she loves her brother, and this betrayal of his trust could end our friendship.

"I know." The words feel devastating as they leave my lips. She squeezes my hands before letting go and turning to head back to the house.

"Taylah." I turn abruptly as I call her name. She stops in her tracks and shifts back to look at me as I scramble for something, anything, to salvage this. "Give me this summer." She tilts her head, giving me a quizzical look. "We're here for the rest of the summer. I promise Tristan won't find out." I know this will only make it harder to say goodbye when summer ends, but I'm incapable of letting her walk away from me.

The silence draws out between us as I watch the battle take place inside her head.

"Okay." That one word fills me with so much hope, before hitting me with that smile. And with that, she turns on her heel and walks away from me. It's only when she's completely out of view that I let a smile fall over my face, and my god, does it feel good.

Chapter Twenty

Taylah

The sun's barely up, but I'm wide awake. The party only ended a few hours ago, and sleep has been a task I've yet to achieve. I disposed of most of the mess in an attempt to distract my mind, but as I toss and turn, there's too much running through my head to switch off. Sliding out of bed, I grab my lace gown to throw over my beige silk pajamas, and head for the music room.

When I step through the threshold, my eyes draw straight to the piano, and heat pulses between my legs. I'm assaulted with vision after vision of Cruz's face between my thighs as the most earth-shattering orgasm swallowed me whole. Goosebumps encase my flesh as I take a seat on the piano stool and slide the keyboard cover open. I let my fingers find their place, close my eyes, and let the melody fill the room. I smile to myself as I feel my mind, body, and soul find their reset in the same place, a few hours prior, I was taken to heaven and back.

I don't know how long I've let myself indulge in the moment, but when I eventually open my eyes, I feel a presence behind me. Glancing over my shoulder, I see Cruz leaning against the entrance, staring at me with those infatuating eyes that make my skin ignite. He's wearing some black gym shorts and a white T-shirt with a pair of Nike runners. He looks... good.

I stay seated as I turn to face him, and he makes his way toward me. The distance closes between us, and I feel my body come alive with want. Just the thought of his mouth back on me has me dripping with need. He drops down into a crouched position, looking up at me as his dark hair falls onto his forehead. He doesn't say anything, letting his eyes roam over my face before he stands back upright.

"I'm off to the gym with your brother. I won't be long." He stands there for a moment assessing me, as if trying to read my reaction at the mention of my brother. I'm still not on board with the idea of running around with his best friend behind his back, but right now, I don't think I could stop myself if I tried.

"Okay," I answer as he leans down leaving a warm kiss to my forehead, and heading for the door.

I managed to get a few hours' sleep in while Cruz was at the gym. But as I slide a white sundress over my black bikini, I know it was nowhere near enough rest since my mind refuses to settle. I head to the kitchen in search of some caffeine but seize up as I enter and see Sam seated at the breakfast bar, with a white coffee mug pressed against his lips.

"Good morning, sunshine." He lowers the mug, and his big, bright smile fills the room. You can't deny how utterly gorgeous this man is.

"Good morning," I respond politely as I play around with the coffee machine.

"You look good, Taylah." The flirtatious nature of his tone doesn't go unnoticed.

"Thank you," I respond as I slide up to the breakfast bar next to him with a hot coffee in hand. "Where is everyone?" I ask, taking a welcoming sip of caffeine.

"Lexi's hungover in bed. Cruz and your brother are at the gym, and Trey is walking that golden retriever. I still can't believe Lexi is okay with having a dog here. Whose dog is that anyway?"

I laugh. "Lexi is not okay with Nugget being here. And he belongs to a family a few houses down. They're away for a few weeks." The conversation flows, and I've always felt so comfortable around Sam.

Did I confuse comfort and attraction with love?

"Can someone get me some kind of pain relief?" Lexi files into the kitchen, looking a little worse for wear. Sam chuckles as I get to my feet and head for the medicine cabinet. "I'm never drinking again," she states, as I hand her some pain pills and a glass of water.

"We were just talking about how much you love Nugget." Her eyes sharpen as her brother continues to provoke her. "If you had to choose between kissing Tristan Barker or that dog, who would you choose?" I'm about to tell Sam to leave her alone when I hear something drop behind me. I turn to see Tristan and Cruz back from the gym, the noise I assume was

Tristan's heavy gym bag hitting the floor. Lexi's face turns an awkward shade of red as Sam pales.

What is going on right now?

I glance at Cruz, who's standing there looking awkward. And as painful silence stretches out between us, the air is filled with so many words that remain unsaid. The moment is broken when an overexcited Nugget stampedes into the room with Trey following behind.

"What did I miss?" he asks taking a seat on the couch.

"Nothing," Tristan snaps, walking into the living room to join him. My eyes trace back to Cruz who's awkwardly running his hand up the back of his neck.

"Cruz, can you go get the things we need for the barbecue tonight?" His eyes leave mine to look over in Trey's direction. He nods, and I turn my attention back to Lexi.

"Is everything okay, Lex?"

"Of course. This hangover is just really kicking my ass. I think I just need some more sleep." She barely looks at me as she shuffles out of her seat and heads off down the hall. I see Cruz turn to leave, and I jog after him.

"I'll go with you; there's some things I need." He doesn't say anything as we head out the front door and over to where his car's parked next to mine. He opens my door, and I slide in, letting my eyes indulge in his tall, muscular body while he rounds the front of the car to the driver's side. He must have showered and changed at the gym because his gym wear is now replaced with a white cotton shirt and a pair of grey cotton basketball shorts.

He slides into the driver's seat, and I'm hit with the familiar clean smell of him. I close my eyes and let my senses run wild. The car rumbles to life, forcing me to open my eyes. I lean back into the comfort of the leather, as I watch how effortlessly he shifts it into reverse and backs out of the driveway.

We head toward town, and I get lost in him, studying the way his hand grips the gear stick as he fluently shifts through the gears. His eyes are on the road ahead, with the other hand gripping the steering wheel. His white shirt hugs his tensed body, and the muscles in his arms ripple and contract with every movement.

Since when has driving a car looked so goddamn sexy?

Rolling the window down, I feel the sun coat my face and I close my eyes, breathing in the salt air. Without warning, he accelerates, and the car comes alive, as the roar of the engine sets my body on fire. I grip onto my seat as the car rides smoothly through the bends. Wind in my hair I take it in, every freeing second of it. My heart is racing, and my body is buzzing, as pure heat fills my core. I clench my thighs together in search of some friction when the car pulls off the road and comes to a stop.

I hear Cruz's belt unlock, and my eyes fall in his direction.

"I thought we were going to the store?" I ask as he slides out of the car and makes his way to my door. It clicks open, and he leans over my body, unlocking my belt.

"We are, but I need to take care of something first." His arms wrap around my waist, and he pulls me out, carrying me the short walk to the front of the car and placing me down on the hood. The warmth from the engine only adds to my scorching hot skin. He places his body between my legs, cupping the hem of my dress, and forcing it up my thighs.

"You think I don't notice how worked up you are?" His hands on my body start to ease me. "Lean back." Resting onto my hands, I let the adrenaline pump its way through my body as he removes my bikini bottoms, dropping them on the hood next to me. His hands slide under my thighs and grip my hips, as he pulls my body to meet his mouth. The heat of his tongue sliding through my folds, mixed with the vibrations of the engine below me, has me writhing beneath him as I search for my climax.

Closing my eyes, I tip my head back and let the sun soak my skin while his hungry hot mouth devours me. Hearing him moan against my pussy has me hurdling toward my peak at record speed. His mouth leaves my body, and the loss is devastating. I open my eyes just as his mouth crashes onto mine. I can taste myself all over his lips as I suck them greedily into my mouth.

His touch between my legs, as a finger rides my clit.

"Come for me." He whispers into my mouth and my climax is instant, my orgasm so intense that white light momentarily steals my vision. I'm a soaking wet, panting mess as he softly kisses me through my high.

Sliding my bikini bottoms back up my thighs, he lifts me into his arms, and places my satisfied body back in the passenger seat. The car turns around, and thunders towards town, while all that's running through my mind is *what the delicious fuck was that?*

"Taylah, this potato salad is to die for," Trey announces going in for a second serving. Everything after what happened on the hood of Cruz's car has been a blur, and I think I'm stuck in some euphoric episode of bliss. I'm glad I have that distraction on my mind because everyone is still acting weird and secretive, and if I wasn't so high on what happened today, the awkwardness at this table would send me insane.

I feel Nugget nudge me under the table, and I'm pulled from my erotic daydream. He licks my leg, and as much as I push him away, he won't budge.

"Jesus, I don't taste that good, do I?" I only realize the content of what's left my mouth when I hear Cruz choking on his glass of water.

"Shit, you alright man?" Tristan pats him on the back as he coughs into his fist.

"So Taylah, are you enjoying Brown?" Sam asks, and I welcome the diversion.

"I love it there. For as long as I can remember, I've wanted to study politics, and Brown was just the perfect fit for that." It feels nice talking about my goals for the future, and a smile warms my face.

"I was thinking of transferring to the New York Fire Department in the fall; maybe you can show me around?" I don't get a chance to answer when Cruz abruptly gets to his feet and storms toward the house.

Chapter Twenty-One

Cruz

Fuck! I pace my room, trying to get a grip on myself, but all I can think about is the moment when summer eventually comes to an end. I know I asked her to give us until the end of summer, but I want all her summers and all her springs, winters, and falls too. I want...

My door cracks open, and I can smell her intoxicating scent before I see her.

"Are you okay?" I watch the way her lips trace every word of that sentence. God, I want her. I want her so fucking badly, it's the only thing I can think about.

She closes the door, clicking the lock, before taking a step toward me. I can't look away as her tongue traces her bottom lip.

"You've never been an easy person to read, Cruz. Talk to me." She makes it sound so easy, but how the fuck do you word, *I've loved you since the moment I saw you, and one summer will never be enough for me?*

My whole world freezes as she closes the gap between us. Her eyes search mine, and I watch them sparkle like the fucking night sky.

God, she's beautiful. Life-changing, soul-meltingly beautiful.

She takes a breath, wrapping her hands around my waist, and my heart thunders away inside my chest. The moment is filled with so many unsaid words, and when she leans in and rests her head against my chest soaking me in a wave of calm, I find the courage to speak.

Taking a breath, I wrap my arms around her, and squeeze her tight. She mimics the movement and tightens her grip around me.

"One summer will never be enough for me, Taylah." It comes out so soft that I'm not sure if she's heard me, and before I can find out, there's a knock at my door, followed by Tristan's voice.

"Cruz, are you in there?" Taylah sighs, retreating from my arms, and backs up against the wall. I head for the door and let Tristan in. He steps through the threshold, followed by Trey. They glance over at Taylah, who's doing her best to look un-bothered.

"Tay, Lexi needs to talk to you. She's in the living room with Sam." Taylah nods and heads for the door, keeping her head down as she passes me.

"We need to talk to you," Tristan states while walking over to my bed and lying down. Heat floods my nervous system, the first thing that crosses my mind is that they know about me and Taylah, and at this point, I'm ready to have that conversation.

"What about?" I ask, leaning back against the wall and crossing my arms over my chest in an attempt to seem unbothered.

"Nugget hasn't been his usual happy self lately." A rush of amusement runs through me, but I keep my laughter contained.

"You need to talk to me about the dog?" Tristan nods, and Trey steps forward.

"We think he might be homesick, so Tristan and I think a few days with him at home might be what he needs. We already talked to the Malcolm's, and they think it's a great idea."

I want to laugh. There's so much going on inside my head that this conversation about a sad dog actually has me lost for words.

"You'll be here by yourself, so feel free to come with," Trey adds.

"I'm not four years old. I'll be fine by myself." They look at each other and then back to me.

"For as long as I've known you, you just get so in your head at times. Match that with being the hardest person to read, and we just wanted to make sure you're okay with being here alone." The sympathy on Tristan's face makes me want to tear my fucking hair out.

"Jesus Christ, I'll be fine." Satisfied, they both head for the door. I walk over to my bed and drop onto the mattress, letting the air rush from my lungs. I'm wound so tight that I think I need to take a drive to silence my mind. I grab my keys from the nightstand when I hear Lexi's voice outside my door.

"I promise it will only be for a few days." I get to my feet and throw on a fresh shirt before stepping into the hall. I see the back of Taylah as she rounds the corner and slides out of view.

"This could be your big break, and I'm happy for you." I follow Taylah's voice down the hall and into the living room. She has her back to me as she faces Lexi, who has a suitcase sitting at her feet.

"You ready, Lex?" Sam walks through the front door, heading in their direction. "I'll take this to the car." I watch as he picks up Lexi's suitcase and turns back toward the exit. He stops in front of me, glancing in my direction. "Maybe I'll see you in New York; you go to school there, right?" I grit my teeth, and I nod at him as the thought of him and Taylah in New York together reignites.

"Are you sure you'll be okay here by yourself?" Lexi asks, bringing Taylah in for a hug. I'm suddenly hit with the realization that everyone is leaving for a few days, except for Taylah and me.

"I'll be here." I don't mean to say it out loud, but when I see Taylah turn to face me, struggling to hide the smile on her face, I'm happy I did.

"Take care of her, Cruz," Lexi states. I nod at her, seemingly satisfying her request, as she takes one last goodbye and heads for the door.

Looking across at Taylah in a now-empty house fills me with nerves.

Why the fuck am I so worried to be alone with her?

I look down at the way she's playing with her hands and avoiding eye contact, and I find some relief that she's nervous too. She glances up at me as I take a step toward her and then another. But before I reach her, she tears her eyes away from me and heads for the kitchen.

"Are you hungry? I'll make us some food." The nervous rattle to her makes me want to wrap her up in my arms.

"Lunch wasn't that long ago, Tay." She freezes as she stands with her back to me in front of an open fridge. She doesn't move while I make my way over to her. Standing behind her, I let my eyes roam the length of her, before wrapping one arm around her waist while the other slides softly around her throat. I constrict her just enough that her head tilts back and rests against my chest, and the way she pants with arousal in my grip has me losing my fucking mind.

"Your heart is pounding inside your chest, Cruz." The way my name is whispered from her lips has me desperate to hear her scream it while I'm buried inside her. Sliding my hand under her white sundress, I run it across her stomach, indulging in the way she leans into me for more while my fingers untie the sides of her bikini bottoms and let them fall to the floor.

"Tell me what you want." I hold her against me, enjoying the way her body trembles with excitement as my fingers trace across her stomach. Her breathing turns erratic when my touch dips closer to where she needs me most. I'm torturing her... I know that, but I want to hear her say it.

Loosening my grip, I take a step away from her when she turns and reaches for me.

"You. I want you." My hands grip her thighs and lift her into me, our mouths colliding together as the moment detonates. I keep her latched to me as I walk to the living room. I drop down onto the couch with her mounted in my lap, and her hands grip wildly onto my hair, anchoring us together, like she's scared I'll somehow float away.

"I'm not going anywhere." I feel the need to reassure her, the words barely leaving my lips as her hands reach under the hem of my shirt and rest against my stomach. Her fingers trace the ridges of my abs as she whimpers breathlessly into my mouth.

"Jesus Christ, Taylah, you moan like that again, and I'll come in my fucking pants." She smiles against my lips as a giggle leaves her mouth before pulling back from me with a smirk.

"You're that close?"

"Yes, I'm that fucking close." She grins, slowly dropping to her knees between my legs. If I thought my heart was racing before, I'm now bordering cardiac arrest. Her hands reach up and dig into the top of my shorts, tugging at them. I lift my hips and help her drag them down my thighs.

I take in the exact moment her eyes find my throbbing cock, memorizing every detail. The way her eyes widen. The deep breath intake. The way her cheeks fill with warmth as she wets her lips.

Looking back up at me, her hand grips the bottom of my shaft. My whole world turns on its axis as I watch her lean forward, keeping her eyes locked on mine as she coats her lips in the pre-cum dripping from the tip of my cock.

Dear god, let me savor this moment for the rest of my life.

I hold my breath when her mouth opens as if not breathing will help me appreciate every delicious detail. But when the warmth of her mouth wraps around me, a growl explodes from my body, and I can't look away as her lips slide down my cock, inch by heavenly inch. Her wet, warm mouth swallows me whole, and I'm a trembling, overstimulated mess in her grip.

Closing my eyes and tilting my head back against the couch, I wrap my fist into her hair as her throat constricts against the throbbing of my cock.

"Fucking hell." I'm sitting on the edge of euphoria as she slides her mouth up and down my cock in slow, torturous movements. The tight suction edges me closer and closer. Opening my eyes I look back down at the way she's swallowing me as her lust-filled eyes stare up at me, and that's all it takes.

"Fuck!" I try to pull back, but she grips onto me keeping me buried inside her hot mouth, as my cum spills down her throat. Waves of pleasure wrack my body, as I watch her mouth milk every drop.

She slowly drags her mouth off me before running her fingers across her swollen lips. I can't move or think straight as I sit there with my shorts around my ankles, and she slowly gets to her feet. Taking the bottom of her white dress into her hands, she slides it off her body and lets it hit the floor. Her bikini top follows until her naked body is on display in front of me. The top of her thighs are slick with arousal, and my mind implodes as I fall onto my knees in front of her.

Chapter Twenty-Two

Taylah

I want him. I know that. The way he makes my body feel is something I don't think I'll ever be able to put into words. And as he follows me down the hall to my bedroom, I take a moment to take it all in.

Stepping through the threshold of my bathroom, I make my way to the shower, glancing at our reflection in the mirror as we pass. Seeing his tall, muscular body behind me sends a shiver up my spine. I reach for the handle, and the minute the warm spray hits my body, I'm flipped around and pressed up against the cold tiles. The initial shock of the chill against my back leaves me catching my breath. But as soon as his body presses up against mine, everything outside of us becomes a blur.

I can feel how hard he is, resting up against my stomach as arousal fills my clit. His hand slides up my throat, guiding its way to cup my chin, as he tilts my face to his, letting our eyes lock in on the moment. I'm captivated as I watch the water drip from his dark hair and run down his face before dropping onto his thick chest. His hands grip my ass, lifting me, and my legs wrap around his waist while I lock my arms around his neck.

"Talk to me, Taylah." I know he's speaking, but the feeling of his cock throbbing against my core has me coming undone at the seams. My chest starts to constrict as the reality of the moment filters through my thought process.

I'm about to lose my virginity to my brother's best friend.

With one hand wrapped thoroughly around my waist and the other running into my hair, I let my hands wander down his torso before slowly running them up his back.

"Fuck." He shivers under my touch, slamming his mouth to mine, claiming me in one delicious sweep of his tongue. I close my eyes as pure ecstasy barrels through my body. Impatience setting in, I run my hand down his body, and take him into my grip, shifting him to my entrance. I feel the change in his breathing as he pants into my mouth.

"Are you sure?" I swallow every word, not allowing his mouth to leave mine.

I want to scream "yes," but the thought of him not being aware I'm a virgin pulls me back. I feel him draw back from me as he cups my face. A worried look passes over his features, as his eyes search mine.

"Where'd you go?" The fear that's spilling down his face is heart-wrenching to witness. I want to just go back to how we were before I got lost in my head and ruined the moment.

"I'm right here." I grab at his body, trying to pull him back, but he's not budging.

"Taylah." The desperation in his tone brings me undone.

"I haven't done this before." It takes him a second to register the words that just came out of my mouth.

"You're a virgin?" I search his features, trying to read his reaction, but he doesn't give anything away as he lowers my legs back to the floor. Drawing his bottom lip into his mouth, he runs his hand through his wet hair. I close the gap between us and wrap my arms around his waist, tilting my head to look at him.

"I want this." His face softens, and a rush of air expels from his lips.

"Not like this, Taylah." He wraps his arms around me before placing one to the back of my head and pushing my face to rest on his chest. We stand there for a moment as his heart beats against me when I hear him speak.

"Please don't think I don't want to press you up against that wall and fuck you until you can't think of anything but what I feel like buried inside you." A vicious rush of heat ravages me with every tortured word that leaves his lips, and I gasp against his chest.

"Fuck." His body tenses right before I'm pressed back up against the cool tiles. "The sounds that spill from this body send me insane." His eyes are hooded and swimming with lust as he leans down and places his forehead against mine. His fingers run down the center of my stomach before dipping between my legs.

I close my eyes as his finger slides through my folds, letting my legs fall open, giving him better access to me. His thumb presses against my oversensitive clit, making my body whimper before he rolls it in slow circles, drawing out my pleasure, before his rhythm picks up, making me buck against his grip. The familiar wave of pleasure heats my core, and I'm about to hit my high when I feel his fingers leave my body. My eyes shoot open in desperation as he drops to his knees, pulling me with him so I'm seated. My back is flush against the wall as he brings my knees to my chest before sliding them apart.

"I want you to watch."

My legs are open, and I'm completely exposed to him while his fingers dip between them. Just like he's asked me, I watch as one finger slowly disappears inside me, the movement so erotic, my body trembles with need.

"Cruz." I'm panting as I watch his finger slide in and out of me, coating him in the slippery, desperate mess I've become.

"Oh my god!" I reach for him, grabbing at his body as if trying to keep myself from floating into the stratosphere. My body is quivering but my high won't let up, and I shatter to pieces right there on the shower floor.

"God, you're beautiful." The raspy tone of his voice only heightens the moment, and he brings his forehead to mine. I lean into him as I come down from my high, his finger slowly leaving me. I barely have time to think as I'm wrapped in a towel, picked up bridal style, and carried to my bed.

Cruz

I'm fucked. There's no coming back from the way this girl makes me feel, but I already knew that. I knew it the moment I met her.

Her soft, naked body is pressed against mine as she sleeps peacefully against my chest. Hours have passed, and the sun has set. I should really get some sleep, but the peace I feel with her body wrapped around me is something I want to revel in. I let my hand slip out of her hair and run down her back. The way her skin feels under my touch is exhilarating, and I can't get enough. I tilt my head so it's buried in her hair, letting the smell of her shampoo wash over me. She wanted me to take her virginity tonight. While the thought of me taking something so special from her creates an ache inside my chest, the idea of anyone else sharing that moment with her almost shatters my heart entirely.

Reaching down, I lift her leg higher, so it rests against my hips as I tighten my grip around her. I know these moments with her are fleeting, and one day, I'll have to say goodbye. But not tonight. Tonight, she's mine.

I'm anxious as I down my third glass of water, waiting for Taylah to wake up. It's approaching lunchtime, and I guess she needed the rest after last night's emotional overload. As for me,

I've barely slept. I slipped out of bed as the sun was rising and went for a run to clear my head. I've showered and put the finishing touches to the afternoon I have planned for her.

The sound of footsteps in the hall kicks my nerves into gear, and I turn as she steps into the living room, my heart pinching when I see she's dressed in a yellow sundress.

"Good afternoon."

She walks toward me with that smile that makes my world turn on its head.

"I guess I was tired." She laughs as she steps around me and reaches for the coffee pot. I walk behind her, not wasting a minute of not having my hands on her and welcome the giggle against my body as I lock my arms around her waist.

"Can we take a drive today?" She stops what she's doing and stills for a moment before turning to face me.

"Where do you want to take me?" The sultry tone of her voice makes me instantly hard, and I have to take a brief moment before I can answer.

"Somewhere special to me." My response isn't what she was expecting, and confusion dawns on her face. I link her hand in mine and pull her toward the door. "I'll get you pancakes on the way."

"Pancakes? It's lunchtime." She giggles as we walk to my car.

"It's never a wrong time for pancakes."

I hold the door open for her as she steps out onto the deck that overlooks the ocean at the Seaside Dock Cafe. There's a scattering of white wooden chairs with matching white tables, and we take a seat at the one closest to the ocean. I stare at her for a moment as the sun heats her rosy cheeks.

"Tell me about Brown."

She glances at me with a smile that steals my breath away.

"Well..."

She's interrupted by the arrival by the pancakes I promised her, thanking the waitress politely, before continuing.

"I want to make a difference in the world; that's why I'm studying politics. Maybe one day, something I do will help someone in such a way that it saves them from whatever darkness they're running from." I pause for a moment. If only she knew how much of her I carried her with me every day, keeping me from slipping too far into the dark. Every violent outburst from my father. Every time my mother would cover her bruises. Every time my father would chip away at my soul in an effort to build a younger version of himself. My memory of her saved me. This girl right in front of me, shoveling maple syrup-covered pancakes into her mouth while the sun glistens over her perfectly tanned skin, and I'm suddenly laced with fear. The fear of not having her in my life forever is almost debilitating, and I need a minute to catch my breath.

"I'll be right back." Sliding out of my seat, I head down the dock as the voices in my head consume me. Staring out at the ocean, the salty air washes over me. The sun, the salt, and the sand are a constant reminder that summer will soon come to a close, and so will Taylah and I.

I feel her arms lock around my waist, and I turn around to face her.

"What're you thinking about?" she asks, and I take a minute to admire the way she looks at me. Something about the way she's staring at me makes me want to tell her everything I feel. But I don't. Instead, I lick the maple syrup from her lips and pull her into my chest as she wraps her arms around me and I take the moment for all it's worth.

Chapter Twenty-Three

Taylah

We've been driving for a couple of hours now along the coastal stretch. I have no idea where Cruz is taking me, and when he turns off onto a dirt road, my curiosity really peaks. Corn fields suddenly surround us as far as the eye can see.

The car starts to slow as he pulls off the road and onto a small grass clearing. Shutting off the engine, he stares straight ahead like he's trying to gather himself. I place my hand on the bulge of his bicep, and he slowly turns to face me.

God, he's beautiful.

Without warning, he opens his door and slides out, and I do the same. He walks to the trunk of the car, pops it open, and reaches for a picnic basket. I see a beige picnic rug rolled the trunk, he slides his hand into mine.

We only walk a short distance into the corn field when it opens up into a massive clearing of yellow daisies as far as the eye can see. I stop in my tracks to take in the fairy-tale-like moment as the sun glitters over the field of yellow.

"Cruz, this is... breathtaking." He doesn't look at me, but he squeezes my hand, tugging me forward. There's a small patch of grass a few yards ahead of us, where he rests the picnic basket on the grass, before taking the blanket from my hand and laying it out in front of us.

He takes a seat, leaning back onto his hands, and I mimic the movement. We sit there in silence for a few minutes, letting the warmth filter across our skin. There are birds chirping in the distance and the sound of running water, but other than that, it's silent.

"So, this is one of your favorite places?" I ask, prompting him to glance my way. He doesn't answer right away; instead, he turns away from me just enough that his side profile is hidden. "Why?"

He clears his throat as if he's about to answer when he leans forward and ruffles through the picnic basket before turning and offering me a sandwich. "Thank you." I take it from his hand and remove the packaging.

We eat in silence as unsaid sentences stretch out between us. I'm confused, and this boy is so hard to read that I'm unsure how to tackle the situation, so I just go for it.

"Why did you bring me here, Cruz?" He stops chewing for a moment, and I watch him swallow. When he remains silent again, agitation starts to creep up my spine. I go to stand but feel his hand grip my arm to hold me down.

"This place reminds me of you." Warmth fills my cheeks at his response. "Being near you brings me peace." He shifts slightly as his eyes scan the horizon in front of us. "You're the sun on all my dark days, with a warmth that gives my broken soul hope."

I feel myself trembling as I look out over the sea of yellow around us. My mind is spinning, and my heart is aching. My body feels heavy and light at the same time as arousal floods me. It takes my mind a moment to catch up to my body, but when it does, I realize I've thrown my leg over his lap, and my arms are linked around his neck. The glow of his warm eyes in the afternoon sun pulls me undone.

My eyes fall to his lips as they part, sending a rush of warm air across my mouth. He slowly slides my sundress up my thighs, the soft movement sends goosebumps skating across my skin.

"Tay—" I slam my mouth on his, smothering the rest of my name from his lips. He moans into me, our tongues finding each other as if searching for all the answers that remain unsaid. I drown in his taste, his scent, his touch. I fumble with the hem of his shirt as I lift it up his body. He grabs at it and pulls it over his head, tossing it somewhere beside us. I take a minute to admire the work of art in front of me, my hands itching to run over the taut pull of his chest and stomach.

"You're perfect." It comes out breathless and needy, and I'm so turned on it hurts. I bring my eyes back to meet his. His messy, dark hair creates a rough edge to his features—a direct contrast to the warmth firing behind those eyes.

"Fuck." His voice is rough and desperate as he grips my hips, pushing me down so my back lays against the blanket, as he positions his body against me. "You are so fucking beautiful,

Taylah." I soak up every word, letting the compliment heat my skin. He rests one forearm next to my face while he uses the other to guide my legs around his waist.

His hand slides up the outside of my thigh and links his fingers into the band of my lace panties. "Tell me to stop." He tugs them slowly down my legs, with his eyes locked on mine, searching for any sign of hesitation.

"Don't you dare stop." My entire body is collapsing with need, and the cool breeze against my naked core drives home just how soaking wet I am. He pulls back, shuffling out of his shorts, and his throbbing cock springs free. Laying his body against mine, he rests his forearms on either side of my head, resting his face mere inches from mine.

I keep my eyes on his while I reach down and take his cock into my grip. The way his hooded eyes gaze down at me, like he wants to ravage every part of me, sends butterflies exploding inside my stomach.

I position the tip of his cock at my entrance, and hold him still for a few moments, getting off on the way his body pulls tight with ravenous hunger.

Taking a breath, I push the head of his cock inside me, feeling the moment he breaks through my purity. He holds his breath, dipping his hips slowly into me. My breathing intensifies, and my body opens up for him. It's hard to focus on the pain when I'm flooded with so much want. I slide my hands slowly up his back, indulging in the ripple of solid muscles under my fingertips.

"Are you ok?" he whispers across my lips as he stills. I can feel the erratic beat of his heart against mine. I nod rolling my hips forward, a sharp rush of air escaping my chest as he sinks all the way back in.

"Fuck, Taylah." His forehead comes down to rest on mine, dragging his hips back so slowly that I feel every inch as it leaves my body before I'm once again filled with him. His mouth finds mine as he repeats the movement, over and over, our kiss turning desperate.

The familiar feeling of an orgasm starts rolling in as my entire body pulls tight. I squeeze my legs around his waist, and my hands form fists with the rug beneath me.

"Oh my god!" A savage rush of pleasure assaults me with so much intensity, stars scatter my vision. Waves of euphoric warmth consume me, and I don't know if I'm floating or falling.

He pulls back from me, and I lock onto him, not yet ready for the loss.

"I'm not wearing any protection." The desperation in his voice is obvious he's almost there.

"I'm protected."

He shakes his head at me. "Are you sure?"

I drag his lips to mine. "Please."

"You are... fuck." His words are a scrambled mess as his body shakes. He sinks back inside me, letting a guttural moan rip through the air between us. I can't tear my eyes away as I watch pleasure consumes him, and for the first time in my life, I *can* read him. I can read every bit of this moment as he falls into me, tightening his hold and anchoring himself against me.

Cruz

Is my body shaking or is it hers? I'm filled with more emotion than I ever felt possible. I'm still buried inside her as I come down from my high. She lets out a deep breath, and I lift my face to look at her.

"Are you okay?" She smiles as her hands grip my shoulders, forcing me backward until my back hits the ground, and she's seated on top of me.

Her body is flush with arousal, and the way she's biting at her lip again has me hard again in seconds. I watch in admiration as she lifts her hips slightly, taking my cock into her hand and positioning me back at her entrance. Watching her in control of the moment is such a fucking turn-on.

She slowly lowers herself down onto me, her tight little pussy contracting as it wraps around me. Her eyes close, and her head dips back into the sun as the sounds of raw pleasure explode from her lips.

Holy fucking hell.

She takes all of me and settles there for a moment, the warm, wet feeling of her consuming me in more ways than one. She drops her head back to face me, leaning forward and taking my wrists into her grip as she lifts them above my head. There's a ring of light around her, as if she's been swallowed by a halo, as her silky blonde hair falls forward, framing her face. But it's when she rolls her hips, and a pleasure-filled moan makes her body vibrate that it sends me hurdling over the edge.

Her spent body collapses against me, and I hold her close as we watch the sun slowly dip behind the cotton-candy-filled sky. It's in this moment, with her naked body pressed perfectly against mine, I feel everything fall into place.

She's the one.

Chapter Twenty-Four

Taylah

Everything feels so heightened on the way back to the beach house. Every star looks brighter. Every breath feels lighter, and every beat of my heart feels like it's beating for a purpose, and that purpose is seated in the driver's seat right next to me. He's wearing a black hoodie that he grabbed from the backseat, but even with the hood up, I can see that gorgeous jawline.

He slides his hand into mine, and it warms my skin as he drives us home, not once letting go of me as he effortlessly switches through the gears.

My body is raw with emotion as I relive every delicious detail of today's events all the way home. And as we pull into the driveway, I can feel the aftermath of the sexual tension that's been building the entire drive back.

He turns the car off and opens his door, sliding out of the driver's seat. I take a minute to catch my breath, watching him round the car and open my door. His arms lock around me as he lifts me and carries me inside.

He places me on my feet in the living room, and I lift my head to look up at him.

"I'm not ready for this day to end." The longer I stare at him, the stronger the fire engulfing my skin becomes. He looks past me, and I watch his brain tick over before his eyes come back to mine.

"Come with me." I smile as he slides his hand into mine, leading me out the back door and down onto the beach.

We walk for a few minutes, until we get to a rock formation that resembles a set of stairs. Reaching the top, I'm met with a rock pool overlooking the cliff edge as a thousand stars glitter across the water. I walk to the ledge and stare out over the ocean, taking in the view.

Cruz's arm wraps around my stomach, and I close my eyes as his palm slides its way up my torso and onto my heart.

"Relax." The warmth from his mouth hits the back of my neck, and I let myself fall into him. Warm kisses slide down the side of my neck, and I feel myself turning into him as my mouth searches for his. His soft lips brush across mine, and I use this moment to breathe him in before our tongues find their way to each other. His fingers dig into my waist as he moans across my mouth.

"I could taste you forever." He pulls back from me and lifts his hoodie off his body, followed by his shirt, as every muscle tenses. He takes another step back as he removes the rest of his clothes until his naked body flexes in front of me.

Jesus Christ.

He steps into the rock pool and walks until he's waist deep, his eyes focused on mine as I salivate at the god-like man in front of me. He nods me over, and I walk the short distance to the edge of the rock pool as I remove my clothes. Sliding my feet into the water, I take a seat on the edge and lean back onto my hands as he makes his way toward me. The moon is reflecting off the water and glowing across his wet body as he places his hands on my knees and pushes my legs open, positioning himself between them. His cold, wet fingers run up my thighs, making me shiver.

"You're not ready for the moment to end? So, tell me what you need." I lose all sense of reality when teeth graze over my nipple, as all rational thought is buried beneath the warmth of his tongue.

"You, god, I need you!" His mouth sucks across my stomach, and I can feel the way my body is begging for it, as my back arches into him. Wrapping his arms around me, he tilts my hips so I can watch him position himself at my entrance. I don't look away as every inch disappears inside me, the word "fuck" expelling from his lungs. He slowly draws out of me, taking a breath before sinking right back in. His hand locks around my throat, making my clit pulse while his warm exhale dances across my collarbone.

"Fuck, you take me so well." His words are fierce as he holds me still and fucks me right there under the stars. "I could watch you take every inch of me for the rest of my fucking life." The gravel in his voice sends me over the edge as an explosion of pleasure washes through me, so savage that I throw my head back and scream his name into the stars.

He pulls out of me and buries his face between my legs, lapping up every drop of arousal that's pouring out of me, and I quiver in his grip. I want to reach out and touch him, but I'm floating through waves of ecstasy, making it hard to see straight. I'm completely at his mercy as his tongue slips in and out of my content body. I try and focus on the stars above to help bring me back to earth when I feel him pull his hoodie over my exhausted body before lifting me against his rock-solid frame.

"That's enough for today, babygirl."

Chapter Twenty-Five

Cruz

Her naked body is pressed against mine as she sleeps peacefully in my arms. Her hair is splayed all around me, allowing me to drown in her scent. I'm watching a storm roll in over the ocean through her bedroom window as I relive every minute of today. Every breath, every shiver, every exaggerated thud of my heart.

I run my hands through her hair as lightning lights up the sky, the grumble of thunder not far behind. I know I need sleep, but I don't want to waste a minute of her. As much as my soul craves the solitude only Taylah has ever been able to provide, I know deep down she deserves a life filled with as much color as she brings to the table, and my cloud-filled days will never be enough for her.

I don't know how much sleep I ended up getting when the warmth of the morning sun heats my face, forcing me to open my eyes. I immediately realize Taylah isn't in my arms or in this bed or in this room. The sound of crashing pots and pans interrupts me, and before I can overthink, I pull myself out of bed and slide on a pair of sweats before finding the source of all the noise.

As soon as I exit the hall and the kitchen comes into view, I see a very flustered Taylah juggling a pan of bacon while trying to flip an egg in another. Her hair is pulled back in a messy ponytail with some stray pieces framing her face. I swallow hard when I realize she's wearing one of my white cotton T-shirts and a pair of my grey cotton basketball shorts. The entire outfit swallows her whole.

"Do you need help with that?" Her face snaps to mine as she realizes I'm walking toward her, and I wait patiently for that smile to hit me like a ton of bricks. I don't have to wait long, and my heart jolts as it fills out her gorgeous face.

"I'm not usually a bacon and eggs kind of girl. I thought maybe you—" I don't let her finish, as an overwhelming need to saturate my mouth with her taste takes over me. Her soft, velvety lips are enough to drown in as her sweet taste fills me, feeding my addiction. I pull back, dragging her bottom lip between my teeth before the smile that forms over my face forces me to let go.

"Holy fucking shit!" Her eyes widen as she stares at me with such raw emotion, it's taking everything in me to not slam my mouth back onto hers. I see a tear break free and roll down her cheek, which I catch with my thumb. She's laughing as more tears roll down her face. "You have no idea how breathtakingly beautiful you are, do you?" The compliment hits me like a freight train, knocking the wind out of me. "I always wondered what it would feel like to see you smile." She wipes at her face as she turns her back to me in an attempt to salvage the burning bacon.

I close the space between us, pressing my chest against her back, as I lower my mouth to whisper into her ear.

"And?" She freezes, and I can hear the wheels turning inside her head as she tries to piece together her next sentence.

"Earth-shattering." The softness of her voice sends me over the edge, and I lean forward and switch off the gas cooktop before throwing her over my shoulder.

"Wait, aren't you hungry?" She laughs as I power toward the living room.

"Ravenous." I drop her onto the couch and, in one swift movement, grab at my shirt she's wearing and drag it off her body. "That's mine." She giggles as I throw the shirt across the room, opening her legs so I can position myself above her. I waste no time taking her mouth with mine as the frenzied kiss turns animalistic to straight-up savage. I break the kiss and suck a line down the center of her body as her hips buck against me in anticipation.

Gripping the top of my shorts she's wearing; I pull them down her thighs. "These are also mine." She lifts her legs out of them hurriedly, and I toss them over my shoulder, grip the inside of her thighs, and push her legs open. My mouth waters as I take in how her soft pink pussy glistens with arousal. I waste no time burying my face between her legs, running my tongue from entrance to bud, enjoying the way she trembles beneath me. I dip my tongue inside her, and her thighs tense up and wrap around my face as her hands find their way into my hair.

"Cruz." The desperate way my name leaves her lips makes my cock ache. I lick my way back up to her clit and lock my lips around it. She's squirming beneath me, but I don't let go. Her hands are now fists in my hair, and the sound of her moans fill the room. Her back lifts off the couch right before she shatters in my arms, her body shaking and jerking as her juices fill my mouth. I'm soaked in the taste of her when her hands grab me by the shirt, dragging me up her body until her mouth finds mine. She whimpers against me as she tastes herself all over my lips, and for a second, I try and think when innocent, virginal Taylah turned into this ravenous, uncaged sex goddess.

Her hands are at the waistband of my sweats as she slides one inside, pulling my throbbing cock out and fisting it in her tight grip.

"Fuck." She pulls me even closer, but I jerk back to look at her. "Baby, aren't you sore?" I brush the loose strands of her hair from her face as she nods at me.

"Yes, but the need for you to be inside me aches more."

Jesus fucking Christ.

I let out the breath I didn't know I was holding and let her guide my cock back to her entrance. I don't bother removing my pants as they sit just below my ass. I need her just as much as she needs me. It's more than sex. It's a connection I'll never be able to put into words. Pushing inside her, I feel her walls clamp around me, and her arms wrap tight around my neck, dragging my mouth back to hers.

"More, I need more." I pull back and drive into her, over and over, as her mouth assaults mine, layering her taste across my tongue and into my soul. "Cruz." My name rips from her throat as the telltale signs of her orgasm crash over her. Hearing her scream my name is all it takes, and my own orgasm comes powering through me. My entire body fills with waves of pure ecstasy so overpowering that my vision shakes. I want to savor the moment until the end of fucking time, but all good things must come to an end. And that end is right now as the sound of a barking dog throws me face first back into reality, along with a very flustered Taylah searching for the clothes I tossed around the room.

We somehow manage to pull ourselves together enough to not look like we just fucked the hell out of each other before Tristan, Trey, and Nugget slide through the backdoor.

"Back already?" Taylah asks as we watch the trio take a seat on the couch in front of us.

"Yeah, the family portraits all over the walls are killing the bachelor summer party vibe," Trey answers.

"Anything happen while we were away?" Tristan asks as he ruffles the fur on Nugget's head, searching for the TV control. We sit there in silence as Tristan looks from me to Taylah and back again. "You two okay?"

"You were only gone one night. What could possibly happen in one night?" I answer, hoping that stops him from probing any further. And judging by the way he pulls his phone from his pocket and starts scrolling, I assume he's done with the line of questioning. That is until something registers, and he glances up, looking directly at Taylah.

"Are you wearing Cruz's clothes?"

I can feel the panic rolling off her in waves, and I scramble for a response for her.

"She lost a bet. That's her punishment." Tristan and Trey laugh, and relief washes over me as the lie lands and sticks.

"Don't be too mean to my sister, Cruz," Tristan says, as he scrolls through his phone.

Pretty sure eating her out until she screams my name wouldn't be considered mean.

The rest of the day goes by in an awkward combination of Taylah avoiding me and me avoiding Tristan. I hate to admit that there's guilt floating around in the bottom of my stomach. Tristan has been there for me through so many fucked-up situations with my father, and hiding the fact that I've been fucking his sister behind his back, doesn't sit well with me. I need a minute to gather myself, so I head for my room.

"Can we talk?" I look back down the hall to see Tristan staring at me. He seems off, but there's no anger in his features, so I'm guessing what he wants to talk about has nothing to do with his sister and me.

"Sure." I back away from the door and follow him out into the living room, where he grabs his beer off the coffee table and heads for the sliding back door. He's silent as we walk down the beach, and I can feel myself starting to sweat.

He stops abruptly, taking a seat on the sand, and I do the same.

"You know I had sex with Lexi, right?"

Relief floods me. "I know."

He lets out a sigh and brings the beer bottle to his lips, taking a long sip as if needing some liquid courage to continue this talk.

"She doesn't want Taylah to know." I nod slowly as what he's just said sinks in. "You haven't told her, have you?" I shake my head, trying to think of a reason why I haven't told her already. It's not like I was purposely keeping it from her. I guess what was happening between us took priority over who her brother was sleeping with.

"I think I like her." He says it so softly I almost don't hear him. He drains what's left of the bottle before dropping it at his feet. "I want to see where this goes before I break her trust, so please just don't say anything to my sister."

I feel instant guilt ripping apart my stomach as I try and piece it all together in my mind. Taylah has me keeping a secret from my best friend and Tristan has me keeping a secret from the girl I'm in love with. What's the worst that can happen?

Chapter Twenty-Six

Taylah

I roll over and look at the clock on my nightstand. 1:11 a.m. I let out a groan while I search through the sheets for my phone I tossed in frustration mere minutes ago. I open up Instagram and notice that Lexi has uploaded a new photo. My heart drops into my stomach, and I launch myself into a seated position as I take a closer look.

It's Meredith White in all her perfectness. They have their arms around each other in what looks like a nightclub. My body is running hot, and I can't think straight, as I hit dial on Lexi's number.

It rings for what feels like forever.

"Taylah!"

"Hey, where are you?"

"Out with Meredith freaking White! She's introducing me to some acting connections in return for a simple favor."

"What's the favor?"

"Bring her back to the house with me tomorrow, so she can shoot her shot and get her man back."

I feel all the color drain from my face, which is soon replaced with raging jealousy, and I fumble to end the call with my hands shaking. Powering it off, I drop it beside me and fall back into my pillows. I hold my breath in an attempt to calm my racing heart as the words "her man" eat away at my self-control.

Meredith, Cruz, and I, all together under one roof. Is there any possible way that this could end with someone's heart not being thrust through a blender?

I wake up with just as much anxiety as I had when I went to sleep. Turning my phone back on, I see there are some missed calls and messages from Lexi, but there's no way I can deal with that situation right now. I contemplate telling Cruz but decide against it. Instead, I head down to the music room and lock myself inside.

I'm on a blissful high when I exit the room, I see Cruz walking toward me. I barely have time to think when his arms wrap around me, and my back is flush with the wall. His body is pressed against mine, and I want to melt into him right there against the wall. His forehead comes down to rest on mine, and I feel his chest expand with a deep inhale.

"God, you smell good." It's all he says before his body is off me, and I'm watching him walk down the hall and out of sight.

I get back to my room and hear the chime of a new message. I know it's from Lexi, and if I keep ignoring her, she's going to know something's up. Picking up my phone, I open the latest text.

Lexi: Call me as soon as you get this.

I click dial and sit down on my bed, bringing the phone to my ear. It barely rings when she answers.

"Oh my god, where have you been? I've been trying to call you."

"Sorry, I've been really wrapped up in the beginning of this romance story."

It's not a complete lie. The day in the field of daisies with Cruz definitely has all the makings of a beautiful romance novel.

"You and your books. Anyway, I just wanted to check in. Meredith and I'll be there by nightfall. Let's go out, all of us. I miss everyone."

I hear Lexi's name being called.

"Sorry, Tay, got to go. See you tonight."

The phone goes dead, and I let out a sigh of frustration. Let's all hang out with Meredith White, who's on a mission to get Cruz back in her life. Fan-fucking-tastic.

I spend the day in my room with my face buried in a book. Of all the books on my shelf, I had to choose the one with the love triangle. One guy, two girls. If that isn't a sign of how my day's going, then I don't know what is.

The sun is setting when there's a knock at my door. Given the time, I expect Lexi to walk in, but I'm taken by surprise when I see my brother standing there staring at me, and I'm surprised at how guilty I feel for what I'm doing behind his back.

"Is everything okay? You've been holed up in here all day." He shakes his hair away from his eyes as he walks toward me, taking a seat on my bed. "I've known you your whole life, Taylah, and I know when there's something off with you. Is it Cruz? Has he been giving you a hard time? I know he can be a little…"

"He hasn't been giving me a hard time." My cheeks flush with heat from the poor choice of wording. I slide my knees to my chest and tilt my face away from him. It's hard not being able to vent my issues with my brother. We've always had that.

"Lexi called me." I lift my head to look at him.

"Are you two on talking terms now?" I ask, but he awkwardly looks away.

"She wants everyone to go out tonight. Apparently, Meredith knows the owner of the new club that opened a few nights ago and will look past you and Lexi being underage." I roll my eyes and go back to resting my head against my knees, hoping that's signal enough that I don't want to talk anymore.

"I want to tell you something," he starts before he's interrupted by the happy girl scream coming from the hall.

"Taylah!" Lexi runs into my room, dropping arms full of shopping bags onto the floor, then diving onto my bed and wrapping her arms around my neck. "Sorry, I'm late. You won't believe the discounts Meredith can pull on Rodeo Drive." My eyes drift over Lexi's shoulder as Tristan silently leaves the room, soon replaced with a tall, slim brunette with cheekbones that could slice through glass and bright white teeth framed by ruby-red lips.

"Hi, Taylah, Lexi's told me so much about you." Her voice irritates me immediately. I give her a small smile and nod.

"Let's get ready." Lexi shouts.

The next few hours consist of Lexi and Meredith trying on different outfits in my bedroom while doing tequila shots and me fading away into the background. I'm riddled with jealousy, which is a foreign feeling for me, and it's hard to decipher where it's coming from. Is it knowing that Cruz's hands and mouth have been all over the girl in front of me who looks like she's walked off a New York runway? Or is it watching my best friend obsess over her?

God, what is wrong with me?

"Do you think this is too much?" Meredith asks, turning to face me with one hand on her hip as she flicks her straightened hair over her shoulder. The dress is red with cutouts revealing the sides of her stomach and waist. It's strapless and sits just under her ass. She looks stunning, that's a fact.

"You look nice," I answer. Because, let's face it, she does, and the old Taylah prides herself on being that girl who builds other women up. I need to find my way back to her. I miss her. So, I smile as I get to my feet and rifle through my wardrobe in search of something to wear.

"Would you stop rearranging your boobs, Taylah." My breasts are three seconds away from spilling out the top of the dress I'm wearing, and I'm regretting every minute of letting Lexi and Meredith choose my outfit for tonight. It's a black backless dress with a bandeau strap that barely contains me. It sits mid-thigh and hugs my body like a glove.

"Uber's here," Trey calls out. Meredith and Lexi throw back one more shot each as I slide on a pair of black red-bottom heels, and head for the door. The boys are already outside waiting for us as we exit the house. I immediately feel Cruz's eyes on me. He's wearing a pair of black jeans and a white button-up shirt.

Damn.

"Let's get this show on the road." Lexi links her arm through mine and Meredith's as she marches us toward the Uber. I watch as Cruz storms in front of them, bringing them to a halt.

"Excuse me muscles, we have an Uber to catch," Lexi says as she attempts to step around him,

"Why are you here?" The anger in his voice as he glares at Meredith makes her stumble over her words.

"I... We..."

"Shotgun," Trey shouts as he heads for the passenger door, and Lexi and Meredith use this distraction to slide into the middle row of the SUV.

"Taylah?" Lexi calls out to me as she taps the seat next to her. I glance up at Cruz as I pass. He doesn't say anything as Tristan walks past us mumbling about the fact he, and Cruz will have to squeeze into the two tiny seats in the back.

The car is weaving through LA traffic, as the whole car starts to drunkenly sing along to a Taylor Swift song. Well, everyone besides the only two people in the car who don't drink. I use this moment to glance back at Cruz, whose lust-filled gaze creates an ache between my legs.

Fuck.

I snap my eyes away from him, focusing straight ahead. My body is screaming at me to crawl into the backseat and seek out some relief. I rub my thighs together and try and swallow, but my mouth has run dry.

Resting my head against the window, I will time to move faster as the space around me suddenly becomes too constricting.

"Oh look, there it is," Meredith announces.

Thank god.

Chapter Twenty-Seven

Cruz

*F*uck me.

I am two seconds away from throwing Taylah over my shoulder and carrying her all the way back to the beach house. I'm seated in VIP on a dark-purple couch with Tristan and Trey, who are currently arguing about who's the hottest Marvel character. They're distracted, and the lighting is dim in here, so I continue to stare at her as she rests against the black marble bar on the far side of the room. The dress she's wearing shows just how long her legs are. The same set of legs that lock around my waist when I fuck her.

I see a guy approach her and nod at the girl behind the bar, heat prickling up my neck as jealousy comes barreling through me. I can't hear what they're saying, but I assume he's asking to buy her a drink. She smiles and shakes her head at him, and I'm filled with relief when he takes the hint and walks away.

"This seat taken?" Meredith asks as she falls beside me with a pink cocktail in each hand before sliding them onto the glass table in front of us. "How've you been?" she asks as she lifts the cherry from her glass and rolls it across her lips.

"Great." I keep my gaze locked ahead as I watch Lexi take Taylah's hand and lead her to the dance floor.

"I'm gonna get straight to the point." Her hand is on my thigh, and it takes me a moment to register. "I miss you." She leans in, and I grab her hand, sliding it off my body. She stomps her gold stiletto on the floor, and I feel a tantrum brewing. "Who do you think you are, rejecting someone like me? No one has ever dared treat me the way you are right now, Cruz." She downs both cocktails and folds her arms across her chest, pouting.

"Well, there's a first for everything, Meredith." I get to my feet and head for the bar in search of some water when Tristan appears beside me. He runs a stressed hand through his hair as he orders another beer. "You, alright?"

He lets out a deep sigh and shakes his head.

"I don't know what's gotten into me, Cruz," he stammers as he takes a sip of his beer, turning his back to lean against the bar as he nods to the dance floor. I follow his line of sight and see Taylah and Lexi, but where Taylah is dancing alone, Lexi has her arms linked around some random guy's neck. "I'm falling for her hard." His drunken confession takes me by surprise. Tristan has always been the overly romantic, love at first sight kind of guy. But with Lexi? All they do is argue.

I go to tell him to relax and that it's an innocent dance, but when I see a guy approach Taylah and her arms slide around his neck, I see red. The entire room disappears, and the only thing I can see is his hands finding their way to her waist as I storm onto the dance floor. My palm hits his chest with such force, he stumbles back falling onto his ass.

"Cruz!" I ignore the shock in Taylah's tone as I grab her wrist and drag her toward the corridor that leads to the bathroom. "What're you doing?" She's clearly freaking out, but I ignore her. Tugging her down the hall, I round the corner at the end, which leads to a locked supply closet. Even though we're still in the club with her brother and our friends mere feet away, it's dark back here, and I take full advantage of that.

Pushing her up against the supply closet door, I grab her wrists and lock them above her head as I press my body against her. Her eyes are filled with want, and it has my cock leaking pre-cum, with the thought of taking her right here against the door.

"Closer" by Neyo starts playing and I almost laugh at the ironic lyrics in the moment.

"We can't." I don't let her finish that sentence, forcing my mouth to hers as she sucks back a breath, taking mine with her. I couldn't care if she stole every breath until my lungs collapsed if that's what she needed.

I feel her hands fumbling with my belt buckle, and when I pull back, she drops to her knees in front of me. I lean my palm against the door, gazing down at her while she unzips my pants, reaching inside and pulling my cock free. She peers up at me through those thick lashes as she leans forward with her tongue out, and I'm not ready for the gorgeous fucking sight of her tongue circling the head of my cock.

"Fuck!" It's a growl that rips from somewhere so deep in my stomach it takes my breath away. She pulls back slightly, running her tongue across her lips, before leaning back in and sliding my cock into her warm, wet mouth. I feel myself sliding down her throat, and my brain is short-circuiting; the need to feel her tight pussy hugging my cock becomes painfully over-whelming. Lifting her to her feet, I push her against the door. Every movement is wild and chaotic as I rip her red silk thong down her legs. I waste no time hitching her leg over my hip, angling her to me. Taking my throbbing cock into my hand, I place it at her entrance, letting her arousal soak me.

Her eyes look down at where my cock sits, and a rush of adrenaline snakes its way up my spine at the thought of her watching me fuck her. I sink into her slowly, letting her watch every inch disappear inside her. She watches me pull back, my cock now coated in her. Her eyes come up to meet mine, and they're wild and frenzied.

"Fuck me." Something inside me snaps when those words leave her mouth, and I slam into her with force. She pulls my mouth to hers as I fuck her hard against the door, whimpering with every thrust. The fact that someone could walk around the corner and see us barely even registers in my brain as I lose myself in her.

"I'm coming, I'm coming," she screams out as her eyes close, and her head falls back, hitting the door. A few more deep thrusts and I empty my release inside her, pulling her into me, and devouring every shake and shudder pouring off her body.

She smiles and starts to laugh, and I can't help but smile back. "What are you doing to me?" I lower her leg to the ground and buckle my jeans back up before dropping down and picking up her thong. Taking her ankle into my hand, I slide her panties in place before re-adjusting her dress. Stepping away, I lean up against the wall and watch her attempt to slick down her *I just got railed hair.*

No longer on my sex-fueled high, I realize I might have some explaining to do.

"I'm pretty sure your brother saw me storm across the room and grab you."

We barely have time to process when we hear Tristan's name being screamed. I turn and run down the hall, where I see a crowd forming around two men throwing punches. It's when I see blood pouring out of Tristan's nose that I feel myself propel through the crowd, grabbing the unknown man off of him and slamming him against the DJ desk. I immediately realize it's the guy who was dancing with Lexi.

"Cruz, we have to go." Taylah's voice cuts through the music, but before I can respond, the cold air smacks me in the face as security escorts me outside.

Tristan is ushered out not long after me, followed by Taylah and Lexi. The ice-cold glare that Lexi buries Tristan with before she turns and walks a short way down the street is enough to freeze hell over.

"I'll order an Uber," Taylah says before she turns and walks off after her friend. I pull my phone out to call Trey to tell him we're leaving when he stumbles out with a very intoxicated Meredith under his arm.

"Is everyone okay?" he asks, taking in Tristan's state and looking down at Lexi, who's wiping tears off her face.

"Fine," Tristan answers, wiping the blood from his nose and onto his white shirt. Trey nods as he struggles to keep a drunken Meredith on her feet. I walk over to him and send off a text to her driver before helping to stabilize her.

"Her driver will be here within fifteen minutes."

After piling Meredith into the back of her town car, our Uber arrives like clockwork. Tristan slides into the passenger seat up front, clearly wanting his space from everyone, while I head for the small space at the back.

"I'll sit with you." I turn around to see Taylah standing behind me, and I glance over her shoulder to where Trey and Lexi are stuck in deep conversation. Sliding into the back, I take her hand and pull her into the small space with me. Lexi and Trey pile into the middle of the SUV, and it pulls away from the curb.

The drive is silent until the patter of raindrops tap against the roof as the sky opens up in a downpour.

"This is the most rain we've ever seen over summer in Cali." The driver tries to make small talk, but I'm no longer listening when I hear a gasp escape Taylah's mouth. I watch her thighs clench together, and she lets out a deep breath.

"What's wrong?"

She turns and looks at me with a smirk that makes me want to drag her onto my lap and bury myself inside her against the backseat.

"I can feel you dripping out of me."

Holy fucking fuck.

I didn't know what was going to come out of her mouth, but that was not it. I watch in awe as she slides her thong from her body and drops it into my hand before guiding my other hand between her legs.

She glides my fingers up the inside of her thigh, coating them in my own cum. Her legs widen as she tilts her hips, pushing my cum-coated fingers inside her. An uncontrolled moan breaks from my chest, leaving me thankful for the clatter of rain that's currently drowning out the noises coming from the backseat.

I withdraw my fingers slowly before shoving them back inside her, watching her body suck the pleasure out of the moment as I quicken the pace. Her hips tip into my hand, and she grabs at my shirt before a gush of arousal explodes all over my fingers.

She's trying to catch her breath as her body convulses in pleasure. I slowly remove myself from her body and hand her her thong.

We went from fucking in a field of yellow daisies in one of the most breathtaking, book-worthy moments of my life to me finger-fucking my cum back into her in the backseat of an Uber.

❧

Chapter Twenty-Eight

Taylah

A couple of days have passed since the nightclub, and with Tristan and Trey devouring all of Cruz's time, we've barely spoken. I asked Lexi what happened that night between her and Tristan, but she's avoided giving me any kind of explanation.

We're both currently curled up on my bed reading. Lexi with her women's lifestyle magazine, reading about the top ten vibrators on the market, and me with my forbidden romance book that's doing nothing but torturing me with thoughts of Cruz.

"Do you believe in true love?" she asks as she rests the magazine on her lap. I'm thrown for a moment before letting out a laugh.

"I'm obsessed with romance novels, Lexi; of course I believe in true love."

She smiles, but it barely reaches her eyes. "What do you think it feels like?" Her words float around in my brain as I sit there and let the question stew for a minute, replaying every romance novel I've read through my head, but nothing feels good enough.

"I think true love is a place your soul searches for, and when you find it, it's like you've finally found your way home."

She sits there for a moment before rolling over and facing me with a smile across her face.

"Guess that means you're my true love then." We erupt into a fit of laughter, and in that moment, I'm thankful I have her in my life. I've never kept anything from her. We tell each other everything. We're there for each other in the lows and celebrate each other in the highs. And as I think about the incredibly high milestones I've just gone through in my life, it suddenly feels wrong to keep this from her.

"I slept with Cruz."

The entire room empties of oxygen as I wait for her to speak, the silence slicing through me like shards of glass. Her eyes widen as she stares at me, a thousand different emotions rolling over her face as she processes. Shock, intrigue, hurt, more shock, and finally, she smiles and laughs, filling the room with a much-needed wave of joy.

"Your first time was not only with your brother's off-limits best friend but one of the hottest boys I've ever laid eyes on. Nice." She raises her palm for a high-five before rearranging herself into a cross-legged seat with her head resting on her hands. "Spill."

After relaying the last few days to her, keeping a few of the more intimate details to myself, like the back of the Uber last night, I watch as she energetically takes it all in.

"Was it book-worthy?" she asks, as I sit there replaying every delicious minute of it all in my head.

'Every single second."

Cruz has been gone for the last week. He left in the middle of the night without a word. Tristan said he's dealing with a family emergency, and in that moment, I felt such a sudden grip of jealousy. Jealous that my brother knows more about the guy I'm in love with than I do.

It's party night at the beach house tonight, and I'm definitely not in the mood to socialize with a bunch of intoxicated and overstimulated boys. I try Cruz's phone again, but it goes straight to voicemail, so I shoot him a text.

Taylah: I'm worried, please let me know if you're ok or if there's anything I can do.

I place my phone to charge on my nightstand before heading for the shower.

"Are you wearing the red or beige silk dress tonight?" Lexi's face appears through the steamed-up glass.

"Whatever one you don't wear, Lex." I respond casually as I rinse the conditioner from my hair.

"I know you miss him, Taylah, but please try and use this night to bring some much-needed laughter into your week. You've been so blah without lover boy here."

I smile and nod at her, and she turns and heads back into my room before I hear her call out, "I'll be the one in red."

Once dressed, I slide on some black, strappy heels and take a look in the mirror. I flick my blonde curls over my shoulder and see Lexi staring at me in the reflection.

"God, I wish Cruz was here to see you in that." She slides a gold hoop through her ear as she walks toward me. "Have you heard from him?"

I shake my head. It's been a week of radio silence. I've even scanned media pages of anything about the Valentine family, and nothing.

I can't shake the horrible feeling in the pit of my stomach as I walk with Lexi into the living room. Tristan and Trey have set up the beer pong table inside and are well and truly on their way to intoxication as Sam walks through the front door with a few of his friends, including Sarah, one of Lexi's friends from acting class.

"Sam! You made it," Tristan calls out, raising a red cup into the air before chugging it back and flipping it onto the beer pong table. The room starts to fill with bodies and the smell of stale beer. The music is so loud that people are yelling over it just to have a conversation, and I need a minute to think. Lexi's at least three shots deep with Sarah, so I don't feel bad as I head for my bedroom.

I'm almost at my door when I feel a hand grip my wrist. My heart soars, and I've never turned around so fast in my life, only to be met face-to-face with Sam.

"Can I talk to you for a second?" I turn back and look at my room before moving to face him, contemplating just slipping from his grip and locking myself in my room for the remainder of the night. "Please?" His voice is soft and sincere, so I stand there and wait to hear what he has to say.

He closes the distance between us, only to be met with my palm against his chest. It registers instantly, and he retreats.

"Sorry, I didn't mean to crowd you. It's just..." He takes a breath and runs his hand across his jaw. "I like you, Taylah, a lot." His eyes scan mine while I process what's just come out of his mouth. "I'm moving to New York to be closer to you." I can hear the words that are coming out of his mouth, but they feel like a scrambled mess inside my brain.

He likes me. He's moving to New York to be near me. This is a mess that needs fixing immediately.

He goes to take my hand in his, and I know right at this very minute I need to attempt to set this straight. I'm in love with Cruz Valentine. Madly, deeply, unapologeticaly in love.

"My heart's somewhere else." He blinks back the initial shock, before nodding in understanding. He turns on his heel and heads back to the party, and I make the final steps to my room, pausing with my hand on the knob. I glance over at Cruz's closed door, and the ache I feel from his absence is becoming too much to bear.

Walking to his room, I open the door. Stepping through the threshold, I'm immediately consumed with his fresh scent. I lock the door behind me and let myself breathe him in. I spot one of his hoodies folded on his bed, and before I can stop myself, I'm stripped out of my dress, and slide the material over my body. I revel in the way it swallows me whole, as I slowly drop to the floor and rest my back against his bed. Bringing my knees to my chest, I let the hood engulf my face as I sit there in the dark and fall into myself.

My phone starts ringing, and when I glance over at where it's lying on the floor, I see Cruz's name flashing across the screen. I scramble to answer it as my fingers shakily tap at the screen.

"Taylah?"

His voice comes through on the other side, and I'm so overloaded with emotion that tears are streaming down my face.

"Are you there?"

That's when I realize I'm nodding, and he can't see me.

"I'm here."

As much as I wanted to hide the fact that I'm midway through a breakdown, the words come out mid-sob.

"Are you okay?"

The panic in his voice is clear.

"I'm fine, I just... miss you."

The line is silent for a few moments, with the sound of his breathing and my sobbing an intermingled mess.

"I'm sorry I didn't say goodbye or tell you why I had to leave."

"Can you tell me now?"

"I can't. I'm sorry."

I feel heartbroken, and I can't explain why. But the thought of him going through something and not being able to confide in me is such a gut-wrenching dose of reality. I'm not his girlfriend; I'm his secret summer fling.

"I have to go, but I want you to promise me something before I hang up."

"What's that?"

"Let your hair down tonight. Have some fun. Enjoy your summer like you were meant to. Spend the night smiling, Taylah."

It sounds like he's telling me to move on. Is this goodbye? My heart is beating so fast in my chest, I break out in a sweat.

"What are you trying to say?"

"I'm sorry."

The phone goes dead, and my body is shaking so badly, I feel like I'm about to be sick. How can something so beautiful, come to such a devastating end. I jolt as my phone starts ringing again, and when I glance down it's an unknown number.

"Hello?"

Chapter Twenty-Nine

Cruz

As soon as I end the call, my heart explodes inside my chest, and an unsettling ache ruptures my soul. It's like someone's turned all the lights out, and standing here alone in the dark. I do my best to pull myself together, sliding my phone into my pocket and running my shaking hands through my hair before getting to my feet and heading to room 217.

My mother's black eyes are healing, and the swelling under her nose and cheekbones has subsided a lot over the last week. Taking a seat on the tanned, leather chair that faces her bed, I do my best to avoid her gaze. One look, and she'll be able to tell I'm falling apart at the seams. My heart is slowly disintegrating inside my chest, as the tears stinging my eyes threaten to roll down my face.

"Did you speak to Taylah?" Her name alone is like a sledgehammer to the chest, and that's when a rogue tear breaks the surface.

"She deserves someone who mirrors the joy she radiates. Who will be that beacon of light for her on her dark days."

"Oh, son, I wish you could see yourself through my eyes. It hurts to hear you think so little of yourself."

I can feel my emotions boiling over as her words chip away at my resolve, and suddenly, tears are streaming down my face. "Crying is a sign of weakness; do you remember those words?" Her face falls as she recollects the moment she said those exact words to me. "That was the day I lost hope. I took every insult, every degrading comment from Dad. But the night he attacked you, I called the police to save your life, and do you remember what you told me?" Tears prick her eyes as I continue. "You told me that was the wrong thing to do. That trying to save your life was the wrong thing to do." My lungs are burning as I try and take a breath through the sobs wracking my chest. "I thought I finally freed you from the nightmare we had to live through, only for you to tell me I did something wrong."

My heart is pounding, and everything I've held inside comes pouring out of me. "Everything I do is to save you from his wrath. I'm tired, Mom." My bones feel heavy, and my stomach is in knots as all the unhealed pieces of my soul fight their way to the surface. I walk over and lean down, leaving a tear-soaked kiss on her forehead. "Get some rest, you need it."

As I approach the wrought iron gates, I'm not filled with the usual dark, soul-disintegrating feeling I'm used to. Instead, anger and resentment have taken its place. I rip the handbrake up and skid across the gravel before launching myself from the car and storming up the familiar cold concrete steps I loathe.

Entering the house, I head for his study. As soon as the door comes into view, my body feels static as liquid heat ravages my veins. I shove the door open with such force it smacks the wall behind it, making my father jump from his chair.

"What the fuck do you think you're doing?" The pure hatred in his voice has little effect on me right now, and I find a sliver of peace for myself in that.

"Your violent, controlling ways are done."

He glares at me, snatching his glass of scotch off the desk.

"I suggest you leave, Cruz, before someone gets hurt." I watch as he reaches down, unlocking the top drawer of his desk and retrieving a black handgun.

"You did everything in your power to make my life as cold and grey as your fucking soul." He smirks at my words as he raises his glass to his lips, taking a slow sip. "But while you were dragging me into the dark, I found someone who makes my world explode with color, and it's fucking breathtaking." I choke on my words as I fill my lungs with air, trying to ease the pain imploding my chest.

"You made damn sure I was so emotionally destroyed, that I'd never be able to love someone of that caliber." I wipe the tears from my face needing a moment to catch my breath. "I might not be half the man she deserves right now, but there's not a chance in hell I'll leave this world without knowing I tried."

Anger flashes behind his eyes as the gun squeezes in his grip. "Your weakness is such a fucking embarrassment."

I take a few quick steps toward him and watch his eyes widen at my close proximity.

"You seem to think I care what some abusive, pathetic excuse of a man thinks of me." It's in the way terror briefly flashes behind his eyes that I smile, a big, genuine, joy-filled fucking smile. But it's short-lived when the sound of sirens bust the moment wide open.

"You called the fucking police?" His panic-stricken voice is satisfying as he races to the window. Blue and red lights flash over his terrified face, and it's in that moment when my father is about to be arrested, that I realize just how small, weak, and pathetic he really is.

I watch the moment he's handcuffed and dragged from his office before climbing the stairs to my bedroom. I stand there for a moment and look around. For years, this room felt like a prison, and right now, hearing my father yell and scream as he's loaded into the police vehicle, I find some peace.

I hear footsteps behind me, and when I turn around, every bit of oxygen left inside my lungs collapses when I see Taylah standing only a few feet away from me. I blink a few times to make sure she's actually there. Maybe this is what happens when you finally lose your fucking mind.

"Your mom called me." Her voice shakes as she plays with the sleeve of the hoodie she's wearing, and it takes me a minute to realize she's wearing my clothes. My white hoodie and my grey sweats. Her eyes leave mine as she scans my room, gradually making her way along the back wall toward my desk. Her back is to me while her hands meticulously skate over my things, as if her mind is trying to piece together parts of me that I've closed off. She tilts her head as she reads through the playlist saved on my laptop, before hitting play.

"Flaws," by Calum Scott starts to play, and she turns to face me.

"I wish I could've been there for you. I'd never let anyone hurt you, Cruz." I don't know exactly how much my mother told her, as I watch her break apart in front of me. Her tear-filled eyes reflect nothing but love as the magnitude of the words in that sentence shatter every wall I've ever built.

I close the distance between us as the overwhelming need to have her close intensifies. Cupping her face, I collect her tears with the pads of my thumbs. She closes her eyes and leans into my chest, wrapping her arms around me as the room slowly fades away. Our battered emotions find their peace as she peacefully sways to the music, buried in my arms.

She tilts her head to look at me and I'm hit with those starry grey eyes shimmering in the moonlight. I lift her onto me, our mouths colliding as we both drown in the taste of our tears. I back up until my legs hit my mattress and drop down with her wrapped around my waist. There are so many unsaid words that drift through the air around us, but I'm taking this moment for all it's worth. I lay back and she falls with me.

"I need to be inside you." I'm so overwhelmed with everything that's happened over the last few hours; my soul is craving the peace that only she can give me.

She shuffles out of my clothes, and I do the same until our naked bodies collide against each other with so much heat, I'm struggling to contain myself. I flip her onto her back and take pleasure in familiarity of the way her legs wrap around my waist. I'm torn between looking into those gorgeous fucking eyes as I push inside her or tasting the rapture through her mouth. I go with the latter, pushing into her and stealing every euphoric breath from her lungs.

My hands are buried in her hair as her cotton candy scent engulfs my senses. Pulling back to look at her, I don't dare look away as I slowly withdraw before sinking back inside her. The way her soft features pull me out of the dark spaces inside my head as my heart collides with my soul, is a feeling I'll never be able to explain.

With every roll of my hips. Every stolen breath. Every beat of my racing heart, I make love to the love of my life in the very place that broke me.

I feel the moment my heart shatters completely when I realize this is the part where I have to let her go. She's my person. I can feel it in my bones. But I'm a broken man, and until I heal myself, I have to let her go. Right now, it's just not our time, or maybe she was never mine to keep. After all, some of the most beautiful moments on this earth are merely just passing through.

I lift my head for one last look at her, knowing this is goodbye. I bring my hands to hold her face, with the feeling of us drifting apart becoming all too real, and she deserves an explanation.

"One day, when my heart isn't so heavy, I'll be able to give you the love you deserve. But we can't be us right now, and I don't know when I'll be ready to give you the love you need from a heart that's barely even capable of beating." The ache in my chest becomes unbearable as tears roll down her cheeks. I wipe them away with my thumbs, not letting my hands leave her face. "I'll never be able to look at another cotton candy sky without being completely consumed by the thought of what we had. I'm in love with you, Taylah. From the moment I laid eyes on you in that yellow dress looking brighter than the sun itself, I knew my heart wasn't mine anymore."

She pulls me closer, resting her head against my chest as she inhales me. "Please don't let me become a memory."

Chapter Thirty

Taylah

I can barely see through the tears that soak my face as I drive through the city toward my parents' house. The beach house is the last place I want to be right now as I replay the final words Cruz said to me. There was no point in begging him to stay, he had checked out. I could see it in his eyes. Those devastatingly beautiful eyes. The hauntingly familiar grey cloud was back, and it had consumed him completely.

I park my car and wipe the tears off my face, pulling Cruz's hood up over my head. As torturous as it is drowning in his scent-filled hoodie, I can't bring myself to take it off. He was everything I didn't know I needed. A part of me I know I'll never get back. I fight back tears as the reality of the situation weighs down on me. Whatever breathtakingly beautiful love story we started, has come to an end. And as much as I try and come to terms with it all, my heart just doesn't want to hear it.

I feel a small token of relief with every step closer to the front door of my parents' house, as comfort washes over me, and I know I made the right decision to come home.

Unlocking the door, I do my best to slip through quietly. It's late, so I don't expect my parents to still be awake. But as I head for the stairs, I hear classical music coming from the living room. I take a few steps, before rounding the corner, where I see my parents slow dancing. My heart warms just watching them as the sweet memory of Cruz and I from earlier tonight sweeps through me. True love, right there in front of me.

Tristan and I were raised with such love and devotion that I never really stopped to think about how detrimental it must be for the human soul to live through what Cruz has had to live through. But after everything his mother told me and witnessing his father being arrested for domestic violence, I can't even fathom the devastation he endured behind those walls.

I understand now why he needs time to heal his soul, and I'm going to respect that. I guess there really is moments of right person wrong time, and I can only pray that one day he finds his way home to me.

Home. I smile to myself replaying the answer I gave Lexi about what I thought true love would feel like as, an indescribable ache bleeds through me. No one prepares you for how devastatingly beautiful finding your soul mate can be, and nothing prepares you for the pain of having to walk away from them.

I hear footsteps in my bedroom right before I'm blinded by light. Squinting, I see my mother fixing the light-pink drapes that house the window that looks out toward the river. I sit up and lean against the soft pink velvet headboard as she takes a seat on the edge of my bed.

"I didn't realize you knew I was home."

She smiles and places her hand on mine. "I'm your mother; nothing gets past me." She's always had such a calming aura about her, and now more than ever, I feel so blessed to be raised by someone like her. "Who's the guy?"

"What do you mean?"

"Taylah, your eyes are swollen from crying, and you're wearing a hoodie that's four sizes too big for you." I don't know why, but at that moment, I feel like I want to burst into tears. My heart feels too heavy to talk about the fact I'm in love with someone I can't have, and after the emotional overload last night, I'm exhausted. She takes my silence as an indicator I'm not ready to talk about it and gets to her feet.

"Stay here as long as you need, sweetheart." She heads for the door, and I want to just pull the blanket over my head and bury myself and my feelings in my bed all day, but instead, I slide out of bed and slip my sneakers on before heading outside for some space to think.

The sun on my back has a calming effect as I make my way toward the river. I see the rope swing come into view and take a seat on the river bank. It doesn't feel that long ago that a twelve-year-old Cruz was here, seated next to me and sharing some cotton candy. I didn't have a care in the world—life was bliss, and now knowing the extent of what Cruz was going through at that time makes my heart feel heavy.

I replay the phone call I had with Cruz's mother over and over in my head. Whilst sparing the more horrific details, she told me enough to know that Jack is an extremely violent man and has been throughout Cruz's entire life.

I'm completely overwhelmed as my mind races, and I lie back on the grass to try and make sense of the scrambled mess in my head. How people like Jack Valentine can live with themselves makes me sick to my stomach. He deserves to be locked behind bars.

It's at that moment that I think about Skylar and her drive for justice. And how, instead of spending her summer relaxing by the ocean, she's out there working toward making a difference in this world. And suddenly I know exactly where I need to be.

My flight back to New York is booked for later tonight, so I have a few hours to head back to the beach house and pack. I head down the coastal strip with the windows down, indulging in the salty air. The entire drive here, I've gone back and forth about what I'm going to say to Tristan, and as I pull into the driveway, I've made the decision to come clean about every-thing.

Getting out of the car, I head for the house, a nervous flutter in my stomach at how Tristan might react. When I step through the front door, I see Tristan and Sam cleaning up after last night's party. Considering the amount of people that were here last night, it doesn't actually look that bad.

"Hey, Tristan, can I talk with you for a second?" His head tilts up to look at me, noticing the serious tone in my voice.

"Sam, can you give us a second, please?"

"Of course." He nods and heads for the back door, sliding it closed behind him.

"You slept with Cruz, didn't you?" It's more a statement than a question.

So much for me needing to explain myself.

"How did you know?"

"After I saw you leave the party last night dressed head to toe in his clothes, everything started to come together. Things I thought I was imagining."

"Things like what?"

"Seeing him smile at you."

Butterflies flood my body as the image of Cruz's evasive smile plays through my mind.

"Are you mad?" I ask, not sure if I'm ready for his response.

"I'm not mad, Taylah." He takes a seat on the couch and lets out a deep breath, and I sit down beside him. "You can't help who you fall in love with." He runs his hand through his blond hair letting out a sigh. "I've been sleeping with Lexi, and I think I might be in love with her."

It was at this point everything collided. All the lies and the secrets and unspoken words. There are only so many shades of emotion one summer can hold.

"Does she feel the same way about you?" I regret the words as soon as they leave my mouth when the look on his face tells me everything I need to know.

"I tried to talk to her about it last night, and she left." He leans back into the couch letting out a deep breath. "Does Cruz feel the same way about you?"

"It's complicated."

He nods at me. I don't know what else to say. It's hard to explain how two people can be so in love, but not be together. "I'm actually heading back to New York tonight," I announce as I too lean back into the couch.

"I'm sorry Lexi isn't here to say goodbye to you." I indulge in the fact Tristan doesn't press me for further questions about Cruz, but it also hurts to see him so down. He's one of the happiest, carefree people I know, and to see him so destroyed breaks my heart.

"Do you need me to stay for a few days?" I ask.

He shakes his head. "No, I'm a big boy, Taylah. Besides, I can see the heartbreak all over your face, and if going back to New York is the first step in finding yourself again, I'll pack your bags myself."

I slept through most of my flight back to New York, and as soon as I exited the airport doors, I felt an immediate wave of calm wash over me, solidifying that I made the right choice. I try Lexi's phone again, but it just goes to voicemail, so I shoot her a quick text to call me back before sliding into a taxi and heading for campus.

Since it's summer break, the residence hall at Brown is eerily quiet. Juggling my room key and luggage bags, I manage to get the door open and flick on the light. My side of the room is exactly how I left it. Light pink comforter tucked neatly into the white bed frame, with a few books stacked onto the matching nightstand. My laptop is on my desk, and I contemplate getting a jump on some research. But when I stifle a yawn, I know I need some sleep. Besides, Skylar isn't here, and I could really use her opinion on where to start.

I take a quick shower before sliding Cruz's hoodie back over my body and crawling under the covers. I need as much rest as I can get because what I have planned for the next few months isn't going to be easy, but I'm hoping it's going to be worth it.

Chapter Thirty-One

Taylah

"Need help burying a body?" Skylar's voice pulls me from my sleep. I open my eyes and see her standing over me, with her head tilted and her hands on her hips. "Who is he?" she demands as her boots tap impatiently against the floor.

"It's not what you think." I sit up and stretch, noticing the paint that's in her hair.

"Why is there blue paint in your hair?"

"No way. You're not changing the subject, Taylah." She takes a seat on her bed that faces mine, folding her arms over her chest. I take a minute to process how much to say; after all, I did come back here wanting her help, so I start at the beginning. I tell her everything. Every heart-dropping, soul-stealing, panty-dropping detail. Until I get to the night that slammed us both face-first into a devastating reality.

I swallow back tears as I watch Skylar process everything, and for the first time since I've known her, she looks absolutely devastated.

"I need you to help me do anything we can to make sure Jack Valentine gets the punishment The deserves."

It doesn't take long for her fire to return, and she's on her feet pacing. "Oh, he'll get it alright. Let's nail his abusive ass to the wall."

My eyes are burning, and I hear Skylar groan as she looks down the barrel of her empty coffee cup.

"What time is it?"

I glance over at my phone. "It's almost 3:00 a.m."

"Let's go over what we've got so far." She shuffles her papers and joins me on my bed. "I've found some sections of legislation that I think might be useful, but we know he's going to have the best lawyers money can buy, and those fuckers always have an answer for everything."

We sit there in silence as our brains work overtime when an idea pops into my head.

"We need to create some noise." She looks up at me with a quizzical look on her face that makes me laugh. "Tell the world what he's done. Let the media outlets drown him in bad publicity. Let them paint the picture of the man he really is. You can't run from that, and once it's out there, it's hard to forget. If he walks out of that courthouse a free man, there'll be an uproar."

"Fuck, Taylah, that's actually fucking genius." She clasps her hand over her mouth as her eyes sparkle with admiration, and I'm feeling pretty good about myself until I see her features change.

"There is something that can happen that will allow Jack to walk away unscathed."

"What's that?"

"If his wife doesn't want to press charges. You said she told you he's being doing this for years? Why isn't he already behind bars?" I feel dread form in the pit of my stomach. I can't make her do this, but what Cruz's father put them through seems to be a huge contributing factor in the broken man he is. So, if this is something that could help the man I love start to heal, it's a conversation I'm willing to have. I mean, she did call me that night. Maybe she's at a turning point too?

"I'll talk to her."

I'm filled with nerves as I walk up the garden path where Cruz's mother is staying. I'm glad she's not at the Valentine Estate anymore, and Florida is only a short plane ride from New York.

I take the gold door knocker into my hand and give it a knock. I hear footsteps, and the wait is making me anxious. The door opens, and there she is, Elaine Valentine. I can still see the remnants of two black eyes, and my heart falls apart inside my chest. Seeing the damage firsthand of what Cruz has had to witness almost brings me undone. But I pull it together and give her the warmest smile I can manage.

"Hi, Elaine. Thank you for letting me come see you."

"Of course, Taylah, come in." She steps aside and welcomes me into her home. It's a cozy cottage on the beach, decorated with a nautical theme. "Would you like some iced tea? We can have it on the deck." She seems in high spirits, and that alone warms my heart.

"I'd love some."

Following her out onto the deck, I take a seat on the wooden chair that faces the ocean.

"You said you wanted to talk about Cruz?" she asks, pouring us both a glass. I take a sip trying to dissipate the nerves eating away at my stomach.

"I went and seen him the night you called me. I was there when Jack was taken away." Her eyes widen and the fear I see resting behind them is gut-wrenching. "He's been through so much, Elaine." The emotion behind that sentence creates an ache in my throat. Tears spill down her face, as her trembling hand reaches for her glass.

"I know." I take a minute, wanting to get my words right. I know this kind of situation is fragile, and I want this moment to be as judgmental free and comforting as I can make it. But there's one sentence running through my heart that's begging for me to say it out loud, and I can't hold it in any longer.

"I'm in love with him." I feel such a rush of relief as the words leave my lips and settle across the room. "I know he's in pain right now and has been for a long time. But I'm going to do everything I can to try and put the pieces of his soul back together."

Her head drops into her hands, and her body shaking as she sits there and sobs.

"You must think I'm a terrible mother." She lifts her tear-soaked face as her bruises and scars peek through her make-up. I get out of my seat and kneel down in front of her, taking her fragile hands into mine.

"I know things are never as black and white as they seem."

She squeezes my hands taking a deep breath. She obviously needs to get this off her chest, and I'm ready to listen.

"I met Jack when I was in a horrible place in my life. Both my parents had died in an accident, and I was a struggling waitress, barely able to make ends meet. I ended up losing my apartment and had nowhere to go; that was until Jack came into my life and helped me." I watch as she sits there for a moment, reliving her memories. "Before I saw the monster under the mask, Cruz was already born. I tried to leave once, and his words haunted me ever since that day." She swallows hard, and the despair in her voice makes my heart pinch. "He told me that I'd end up on the streets where he found me, making it easy for him to take our son and never let me see him again."

I feel the moment my heart breaks in half. "You know that you have a chance here to hold the power for once. You can put that man behind bars for everything he's done to you and Cruz. I'm doing everything I can, but I need your help, Elaine."

"Jack's cut me off from the family money. He would've taken this house from me too, if his lawyer didn't advise him against it. Apparently, taking everything from your wife and having her live on the streets would do too much damage to his reputation." She rolls her eyes and takes another sip of her iced tea. "I can't even afford a decent lawyer; meanwhile, he has LA's finest burying me in paperwork."

"Please let me help you with this. I don't plan on going down without a fight."

She nods at me as she wipes the tears from her face. "My son's lucky to have you, Taylah." She smiles as her fragile hands grip onto of mine. "I'm ready."

And that's the moment I witnessed Elaine Valentine's heart shatter into a million pieces as she finally let herself grieve every moment that she was never there for a boy who deserved so much more than this life had given him.

Chapter Thirty-Two

Cruz

It's been three months, sixteen days, twenty-four minutes, and eight seconds since I saw Taylah walk out of my room and out of my life, and yet her scent here is still so prevalent. It's one of the reasons I haven't been able to leave this place.

I took a leave of absence from my studies to get my head together and have been staying at the Valentine Estate since. I'm here, Tristan's back at school, and Trey's in Canada with his brother.

It's a weird feeling being in this house by myself, while my mother stays in Florida. I've only seen her once since she was able to leave the hospital. But if anyone can understand the need for space right now, it's me.

I've been keeping my mind busy by working on my car, but even as I stand here with my grease-covered hands resting on the open hood, I'm sent down a spiral of memories of her.

"I hope it's okay that I'm here." I'm slung back into reality at the sound of a female voice behind me. I look over my shoulder and see Meredith. "I come in peace; I promise." She waves her white Prada handbag as if waving a white flag of surrender. I close the hood of the car and grab the cotton rag beside me to wipe my hands as I turn to face her.

"What do you want?" I ask disinterestedly.

"I heard about what happened with your father, and I want to apologize." For the first time in my life, it appears as if she actually cares about someone other than herself.

"Do you want to come in? I don't have long; I have to be at the airport in an hour."

She nods, and we make our way toward the house.

"Where are you flying to?" she asks as I open the front door motioning her in.

"New York. I have a meeting tomorrow morning with the headmistress to discuss my future at Colombia. If I don't transfer to a new line of study, I will forfeit my place and will be asked to leave."

I nod her toward the living room. "You can wait in there; I just need to clean myself up."

Washing the rest of the grease from my hands and face, I throw on a clean shirt before heading back down to the living room. As I enter the room, I see her standing at the mantle with a framed photo in her hands. As I get closer, I see it's a picture of me at my high school graduation, looking as detached and stoic as ever.

"I've never seen you smile," she states, placing the photo back where it was. She looks at me and lets out a breath. "I really am sorry. Especially your father's birthday night with the kiss. He was telling me you missed me, and I should make the first move and..."

"It's okay. I know exactly what he's like." I cut her off and let her breathe. "I know what being manipulated by him feels like. And as shit and shady as your actions were that night, I understand what it can be like to be caught up under his control."

She nods at me before glancing down at her watch. "Can I drive you to the airport? It's the least I can do."

I go to pass her up on the offer, but something about getting all this out in the open feels somewhat healing. "Sure, I'll just grab my bag."

I head into the hall and jog up the stairs toward my room, grabbing the duffle bag off the floor. I'm rooted to the spot for a moment as the smell of Taylah drifts through the air, and I feel the smile slide across my face at the thought of her. Taking a deep breath in, I coat my lungs with her, and head back down the stairs where Meredith is waiting by the door.

I draw my hood over my head as light rain trickles over me, the pathway littered with a scattering of yellow, orange, and brown leaves. I get to the building with a few minutes to spare and head for Headmistress Jennings' office.

The door is open, and she lifts her head when she hears me approach. "Oh, please come in, Cruz." I close the door behind me and take a seat in the chair facing her desk. She looks down at me over her round Harry Potter-style glasses, her neat grey hair framing her face. "There's something I want to talk to you about, something I think you might be interested in."

I find her warm smile comforting. "What's that?"

Leaning back in her velvet throne-like seat, she clasps her hands out in front of her.

"We're aware of the court case against your father, and well, given the details, I can only imagine what you must have gone through."

I almost get up and leave as every word drips with sympathy, as the familiar heat of embarrassment nudges up my spine. Instead, I take a breath and listen to what she has to tell me.

"A professor who used to work here is running a program that we think you would be an excellent candidate for." She adds, sliding a red manila folder off her desk, and getting to her feet. "Instead of me explaining it to you, all the information is in here." I take the folder from her hands and place it in my lap. She smiles at me as she leans against her desk. "You're moving and living expenses will all be taken care of."

"Moving?"

She nods. "This program is located at Chicago University. Now, I know it's not Ivy League like Columbia, but I can assure you that this kind of career can be extremely rewarding."

I grip the folder in my hands, curious as to its contents. With everything going on right now, a move like this could be the step in the right direction I've been searching for. Waking up every day in this constant state of emptiness I feel without Taylah is agonizing, like my body is going through waves of continuous withdrawal. A withdrawal from her light, from her smile, and from her love.

After we parted ways that night, I changed my number and deleted all my social media so I wouldn't be tempted to contact her. Those moments when the pain of her absence becomes debilitating, are the hardest to keep my distance. But I'm determined to become someone who can offer her the same amount of love and peace she provides me.

I open the folder and scan the first few pages, and within five minutes, I immediately know the answer to my decision.

Heading for the residency hall where Tristan is staying, I muse over my quick decision. But the more I think about it, the more I want to go. The door's locked, so I knock and wait. There's some banging and whispering, and when a disheveled Tristan opens the door like a deer in headlights, I know I've just caught him mid-fuck.

I raise my brows at him, as he stands there mouth agape like he's seen a ghost.

"Everything okay?" I've seen him with women more than once, multiple women at that. Something about this feels off, as a phone rings out in the background.

"I need to call you back, Taylah." Hearing her name sends my heart slamming into my rib cage. I push open the door and see Lexi wrapped in a sheet, scrambling for her clothes. She sees me and slowly takes a seat on Tristan's bed. "Hi, Cruz."

I walk into the room as Tristan closes the door behind me. All I can think of is Taylah, and I'm struggling to rein myself in.

"How is she?"

Lexi looks at Tristan and back at me as if there's something she's not sure about saying, and my heart slides into my stomach, as I break out in a cold sweat. I know they know about me and Taylah. I was surprised when Tristan brought it up and was somewhat easygoing about it. I guess when you're banging your sister's best friend, it would be pretty hypocritical.

"Is she seeing someone?" I feel the quiver of my lips as the words scarcely make it out of my mouth.

I'm three seconds from passing the fuck out when Lexi says, "No, she's not seeing anyone else."

A wash of relief settles over me, but the room is still filled with words that remain unsaid, and at this point, all I care about is knowing if she's alright. So, I ask again, "But is she okay?"

Lexi smiles at me and nods. "She's okay, Cruz."

Closing my eyes, I drop my head, willing the ache in my heart to stop.

"What about you? Are you okay?" Tristan asks, gripping my shoulder in an offer of comfort. I nod and clear my throat. I want to say that every day since we walked away from each other, I'm haunted by the memory of her. Every day that goes by, my world slowly encases itself back into shades of grey, and the hole in my chest where my heart used to reside is eating me alive. But I don't say any of that, instead I say...

"I will be." And as I explain to Tristan and Lexi about my decision to move to Chicago and the details of the program I've accepted, for the first time in my life, I actually do believe I will be okay.

Chapter Thirty-Three

Taylah

I turn off the news and throw the remote across the room as Jack Valentine's lawyer delivers a speech to the press about how much of a moral citizen he is. He's out on bail and staying at the Four Seasons Hotel in LA. As part of his bail conditions, he's not allowed within five miles of the Valentine Estate where he was arrested.

"He'll get what's coming to him," Skylar says as she takes a seat next to me on my bed. "By the way, I have something to tell you."

I turn to face her, and her devilish smirk makes an appearance. "Why does that grin always make me so nervous?"

She laughs and takes my hands in hers. "My father has offered to meet with you to discuss the case against Cruz's father."

"Wait, as in the mayor of New York City?" There's a tremble in my voice, and I'm not quite sure if it's from the emotion that's flowing through me or the excitement.

"I told him a few things about the case, and well, this could potentially be a platform we can use. You could really make a difference here, Tay."

Words? There are none. Having the mayor do this could potentially change the lives of men, women, and children in domestic violence situations and is game-changing, to say the least. I jump to my feet and grab my laptop as I pace the room.

"I have so much to plan and research." I'm a flustered mess, but the thought of presenting something to the mayor is intimidating the hell out of me. There's so much at stake here.

"Would you relax." I didn't even notice Skylar get up and walk to me, but as her hand rests on my shoulder, I take a centering breath. "You didn't think I'd let you try and do this alone, did you?" There's a knock on the door, and she slips past me to open it. "Thank god you're all here, she's freaking out." The door widens, and suddenly, my erratic nerves are replaced with gratitude when Tristan, Lexi, and Sam walk into the room.

"So, a date with the mayor, huh?" Tristan says as he wraps me up in a hug. "Lucky the smart sibling is here to save the day." He laughs as I wriggle out of his grip. Lexi steps in next, hugging me like she hasn't seen me in years. I mean, it has been a few months, and in our friendship, that's the longest we've ever gone without seeing each other.

After I left the beach house, she called me to tell me about Tristan and her and if I was okay with them seeing each other. I had to laugh at the irony of it all. After all, you can't help who you fall in love with.

I feel Skylar pull us apart. "Okay, enough hugging. Let's get to work. I'll get the coffee; it's gonna be a long night."

It's 4:00 a.m., and it's just Sam and me reading through case law. Tristan didn't last long, but as an already sleep-deprived med student, he did pretty well. Lexi is curled up in my bed, leaving room on the pullout couch for Sam to jump in next to Tristan. Skylar left about an hour ago to god only knows where. That girl has so many secrets and connections—you would send yourself crazy trying to figure her out.

"So, he's the one?" Sam asks with his head still buried in the mountain of papers scattered across my desk. He looks up and meets my gaze. "Cruz Valentine?" He raises his brow at me in question, and just hearing Cruz's name sets off an explosion of butterflies through my stomach. I nod and look back down at the paperwork in front of me. "How do you know?"

I think about his question for a moment, but this one is easy to answer. "He feels like home."

My hands are shaking as I walk the marble staircase toward the upper level where Mayor Rhodes's office is located. I'm a nervous wreck, to say the least. It's been over a month since Skylar told me about this meeting, and every spare chance I've gotten between classes, I put into this presentation. Skylar's been a godsend to me; after all, she's the one with all the experience dealing with corrupt assholes. Tristan has dropped in when he could, but there's not much spare time when you're studying to become a doctor. Lexi is in acting school back in LA, so I haven't seen her as much as I'd like. And Sam did transfer to the NYFD and has dedicated his time off to helping me.

"Miss Barker?" I hear my name and glance up to where a tall, elegantly dressed woman eyes me over her square-framed glasses.

"Yes, that's me." I get to my feet and straighten my black pencil skirt before adjusting my white silk blouse. Our heels click in sync along the marble floor as I follow her down a long corridor. We stop at a double mahogany door, and she lightly taps against it. The door buzzes, and she pushes it open, nodding me through.

"Good luck, Miss Barker."

I smile as I enter the room, doing my best to hide the panic when I see Skylar's father seated in a dark, throne-like chair behind his walnut-colored desk. He offers me a warm smile, and for a moment, I'm thankful he doesn't house the infamous Rhodes's smirk that Skylar uses to unnerve people. I smile back, take a breath, and count to three.

"Thank you for taking the time to meet with me regarding such an important topic, Mayor Rhodes." He holds his hand up and I stop speaking, as he gestures me to take a seat in front of him.

"Please continue, Miss Barker." I smile at his warm tone and resume.

"While some of the things I want to talk about with you today involve the Jack Valentine case, which isn't based in New

York City, so much of it can be applied to many other cases, especially here in New York."

After boring him with some case law and statistics on domestic violence, I get ready to land my final statement. All the late nights, early mornings, and library cram sessions have led me to this moment. And breathe.

"Jack Valentine abused his wife for years. When she was finally brave enough to stand up for herself, he cut off all her access to the family money in the hope she would come running back. She can't afford a decent lawyer while he's surrounded by some of the best Los Angeles has to offer. I'm hoping that something can be drafted that in the event of a domestic violence case, the victim has access to adequate legal representation on the same level as the perpetrator. Any perpetrator using money, high status, and power to gain an advantage over a victim needs to be dealt with. Now, I know that any bill passed here won't affect the current laws in LA with respect to the Valentine case, but I'm hoping it could be a platform to start that conversation. I want that asshole to know I'm serious, and I'm not going to stop until I see justice served."

The speech has turned personal, and I hope I haven't ruined my chances. He sits there for a moment, running his hand over his chin as silent minutes drag by and dread starts to creep across my conscious state.

"I'm sorry, I didn't mean to get personal, I just..."

"You sound a lot like my daughter right now." He laughs and I'm flooded with relief. "The City Council is meeting together on Tuesday. I think your ideas deserve a discussion. Leave it with me."

It's not until I get back to my room, lie on my bed, and cover my head with my comforter, that I feel like I can breathe again. I laid it all out on the table, and now it's a waiting game. I have final exams coming up before winter break, and I should really be studying, but the anxious mess inside my stomach has me breaking apart at the seams.

I hear the door open and shut, and I know it's Skylar from the sound of her boots.

"How did it go?" The bed dips as she tugs the comforter off my face. "Tay?"

"I have no idea." I sit up and lean against the bedhead. "It just means so much to me, Skylar."

She rests her hands on mine and smiles. No smirk, this time a genuinely warm, sunny-day-filled smile. "The presentation you prepared was amazing, and if they don't see the goodness you're trying to achieve, I can only assume they're all corrupt idiots and need to be dealt with."

I laugh, but I know she's serious. "Are you going to go all vigilante on your father too?"

She smiles even wider, with her perfect white teeth on full display. "Oh, I'll take him down first."

I exit the exam hall after just finishing my last final exam before winter break. My phone vibrates in my pocket, and when I slide it out, I see Sam's name flash across the screen. I juggle my bag as I place it to my ear.

"Hey, Sam, how are you?"

"I'm good. How did your exam go?"

"I think I did fine. I never can tell."

"Do you have time for a coffee before you take off to the airport?"

I glance down at my watch.

"Meet me on campus at the cafe next to the library?"

"Be there soon."

Sliding my phone back into the pocket of my jeans, I head for the coffee shop.

As I step inside, I shrug off my white woolen coat and take a seat in the booth at the back. I still haven't heard anything about my meeting with the mayor and what was discussed with City Council, so I check through my voicemails and emails while I wait. Nothing.

"Have you ordered yet?" Sam asks, sliding into the booth.

"Not yet."

He signals the waitress and orders two coffees before he turns his attention back to me as he lets out a sigh. We've spent enough time together over the last few weeks that I feel like I can read when something is off with him.

"Is everything ok?"

He scans my eyes for a second before scrubbing his hands down his face.

"I just have alot on my mind right now."

"Do you want to talk about it?"

There's a few moments of silence between us and I can see the war he's having with himself right now.

He shrugs. "Maybe New York isn't for me." He glances out the frosted window and I take a minute to pick my words wisely.

"Is there anything I can do to make you smile?" I ask attentively.

He chuckles to himself and shakes his head.

"Are you excited to go home and see your family for Christmas?" he asks in an effortless attempt to change the subject.

Our coffees are placed on the table, and I wrap my hands in its warmth.

"I was hoping to have heard some news about the bill by now. I wanted to stop in and see Cruz's mom first."

"You should go there anyway; it saves her being alone at Christmas time." He takes a sip, and I'm thrown for a moment.

"You don't think Cruz will be with his mother for Christmas?"

He gives me a confused look as he places his coffee back down on the table.

"Taylah, you're aware Cruz moved to Chicago, right?"

I freeze for a moment, not quite registering what he's saying. Cruz wouldn't have moved away without telling me. I know he needs time, but shutting me out and moving away feels like a kick in the stomach.

"When did he leave?" The words barely make it past the lump buried in my throat.

"I'm not sure, maybe a month or so ago."

I sit there in silence as I try and fight the tears that are threatening to roll down my face. Talking about him brings up too many emotions that I'm not ready to deal with.

"I'm sorry, I have to go." Slipping out of the booth, I head out the door. I pull out my phone to order an Uber to the airport when it starts ringing in my hand. My heart drops when I see it's the number for the mayor's office.

"Hello, Taylah speaking."

"Hi, Taylah, it's Charlie Rhodes here. Do you have a minute?"

"Of course."

"I wanted to personally update you. The bill has been approved, and I signed it today. Your work has been noticed by other local governments, and there's even talk that the White House has had a brief discussion."

I feel myself dropping to my knees as my world tilts on its axis.

"You wanted to create some noise, Miss Barker. Mission accomplished."

Chapter Thirty-Four

Cruz

"You can do better than that," I tease as I block James's jab. I'm standing in the middle of a boxing ring, gloved up, going round for round with one of the boys here at the teenage rehabilitation center. It's a newly established facility at Chicago University that forms part of the program I was accepted into. And right now, as I take a left hit to the jaw, and see James smile for the first time since we met, I'm filled with pride.

"I told you that you can do better than that." We knock gloves before stepping under the ropes and grabbing some water.

"Cruz, can I ask you something?" I stop mid-swallow. We've been meeting here every Sunday morning for the past three weeks, and this is the first time he's spoken to me.

"Sure," I answer, placing my drink bottle back into my gym bag.

"Does the pain ever go away?" The hope in his eyes makes my heart squeeze inside my chest. James is one of the many teenage kids who attend therapy lessons here for kids from an abusive home. They've found that kids are more likely to open up to people who have been through similar circumstances, and so my part in this program is to be that comforting, safe space. Admittedly, seeing how strong these young kids are through everything that they've been through has helped me more than I ever thought possible. There's still so much I need to work through, and my weekly therapy sessions have definitely given me skills to navigate some of the carnage. But it's in the moments when I sit and think about Taylah that I push myself forward, toward the man I'm trying to become.

Looking back at James, I nod. "With the right support system and self-belief, you will find your way back to yourself." He smiles, and I ruffle his shaggy dark hair as I lift my gym bag over my shoulder and head for the door. "You better bring your A-game next Saturday; I'm not letting you get one over me that easily again." I hear him laugh as I exit through the gym door and head to class.

Winter has definitely peaked as a bone-chilling gust of wind whips across my face. I stare down at the snow crunching beneath my shoes as I head to the recreational center. Classes have finally wrapped up for winter break, and most students have left to spend Christmas with their families. But as I walk into the hall and see the smiles on the boys' faces, I know I made the right decision to stay.

"So, you decided to stay here in this blistering cold with us?" Brandon calls out from the back of the room as he bounces a basketball. "I thought students went home for Christmas," he adds, flicking his hair out of his eyes.

"Such a nice way to say you're glad to see me, Brandon." He smiles and shakes his head at me while he tosses the ball through the hoop at the back of the room. "Now group up and pick an activity." They scatter as some head for the basketball court and others head for the gym. I take a few steps toward the office when I see James leaning up against the brick wall, looking down at his phone. His face is unreadable, so I decide to make my way over.

"Everything okay?" He looks up at me, letting out a sigh before leaning his head back against the wall.

"There's this girl." The way that sentence leaves his mouth and hits me like a ton of bricks is enough to drown me in visions of Taylah, and suddenly, this icy day feels a little less numbing for a minute.

"What's her name?" I ask, leaning up against the wall next to him.

"Alison," he answers as a grin slides across his face.

"What do you like about her?"

There's silence between us for a few minutes as I watch him run through it in his head.

"The way she makes me feel." His answer makes me smile. "Like for the first time in my life, I feel hope. Like the world doesn't have to be so dark all the time." I watch the way his face lights up with every word, and I'm flooded with pride. I lift off the wall and place my hand on his shoulder.

"Don't let her go." He beams up at me with his bright white smile, and I can see how much he's changed from the sad, withdrawn boy I first met. I turn and walk away when I hear him speak.

"What's her name?" His question throws me off balance. I stop walking and look back at him over my shoulder.

"What do you mean?" I try and throw off, but since joining this program and meeting these boys, I'm finding it a lot harder to bury my feelings these days.

"Well?" He stares at me with his brows raised.

"Taylah." Her name leaves my lips, and my heart skips a beat.

"Do you love her?"

I suck in a breath as I try and calm my heart from the savage beating my ribs are receiving, before I answer. "More than life itself."

"How did you know?"

Usually, a question like this would make me want to shut down, but talking about her right now is bringing me some much-needed comfort. How did I know I loved Taylah? Where do I even start.

"Before her, I was a broken soul merely existing. But after her..." I take a moment to catch my breath. "After her, I finally understood the beauty a single moment can hold."

His eyes widen as he lets out a long breath before a smirk brightens his face.

"She fell for the Mustang, didn't she?" He laughs as he opens up the notes app on his phone. "Note to self: girls like cars."

I take the phone from his hand and add, "They also love cotton candy."

It's the day before New Year's Eve when I step out the doors of LAX and welcome the California sun. My Uber is already waiting, so I throw my bag in the trunk and slide into the back seat. Being back here fills me with memories of her, and I let myself get lost in them as I head into the city. Turning my phone off flight mode, a text message chimes through.

> **Skylar:** Are we still on for today?

> **Cruz:** I'm about fifteen minutes away.

Skylar reached out to me a few days ago, wanting to meet specifically at Valentine Enterprises. I was hesitant at first, but she's a hard person to say no to. The Uber pulls up against the curb, and I thank the driver before grabbing my bag and heading through the doors of the building.

Scanning the foyer, I see her seated on the black couches off to the side of the main entrance, scrolling through her phone. Making my way over, I take the seat in front of her, and drop my bag at my feet. She looks up from her screen and places her phone on the square steel table between us. My eyes catch a glimpse of the phone background, which is a picture of her and Taylah laughing, and my heart implodes.

"I want to show you something." I draw my eyes away from the phone screen as Skylar hands me a black file.

"What's this?" I open it and scan the pages, having no idea what I'm looking at.

"This... is a fucking game changer." She leans forward and flicks a few pages before dropping her manicured nail over a highlighted paragraph. "Here."

I read through the paragraph that talks a little about my father's case and how he cut my mother off from accessing funds to be able to get competent representation. I read a little further and see everything Taylah has been lobbying for in the months we've been apart, and I just want to hold her in my arms and tell her I'm proud of her.

Looking back up at Skylar, a sudden realization floors me. "My father owns this entire fucking Fortune 500 company we're sitting in, and yet my mother can't get enough money for a fucking decent lawyer."

I watch as a grin forms across Skylar's face as she hands me another file.

"Why do you think I asked you to meet me here."

Chapter Thirty-Five

Taylah

"Wet pussy, quick fuck, or screaming orgasm?" Skylar asks, tapping the shot menu with her fire-red nails as we stand at the bar in a New York City nightclub called The Vault.

"I'll take a screaming orgasm, please," Lexi interjects, the bartender nodding in acknowledgment.

"Make it three," Skylar adds, winking at the bartender as she slides the menu back across the bar. It's New Year's Eve, which also doubles as my birthday, and the girls are on a mission to celebrate my twenty-first birthday sexualized-shot style.

"Three screaming orgasms," the bartender states, sliding the shots toward us, and flicking his long dark hair from his eyes.

"Happy Birthday, Taylah!" Skylar shouts, throwing one back. I look at Lexi, and we both count down from three before tossing them down. "I'll order us some more." Skylar turns back to the bartender, leaning across the bar in her tight little black dress as Lexi and I head back to the VIP section.

We take a seat on the soft emerald-green couches that crowd around a rectangular metal table. I push my hair off my neck and readjust the strapless baby-pink dress that's sticking to my body as Lexi smiles over my shoulder.

"There's the birthday girl." I snap around when I hear Trey's voice behind me.

"Trey!" I jump out of my seat and throw my arms around his neck, dragging him down to sit next to me. Skylar comes into view with a tray of shots and lowers them onto the table. She takes a seat across from us, and if looks could kill, Trey would no longer be breathing.

"I haven't seen you since the beach house! How are you?" I do my best to redirect the moment.

"School and hockey," he answers casually, leaning forward and taking a shot off the table, before throwing it back.

"I don't recall buying that for you." Skylar states aggressively, and I'm immediately taken back to the moment they met at the beach house.

"That was delicious. What was that?" Trey asks as he licks the shot residue from his lips.

"A quick fuck. Probably the only fuck you'll be getting tonight." The heat coming off Skylar is palpable, and when I see Tristan enter the room, I'm thankful for the reprieve.

"Finally old enough to drink." He hands me a purple cocktail and takes a seat next to Lexi. "Taking on the infamous Jack Valentine? No wonder you're Mom and Dad's favorite." He smiles as he wraps his arm around Lexi. "When's the court case?"

"March." I take a sip from the purple cocktail in my hand to help settle the nervous roll in my stomach as I think about it. Trey and Tristan bump fists as they fall into conversation, and seeing them together like this makes me think of Cruz. I know we've been out of contact, and I know he needs time and space, but I really thought he'd be with me to bring in such a milestone birthday. The ache in my chest is still so raw, that I fear I may never fully recover from the night we walked away from each other. The no contact is the hardest part for me. Not knowing if he's moved on with his life without me or if he's missing me just as much as I'm missing him. Is he waiting for me, or has our time come to an end? I'm constantly haunted by the last words I said to him, "*please don't let me become a memory,*" and as each day passes, I'm terrified that's exactly what I'll become.

"Did I mention I play hockey?"

I'm brought out of my thoughts when I hear Trey and Skylar going at it again.

"How riveting?" Skylar is clearly less than amused.

"I'm happy to sign something for you, I plan on going pro." Trey smirks as he steals another shot off the steel tray. I watch on warily as Skylar slowly gets to her feet, snaking Tristan's beer from his hand and dumping it across Trey's lap.

"Do I look like a puck bunny who gives a fuck? Get a fucking clue." She forcefully flicks her curls as she passes him while he sinks back into the seat beside me.

"When will you learn?" I laugh as I get to my feet and follow Skylar to the dance floor.

The lights are flashing as the bass vibrates over my skin, and the alcohol has calmed my state of mind. Flipping my hair, I dance to the quickened beat of the music as my mind trails off to thoughts of him. It's moments like these when I want to pick up the phone and ask how he's doing, and knowing that I can't affects me the most. I just hope wherever he is tonight welcoming in the New Year, that he's happy.

There are five minutes until midnight, and I'm at the bar ordering the last round of shots before I call it a night. That means there's only five minutes left of being the birthday girl. The shots are laid across the tray in front of me with only a few minutes to spare.

"I was asked to give you this," the young man behind the bar states, sliding a light-blue box wrapped in a yellow ribbon toward me. I take it into my hands and untie the ribbon as the countdown sounds out behind me.

"Ten."

"Nine."

I open the lid, and can't believe what I'm looking at. There, in my hands, is a necklace affixed with a yellow daisy charm.

"Who gave this to you?" Tears sting my eyes as I search the bartender for answers. He just shrugs and points to the exit door off to the side of the club.

"Four."

"Three."

I push through the door with my heart thundering in my chest. Fireworks explode around me as it ticks over into the new year. I hear his car before I see it, and as my eyes trail down the busy stretch of road, his taillights round the corner and disappear into the night. I choke back tears as I gaze down at the necklace in my hand, tracing a finger across the daisy pendant.

"There you are." I hear Skylar's voice behind me, and I wipe my hand across my face. "Shit, are you okay?" Her comforting arms wrap around me as she waves down a taxi. "Let's get you home."

The drive home is a blur and as I sit on the floor of the shower with my knees to my chest, I slowly pull myself together. Changing into some comfortable clothes, I step back into the room and see Skylar seated on my bed.

"Is this from him?" My heart squeezes when I see the necklace in her hands, and I take a seat beside her, letting out an annoyed breath.

"I'm so over the confusion, Sky. He's such a god damn enigma." I can feel the frustration starting to build, as more tears threaten to fall. The no contact is getting to me, and I feel defeated. "He's the hardest person on the planet to read. I really thought he'd be there with me to celebrate my birthday. Maybe this necklace is his goodbye. He was right there, and..."

"Oh my god, are you serious? That boy is infatuated with you." I hear her words, but right now, I don't know what to believe. "I need to tell you something." She shifts behind me, linking the necklace around my neck. "I saw him last week."

"What?" I turn my head to face her as she finishes locking the necklace in place.

"I've spent the last few weeks digging through information to help Elaine and Cruz get back what's rightfully theirs."

I shift so I'm facing her completely as I try and piece together what she's confessing to me. "What do you mean, exactly?"

"I mean, Valentine Enterprises. I came across documents that were signed by Jack that place all his assets in Cruz's name to avoid tax penalties with the IRS. Cruz owns everything, and with being a major shareholder of Valentine Enterprises, he can overthrow the current CEO, who is Jack." She takes a satisfied seat beside me, enveloping my hands in hers. "He fired his father's ass and turned the company over to his mother, then walked out the door."

A warmth fills me, and I feel myself smiling at how amazing that must have felt for him. But there's one question I need to know the answer to. Something that crosses my mind every single day. "Is he happy?"

She looks at me and sighs, as if contemplating what to tell me. "Happy wouldn't be the word I would use, Tay, but he is healing."

Chapter Thirty-Six

Taylah

I frantically search the room for my black Jimmy Choos as I finishing locking my bra in place.

"Taylah, you need to calm down," Skylar orders as she hands me a mug of coffee and my shoes.

"The verdict will be out any minute," I shout frantically, silently thanking her for the caffeine fix I'm throwing down my throat.

I slide on my black pencil skirt and tuck in my white blouse, taking a seat on my bed and gulping down the rest of my coffee. Elaine pleaded with Cruz not to be present at any of the court dates. She wants this opportunity to right her wrongs in his life, but there's a little part of me, a selfish part that wishes he was there to see everything we've been working on come together.

"Your Uber has arrived."

"Shit." I place the empty mug on my nightstand and slip on my heels, grabbing my handbag, and heading for the door.

Stepping out of the black sedan, I make a run for it up the concrete steps. There's paparazzi to the left of me, presumably waiting to get a photo of Jack's arrival.

"Jack, Jack!" I hear them shout his name and frantically grab at their cameras as they race past me. My stomach is a nervous wreck, but I do my best to hold my composure as cameras flash repeatedly somewhere behind me. Before he can get anywhere near me, I slip through the marble archway and head inside.

"Taylah." I turn and see Elaine, dressed in a two-piece navy-blue suit, standing with her new lawyers. I race over as my heels click annoyingly against the floor.

"Is the verdict out yet?" I ask, trying to catch my breath.

"Not yet." She takes my hands in hers, and I see her eyes focus on the daisy pendant that's sitting against my chest.

"Nice necklace."

I smile as I run my finger across it.

"Thank you."

"Let's go take a seat." We head down the corridor toward an empty sitting room reserved for family members. In the middle of the room, there's a wooden table with a pitcher of water and some round glasses. To the left of me are some singular red upholstered chairs, and to the right is a long wooden trestle table that houses an array of brochures and business cards.

Elaine pours me a glass of water, and we make our way over to the seating on the left.

"I heard about what happened at Valentine Enterprises."

She smiles at me as she brings her glass of water to her lips.

"I'm in the process of hiring and firing. I'd love to see Jack's face when he finds out I've brought some incredibly intelligent women on board." We clink glasses, and I can't help but look at her in absolute awe. Her bravery and unwavering attitude to see this through is something Elaine Valentine from a year ago would not have been able to do, and I'm so proud of the woman she's becoming.

"Cruz didn't want any part in it?" There's an ache in my chest just mentioning his name.

"He has his hands full with this project he's been putting together." The way she smiles when she talks about him makes my heart melt. "He loves you, you know. I was not the mother he needed when he was growing up, and I know that." Her eyes are glassy, and the raw emotion of the moment brings tears to my eyes. "But he always had you."

I feel a tear roll down my cheek, and she lifts her hand and brushes it away. "Something about you helped him through some of his darkest moments. You're always with him, Taylah, even when you're apart like this. I just wanted you to know that."

I'm flooded with emotion and I struggle to keep it together. "I miss him, Elaine."

She opens her purse and hands me a handkerchief. "I know, sweetheart. Just give him time."

There's a knock at the door before it clicks open, and a police officer enters the room.

"Sorry to interrupt, but the verdict is in."

Cruz

Guilty. Justice has been served. Not only did I get to fire my father from his own company, but I'm currently sitting in the visitors' waiting room of the jail he's being held in to finally let go of everything I've been holding onto. After everything I've done to heal myself, this is the final step I need to take in order to put this chapter of my life behind me. It's time to confront my father with the new man I've become and the dreams I have for my future. A future he controlled not so long ago. I shudder thinking about how dark that period of my life was, but when I see him being led into the room in cuffs, looking haggard and disheveled, that hold he had over me for most of my life is gone.

"Son." He nods at me as he sits down in the metal chair in front of me. I lean against the metal desk positioned between us, the cold sending a chill through me. We stare at each other for a few silent minutes as I bask in the moment. Seeing him here like a caged animal with no control over his life.

How fucking ironic.

Leaning back against my chair, I hold my head high. I have so much to say to him that I don't even know where to start.

"How does it feel to be out of control of your own life?" I start with the easy questions because by the time I say everything I need to, he's going to know just how much of a fucking disappointment to him I can be.

"It's only for a few years. You think your mother has any hope of running a successful company?" He scoffs at me as he struggles to hide just how irritated he really is.

"I'm sure all those intelligent women she's hired will cope just fine." I watch his face turn a few shades of red before I continue. "Mom owns everything now, well, everything except the Valentine Estate. I can't wait for you to see what I have planned for that." Satisfaction rolls down my spine as he visibly shakes.

"I want you to know what I have planned for my future." Getting to my feet, I walk around the table to stand above him. "I'm going to love someone with everything I have to give. To spend my days worshipping the ground she fucking walks on. To stand behind her and cheer for her wherever her brilliant mind leads her. But also, be the man she can turn to for comfort and understanding on days when life gets tough."

"The Valentine name won't be tainted with weak men!" he shouts, getting to his feet as we stand face to face. He's vibrating, and his nostrils flare in rage, and I can't help but smile as I lean in closer.

"You want to know the best part? One day I plan on marrying the girl responsible for bringing you to your fucking knees and thank her every minute of every day for healing a heart she never broke."

And with that, I turn my back to him, letting the door slam closed on a life I no longer have to live.

"Are you sure you want to demolish everything inside?" My contractor Rex is walking toward me carrying a clipboard of documents.

"I want the place gutted," I reply, letting my eyes drift back to the Valentine Estate sprawled out in front of me. Rex signs off on some of the paperwork before handing it over to me for my final once-over. I read through the plans with a grin on my face as I sign my name at the bottom of the page and hand it back to him. He nods at me and heads back to his crew of workers.

"Cruz Valentine." I hear my name and turn around to see surfer boy Brad walking up the gravel driveway toward me. I meet him halfway.

"Thank you for meeting with me."

Chapter Thirty-Seven

Taylah

6 **Months Later**

I glance down at the prompt cards in my palm, seated at my mirrored makeup vanity. I look back up at my reflection and break out in a nervous sweat.

"Thank you for being here tonight. I am honored—fuck." I drop my head onto my arms and let out a groan.

"Taylah, are you almost ready?" My mother's voice echoes from the other side of the door, and I lift my head to respond. "I'll be five more minutes."

I hear her retreating footsteps down the hall as I take a deep breath and once again take in my reflection. My hair is in a messy braid with a scattering of fresh yellow daisies. My dress is a pale-yellow gown that hugs my body all the way to the floor. It's strapless, and resting right against my chest on full display is my yellow daisy necklace.

Getting to my feet, I take one last look over my outfit before heading out the door.

"There she is," my father announces as I step into the foyer. He raises his camera and clicks a few photos as my mother does her best to hold back her emotions.

"Oh, Taylah. We are so proud of you." She dabs her handkerchief at the side of her eyes before closing the distance between us and pulling me in for a hug. My father soon joins, and I embrace the moment. My family has always been close, and after everything that I've seen over the last few months, I couldn't be more thankful for what I have.

"We better get on the road." Breaking apart, I take one final deep breath before we head out the door.

It's dark out, and the city lights flicker by as we wind in and out of LA traffic. Rain starts to fall, and I concentrate on the way the drops glitter the pavement in an effort to distract myself and calm my nerves. The sound of the rain hitting the top of the car brings me back to a very erotic memory, and I feel my entire body heat up as I rest my head against the back seat and smile, bringing my fingers up to play with my necklace.

"We're here." My father's voice brings me out of my head and back to reality, where I'm rattled with nerves. The door opens, and a chaperone awaits, holding a large black umbrella.

"Miss Barker." The tall gentleman in a penguin suit holds out his hand and helps me out of the car. Cameras flash as we walk the red carpet together, heading up the staircase before he nods me through the glass double doors. We head down a corridor encased in large gold frames. I glance at a few and see that some are of past presidents and a few other influential people of years before.

At the end of the corridor, it opens up into a ballroom. There's some jazz music playing, and the only light is coming from the crystal chandelier in the center of the room and a scattering of candles immersing the room in warmth. Down the far end of the room is a large stage with velvet purple drapes and gold detailing. There are several round tables with gold and beige chairs surrounding them, and I scan the room until I see a table that houses a few familiar faces.

"I'll be right back." I leave my parents to mingle as I head to where Tristan, Lexi, and Trey are seated. As soon as Lexi spots me, her eyes fill with tears as she jumps out of her seat.

"You look stunning, Taylah. She brings me in for a quick hug before pulling out the vacant seat beside her. "Try the quiches; they're to die for." She pushes a plate in front of me, but the thought of eating anything with a stomach full of nerves isn't what I had in mind.

"Nervous?" My brother watches me as I politely slide the plate away from me.

"A little," I answer honestly.

"Good, because there's literally like a thousand people who are meant to show up."

"Tristan!" Lexi playfully slaps at his chest. "What's wrong with you?"

I laugh as I reach for the glass of water in front of me and take a sip.

"All your hard work has led you here, Taylah, and we're all so proud of you." Trey's warm tone creates a soothing effect on my nerves.

"Sorry, I'm late." A flustered Skylar drops down into the seat across from me, taking a glass of champagne into her hand. "Please tell me I didn't miss it." I laugh as she downs the entire glass.

I shake my head. "You didn't miss anything."

The room darkens, and a beam of light focuses on the center stage as a lady walks out in a long black gown. She's older with a sleek black bun and piercing blue eyes. She carries herself so gracefully as she plucks the microphone off its stand.

"Thank you all for coming here tonight. My name is Alyssa Reynolds, newly appointed Los Angeles County District Attorney." I'm doing my best to keep my eyes on the stage, but my line of sight keeps drifting to Skylar, who's distractedly searching the back of the room.

"It's my pleasure to present this year's Inspirational Member of Society Award to Miss Taylah Barker."

I hear my name, and the room erupts into applause as I get to my feet. A spotlight follows me as I make my way toward the stage, lifting my dress slightly as I ascend the steps in an eager attempt not to fall flat on my face. Alyssa's eyes are on me, her face creasing into a soft smile as I approach.

"Congratulations." She hands me an open navy-blue box housing a gold medal with the scales of justice and my name engraved into it.

"Thank you." I place the medal onto the podium and adjust the microphone. I take a moment to stare at the medal sitting in front of me and I'm filled with immense pride. Taking a deep breath, I count to three and glance up.

"I'm so incredibly honored to be here tonight accepting this award. To be described as inspiring and influential takes my breath away. I..."

There's movement at the back of the room, and my eyes draw to where one of the mahogany doors opens as a man steps through the threshold. The dim lighting makes it hard to see, but as soon as he lifts his face, my heart takes a nose-dive into my stomach.

Cruz.

His eyes are on mine, and I can't find my next breath. I'm flooded with so many different emotions at once that my mind is a chaotic mess. A sea of eyes are burning into me as I stand there in silence, trying to find something to stabilize myself. That's when he smiles, and my entire world collapses in on itself.

"I'm sorry."

By the time my mind catches up with my legs, I'm three seconds away from the exit doors that lead out into the gardens behind the conference hall. My heart is beating so fast I can hear it in my ears as I barge through the metal door.

I'm doused in rain as soon as I step outside. Lifting my dress, I race down the steps before slipping out of my heels and leaping onto the grass. I have no idea where the fuck I'm running to as the rain stings my face and soaks my skin. Images of Cruz barrel through me like a freight train, causing my chest to pull so tight I can barely breathe.

"Taylah, wait." His voice lights up every nerve ending in my body, and I've never felt so lost yet so found in my entire life.

Chapter Thirty-Eight

Cruz

I call out her name, and she stops in her tracks. She's wearing a backless yellow dress, and I can't pull my eyes away from watching the way the rain skates down her spine, as the wet material clings to her tanned skin.

She keeps her back to me as I close the distance between us. Her sweet perfume consumes me, and my heart aches with how much I've missed her. I stand there for a moment, breathing her in as the rain falls over us. I had so much planned to say, and now, as I stand behind her, mesmerized by the yellow daisies in her hair, I've lost the ability to speak.

Reaching out, I take one of the flowers from her braided hair and slide it slowly down her neck and across her shoulder. She shivers at the touch, and I continue to guide the soft, yellow petals down her spine until I meet dip of her back. She's trembling and I pull her against my chest, linking my arm around her, and lowering the daisy down the center of her face. Her eyes close and I watch the way the rain glides across her mouth.

"Come here." I turn her so she's facing me, and the emotion playing out behind those metallic eyes knocks the wind from my lungs. "Fuck, you're beautiful."

I bring the flower to her lips, enraptured in the way they part as I brush the petals across her mouth. I want to kiss the life out of her, but it's been so long that I have no idea where her head is at. I gently tuck the flower back into her hair, and when my eyes come back to her face, tears are rolling down her cheeks.

She takes a step away from me, and my heart aches for her.

"Don't be here if your heart isn't ready because I'm not capable of watching you walk away from me again." The pain in her voice stabs through my chest. She's sobbing and I reach for her, but she takes another step away from me.

"Please, let me hold you." Watching her fall apart is killing me.

"I can't." She turns to leave, and I reach for her, as distress creeps up my spine at the thought of her walking away from me.

"I wouldn't be here if I wasn't ready to give you my everything, Taylah." She stops walking, keeping her back to me, but I continue. "You healed a heart you never destroyed without even knowing it, and I'm ready to appreciate the fuck out of you until my very last breath."

"I lo..." The words don't get the chance to leave my lips as she turns and leaps into my arms. Our mouths collide with so much desperation, I see stars. Her taste coats my mouth, and the urge to devour her is overwhelming.

"I've missed you." It's a desperate whisper into my mouth and is enough to obliterate my heart. The salt from the tears that are streaming down her face coats my lips as she falls apart in my arms.

I pull back from her, gasping for air, and scan the meadow around us. There's an old barn to the right of us, and I lower her back to her feet, removing my jacket. Throwing it over her shoulders, I slide my hand into hers and make a run for it.

"Let's get you someplace warm." Her grip tightens in my hand as we race toward the old oak barn in the distance. Only just making it inside before the first clap of thunder. She scans a few of the stables while I shake the water from my hair. There's dim lighting coming from a round, copper light that's hanging in the center of the barn. Dark, wooden stable doors line either side, and there's a wooden ladder to the left that leads to the loft above us.

"It's empty." She announces as a nervous smile cross her lips. I watch as she walks toward the ladder that leads to the loft, and as she starts to climb, it's as if an invisible string pulls me toward her and I follow.

The wooden floor is covered with straw, a small pile accumulating just under a large rectangular window, another window on the ceiling looks up at the night sky. I glance over at Taylah, who's still wrapped in my black suit coat while she stares up out at the rain pelting the glass above us. Standing here watching her like this creates a nervous hum across my skin as a flood of memories consume me.

I take a few steps toward her to stand behind her and lift my jacket from her body. Leaning into her, I run warm kisses up the back of her neck and wrap my arms around her waist, bringing her close to me.

"Do you remember the night at the club? We left in an Uber and…"

"Yes," I whisper against her skin.

"How much do you remember about that night?" Her voice shakes as I run my tongue up the side of her neck, resting my lips at the base of her ear.

"Every single cum-filled detail."

A moan escapes her body as she turns to face me, fisting my shirt and pulling me into her. I wrap my arms around her as her erratic breathing pants into the air around us. Bringing my lips to hers, I suck back every breath as I tug her dress off her body. Using one hand, I unclip her bra and let it fall.

"Fuck, I've missed you." That sentence carries so much weight, it's pure relief the moment it leaves my lips. The kiss turns frantic as I carry her to the window ledge and sit her down with her back against the glass. Linking my fingers into her silk panties, I slowly drop to my knees, and slide them down her legs.

Throwing one leg over each shoulder, I smile up at her, and sinking between her thighs as I run my tongue over her clit. Her body jolts, and she tilts her head back against the glass as I suck her throbbing bud into my mouth. I get lost in the taste of her, until the telltale signs of her impending orgasm come barreling through.

"Oh my god." Her breathless moans only feed my endless hunger as I drown myself in her juices, letting her body tense and shake beneath me. I don't let her catch her breath as I get to my feet and crash my mouth against hers, letting her taste herself all over my lips. As our mouths search each other, her hands unlock my belt before unzipping my suit pants and freeing my throbbing cock from my underwear.

She wraps her legs around my waist, pulling me closer, and placing me at her entrance. The heat from her wet pussy is sucking me in, and I lose all ability to think of anything other than how much she consumes me as I bury myself inside her.

"Fuck, Taylah."

I've missed her. My god, have I fucking missed her.

Her hands run under my shirt, dragging her nails across my back as I plunge in and out of her. Taking her wrists, I lock them above her head and I pound into her with intent as the glass window behind us fogs over. The sound of the rain and her breathless cries are so overstimulating, and when I feel her coming on my cock as she screams into my mouth, my orgasm crashes through me like a euphoric wave of heat. Letting go of her wrists, I lift her spent body off the window ledge, and bury us into the pile of hay, filling her with everything I have to give.

Her hands roam my body as I kiss my way across her breasts, before tugging an oversensitive nipple between my teeth, making her whimper. I'm not done with her yet, and I don't let go until she's a frenzied mess beneath me.

Pulling back, she reaches for me, and I take her hands into mine, bringing them to my lips, and laying hot kisses across her fingers. I smile against her fingertips and watch her fall apart.

"Cruz." Her breathless gasp around my name makes my cock ache.

"Who knew one little smile could bring you so undone."

Her eyes roam over my face, down to my lips, and back up to my eyes as pure love detonates behind her starry gaze.

"I could lose myself in the way you look at me, until the end of time." Her words rock me, as a flood of emotion rips through my heart. I don't realize I'm crying until her finger wipes a tear from my face.

Slamming my mouth to hers, I search her, like the missing pieces of myself might be buried somewhere inside her soul.

Sliding back into her, I suck every gasp from her lungs. There are no words that could ever come close to describing the peaceful feeling that settles over me when we're together. She's my soul mate. And I'm thankful for every scar, every battle, and every soul-shattering moment that led me to her.

Chapter Thirty-Nine

Taylah

I open my eyes as the warmth from the morning sun filters through the window. My head is resting against Cruz's chest, and judging by his shallow breathing, he's still sleeping. I slowly slide out of his grip and get to my feet, throwing his jacket around my naked body as I search my purse for my phone.

I tiptoe past him and descend the ladder. The barn is still empty, thank god, and as I slide the door open, I take a breath and power on my phone. I'm not ready to face the aftermath of running off stage last night, but I'm not the type of person who can just leave things and hope for the best.

My phone turns on, and a few messages chime through. One is a congratulations from Sam and an apology for not being there, and one is from Skylar.

> **Skylar:** Everything has been taken care of. Let him in, Taylah, and don't let him go.

I stare at the text blinking back tears, and that's when it hits me. She knew Cruz would be there last night; that's why she was constantly scanning the back of the room. I smile as I type back a thank you and slide my phone back into my purse.

The door slides open behind me, and I turn abruptly to see a very shirtless, disheveled Cruz standing there in a state of panic. He chokes on whatever he's trying to say before grabbing me and pulling me against his chest. My face rests against his bare skin, and I can feel his heartbeat pounding against my face.

"Fuck, Taylah, I thought you left me." Realization dawns on me as his body shakes beneath me. Pulling back, I tilt my face up to find his.

"I'm not going anywhere." I reassure him.

He smiles, bringing his hands up to cup my face, and running his thumb across my bottom lip.

"I love you, Taylah."

My heart jolts out of my chest, clearly unprepared for those words leaving his lips.

"I love you too." He smiles and I leaning in closer, resting my chin against his chest, as I quietly admire the man who's had my heart for longer than he realizes.

His heart finally returns to a normal rhythm, and I tighten my grip around him, never wanting to let go.

"Cruz?"

"Yes?"

"Take me home."

After sliding back into my evening gown, we head to where Cruz's car is parked, praying no one is around to see the disorderly look we both seem to be rocking after a night of *I finally have you back in my life sex.* When his silver Mustang comes into view, my heart skips a beat. The memories we made in and on that car alone are enough to send red-hot heat between my legs.

"What're you thinking about?" He questions, and I glance over at him as the sun beams across that heart-melting grin.

"Just memories." I nod toward his car and hear him chuckle beside me. He opens my door, and I want to slide inside, but I can't take my eyes away from his newly found smirk that makes my panties disintegrate.

"Which memory is your favorite?" he asks as desire drifts across his features as if he's currently sitting through a replay of events.

"All of them." I run my hand down his white button-down shirt and slide into the car.

"Great answer." He lets out a long, staggered breath as he closes my door. I keep my eyes on him as he rounds the front of the car and slides into the driver's seat, still untangling the fact he's right there in front of me. Everything about him makes my heart happy, and as he intertwines his fingers with mine, I feel my soul light up, knowing the love of my life has finally made his way home to me.

I'm in a blissful daze, watching the scenery pass me by, until a sudden realization of where we're heading hits me like a ton of bricks. We are currently driving up the hill that leads to the Valentine Estate, and I'm instantly filled with a rush of apprehension. He must notice the change in my demeanor when I feel his hand squeeze mine.

"I want to show you something." The soft vibration of his voice calms my nerves, and when we pull up to the white wooden fence that has replaced the unwelcoming wrought iron gate, I'm filled with curiosity. He punches a code into the silver box that's nestled nicely against a green hedge, and the gate starts to slide open.

As soon as we start the drive toward the house, my heart drops into my stomach as uncaged butterflies dance across my soul.

"Yellow daisies?" I choke on the words as they leave my mouth, turning to look at him as tears of overwhelming joy stream down my face. The driveway to his house is now white gravel, with rows of endless yellow daisies lining both sides. Rolling my window down, I close my eyes, and take in the scent. Letting the memories of that day take me to a blissful euphoria I never plan on leaving.

The car stops, and the engine switches off as I open my eyes, and it takes me a minute to understand what I'm actually looking at. The house is now white with a gorgeous wrap-around porch. A tall, lean young boy with dark hair descends the front steps with his hands in his blue jean pockets.

"Who's that?" I ask as he approaches my door.

"That, is James." Before he can explain to me exactly who "James" is, my door is open, and I'm face-to-face with the teenager.

"Holy shit, you finally got the balls to go and get her."

"Language." Cruz laughs as he lays his head back against his seat. "Can you give us a minute, please?"

The young boy looks from me to Cruz and back again before smiling to himself and closing my door.

"Sorry about him."

"So, you finally had the balls to come and get me, did you?" I laugh as Cruz closes his eyes and shakes his head.

"There's a lot more boys just like him in there." He nods to the house, and I do my best to decipher what he's trying to say. "When I moved to Chicago, I was part of a program to help people like me heal from things kids should never have to go through. The program also teaches us the importance of opening up and talking through the demons that haunt us. That way, whatever we have buried no longer holds residence, and fuck me, Taylah, is that a freeing moment."

I can see the emotion in his eyes as he swallows hard before continuing. "This is a safe place for those young people, a lot like me, who are trying to become better versions of themselves for the people they love." The pride he holds behind every word makes my heart swell.

"Cruz, I don't even know what to say." He smiles as he takes my hand into his and brings it to his lips.

"Come see what you helped create."

"What I helped create?"

"If you never walked into my world and showed me how beautiful life could be, I would have lost myself to the darkness a long time ago, Taylah. You're the reason for all of this. You're the reason my heart keeps beating."

Every word fills me with warmth and I'm at a loss for words. He lets go of my hand and gets out of the car. I do the same, and we reach for each other as we head for the steps that lead to the main entrance. As I step through the threshold, I'm overcome by how much light now filters through the foyer. The walls are all painted white and there's a scattering of vases down the main hall and throughout the foyer of daisies and sunflowers. We head down the hall toward the staircase as he explains each room we pass.

"The dining hall, games room, music room." The mention of the music room has me stopped in my tracks. I peek inside and see an array of different instruments, including a grand piano. We keep walking until we're at the bottom of the staircase. "Up there are just rooms and bathrooms, but out here…" I follow him around another turn and out a set of glass sliding doors that lead outside. To the left of us is a basketball court where some kids are having a game. To the right, there are garden beds of fresh produce being tended to by some more kids, and down the back of the yard is an outside gym where a few more kids are working out.

"Hi, Taylah." I turn around to see the last familiar face I expected to see walking out the back of the house.

"Brad?" He smiles and brings me in for a hug before turning to Cruz.

"All six accounted for," he states as a group of young boys file past us. He falls into conversation with Cruz, and I stand there in a state of confusion.

"You two work together?" I ask as I try and put the pieces together. Brad turns back to me and nods.

"Cruz asked me if I could help out some of these boys with some surfing lessons. After I saw everything he had put together, it didn't take a lot of convincing. Anyway, I'd best be off; same time tomorrow?" Cruz nods and Brad turns to leave, waving us goodbye as he disappears back around the side of the house.

I stand there for a moment as I take everything in. "Cruz, this is—wow." I'm incapable of finding the right words to say because what he's achieved and what he's doing for these young kids is as breathtaking as it comes. And as he turns to face me, with that soul-stealing smile, his silhouette drowns in a halo of sunlight, and I see my entire future flash before my eyes. He's everything I could have asked for and more, and the way he's looking at me right now, with a smile that literally steals the breath from my lungs, is the way I hope he looks at me until the end of time.

$$\sim\!\!\mathcal{Z}$$

Cruz

2 ***Years Later***

The sound of crashing waves wakes me, and I roll over and notice I'm in bed alone. I lie there for a minute when I hear Taylah's piano and smile to myself as I slide out of bed. Making my way down the hall, I head straight for her, but even I wasn't ready for the vision that's laid out before me. There, seated at her piano that faces the ocean, as the morning sun encases the room, is my wife with our daughter seated on her lap.

"Wow." I will time to stand still as I take a mental picture of the very moment my heart falls out of my chest. Taylah glances over her shoulder and smiles at me, and I lean my back up against the wall and indulge in the moment.

We bought this beach house in Malibu after Taylah graduated from Brown. Not only did she graduate top of her class, but she was offered a highly coveted job handling political conflicts alongside Alyssa Reynolds, at the Los Angeles County District Attorney Office. And she managed all this pregnant with our daughter Daisy. While she's our beautiful little surprise, she's the piece of the puzzle we didn't realize was missing. Taylah's sheer determination and ambition in life are admirable, and I just know the little girl in her arms is going to be just as fierce.

A month before Daisy was born, we eloped down on the beach behind our house. The image of my pregnant wife standing in front of me, promising me forever as the sun disappeared behind her, is a moment I'll cherish for the rest of my life. Seeing my girls together is my proudest accomplishment, and I'll never for one second forget how blessed my life turned out to be.

"Where is she?" And the moment's gone as James bursts his way through the door, stealing Daisy from Taylah's arms and heading for the kitchen. We've become close over the last few years. I brought him out here to LA to help me with the program I run out of the Valentine Estate.

I hear him asking Daisy what she wants for breakfast, and I use this moment to say a proper good morning to my wife. Lifting her into my arms, I bring her mouth to mine as her hands run up my neck and into my hair.

"Taylah." Skylar's voice sounds out behind us as she walks into the room. "Ew, I did not want to see that before I had my morning coffee."

"Then maybe you should leave before you see what I plan on having for breakfast."

An unamused look surpasses Skylar's face as she folds her arms over her chest. "Unless you both plan on helping me bury a dead body, I really need her to talk me down." She points at Taylah, and I lower her to her feet as we both surrender to defeat.

"Who's the unlucky guy?" I ask as we head for the living room. I see James on the way, FaceTiming with his girlfriend Alison, who's still back in Chicago, and I manage to steal my daughter back, taking a seat on the couch opposite the girls.

"Elliot Drake," she announces as anger floods her face.

"As in, multi-millionaire and owner of Drake Media?" I ask. Her head tilts my way, and her eyes narrow into daggers.

"Don't get too excited, I dumped coffee over him in front of his shady-as-shit office building in Manhattan last week, and apparently, he wants to press charges. Can you believe that?" We're saved from answering when her phone chimes with a text message. Her eyes widen as she reads the text, getting slowly to her feet.

"Is everything okay?" Taylah questions.

"I have to fly back to New York. My father wants to see me immediately. There's a plane waiting... I'll call you." And with that, she turns and races for the door.

"Was that weird?" James asks, dropping onto the couch beside me.

"There's not a lot that can rattle her cage, so yeah, that was weird," Taylah answers.

I've spent the day in my office with James, going over the next few months of activity programs. And by the time he walks out the door, I'm exhausted. I find Taylah standing on the back porch that faces the ocean. The glow of the sunset surrounds her as her yellow sundress picks up in the breeze.

I can't breathe as I stand there and take her in. And with each step toward her, I feel that familiar wash of peace she gives my soul. Wrapping my arms around her waist, I pull her body against mine. We stand there and watch as the sky scatters into shades of pinks, purples, and blues, creating a perfect cotton candy sunset.

"Thank you for saving me," I whisper into her hair, drowning in the sweet smell of her skin. She slowly turns to face me, and I'm hit with those sparkling grey eyes our daughter also inherited. They glitter with tears as she wraps her arms around me, holding me close.

"I'm just happy you found your way home to me. I didn't know if I'd ever get to keep you."

The way that sentence leaves her mouth makes my heart burst, and I lift her into my arms.

"Home was never a place; it was always a person, and I was always yours to keep."

Acknowledgements

Firstly I want to thank my readers for taking a chance on my debut romance novel. This story holds a special place in my heart, and it's surreal that it's out in the world forever.

To my daughter, who was the creative mind behind the MMC's name, it suits him perfectly.

To all my amazing ARC readers, thank you for your time and love with my debut book baby.

To my girls on Instagram, you all know who you are. I could not have done this without each and every one of you. You girls are such a rock in my support system and I could never thank you enough.

To my best friend, where do I even start. You've seen me through some of the hardest moments of my life, and I wouldn't be the person or the author I am without you by my side.

To the love and heartbreak that influenced this book, thank you. It really wouldn't be the love story it turned out to be, without it.

To my family for being there through the highs and lows of this entire journey to becoming a published author. You kept me focused on making my dream a reality.

And lastly, to my grandmother, who showed me the true meaning of strength and resilience. I did it. I wrote a fucking book!

his
to
tame

Book Two in the
Tortured Hearts Series

Skylar Rhodes & Elliot Drake

Coming to Amazon in 2025

About the Author

L C Hezemans is a spicy romance author who lives for those heart-clenching, passion driven, toe curling moments. Her characters are written from the heart, and she's a sucker for a happily ever after.

If you would like to connect with her, she's most active on instagram, @lchezemans.author

9 781763 839625